Praise for *The Trouble with Patience*

"Brendan delivers a charmingly quirky and endearing romance that reveals how love and faith can heal two damaged souls."

—*Library Journal*

"This is a sweet love story with plenty of nods to the iconic Old West, complete with rough gunslingers, vigilante posses, and breathless shootouts."

—*Booklist*

Praise for *A Sweet Misfortune*

"Historical fiction readers will love this tale of finding oneself and figuring out what is truly important in life."

—*RT Book Reviews*, 4 stars

"Brendan gives readers a delicious taste of the expansiveness and the demands of life and love on the frontier."

—*Booklist*

"[Brendan is] a true master of the Romance Fiction genre. *A Sweet Misfortune* is very highly recommended."

—*Midwest Book Review*

Books by Maggie Brendan

HEART OF THE WEST

No Place for a Lady
The Jewel of His Heart
A Love of Her Own

THE BLUE WILLOW BRIDES

Deeply Devoted
Twice Promised
Perfectly Matched

VIRTUES AND VICES OF THE OLD WEST

The Trouble with Patience
A Sweet Misfortune
Trusting Grace

Trusting Grace

A NOVEL

MAGGIE BRENDAN

Revell

a division of Baker Publishing Group
Grand Rapids, Michigan

Published by Revell
a division of Baker Publishing Group
P.O. Box 6287, Grand Rapids, MI 49516-6287
www.revellbooks.com

Printed in the United States of America

Library of Congress Cataloging-in-Publication Data
Names: Brendan, Maggie, date, author.
Title: Trusting grace: a novel / Maggie Brendan.
Description: Grand Rapids, MI : Revell, a division of Baker Publishing Group, [2017]
   | Series: Virtues and vices of the old West ; 3
Identifiers: LCCN 2016050304 | ISBN 9780800722661 (pbk.) | ISBN 9780800728915
   (print on demand)
Subjects: LCSH: Frontier and pioneer life—Montana—Fiction. | Man-woman
   relationships—Fiction. | Ranches—Montana—Fiction. | GSAFD: Western stories.
   | Christian fiction. | Love stories.
Classification: LCC PS3602.R4485 T78 2017 | DDC 813/.6—dc23
LC record available at https://lccn.loc.gov/2016050304

17   18   19   20   21   22   23   7   6   5   4   3   2   1

For those who suffer with CIDP—may you always keep the faith and look forward to your new, imperishable body that awaits you in heaven.

Love is patient, love is kind and is not jealous:
love does not brag and is not arrogant.

1 Corinthians 13:4 NASB

1

Gallatin Valley
Montana Territory
Spring 1866

Grace Bidwell pushed her way through the busy mercantile store in the bustling town of Bozeman, certain that it would be the most beneficial place to post a Hired Help sign for everyone to see. She had no choice in the matter—if Bidwell Farms was to remain in operation, then she must have help. Otherwise they'd lose the small potato farm. On her way to find Eli, the store owner, several men moved aside to allow her room, grinning at her like young schoolboys. She felt her face burn with their obvious stares and the tipping of their hats, mindful that other ladies in the store also turned to look at her. But she marched past, giving a brief nod to the ladies, most of whom she didn't really know. Grace hadn't much time to entertain or be involved with the ladies' social circle, or anything else for that matter, since her father had fallen ill.

The mercantile was filled with everything anyone could need, from farm implements and pots and pans to ready-to-wear clothing, fabric, and household staples. Grace savored the mingling smells of the various items—neatly stacked or in barrels—and the scent of burning wood from the stove.

On her way to the counter, she couldn't help but notice a band of three grubby children standing near the glass case and peering at the delectable candy displayed inside. They looked to be ranging in age from four to eleven, if she had to guess, but since she had no children of her own—a huge void that pained her sorely—she wasn't the best judge of ages. The smallest one, a petite girl, wore a faded, dirty plaid dress, her hair a mat of tangled, golden curls.

Grace held her reticule tightly, along with the notice she'd written, and watched the children. The middle child, a slightly older girl, didn't look much better. Her worn dress barely covered her calves and her shoes revealed cracked leather and dried mud around the edges. The boy—maybe the girls' older brother—yanked on their arms in frustration while tucking a package beneath his thin arm. "Come on! We've got to leave now." His dark hair covered most of his eyes and was badly in need of a haircut, and his pants, supported by suspenders, were extremely short. He wore no socks with his brogans.

"Please, can't we get at least one peppermint stick to share?" the littlest one whined.

The older girl shrugged her thin shoulders. "Sarah, you already know that we don't have any money left, so not unless you intend to stay and sweep the floor for the owner of this establishment," she said wryly, pulling her arm from the boy's grip.

"Maybe next time, Sarah, I promise—but not today." The boy clamped his jaw tight, dropping Sarah's arm.

"You have your package now, so you kids run along," the clerk said, and shooed them in the direction of the door, nearly pushing Grace to the side and sending her rocking in her sturdy pumps.

Grace quickly steadied herself and felt compelled to step in. "Please, let me buy the children each a stick of peppermint." The three stood motionless, staring at her with large, disbelieving eyes.

The clerk paused, turning toward her. "Mrs. Bidwell, I . . . uh, didn't see you there. I'm sorry—"

His weak apology was completely dismissed by Grace, who reached into her reticule and handed him a few coins. Turning, she smiled at the children.

"We can't let you do that," the young lad protested through narrowed eyes. From his shoulder bones poking up through his shirt, it looked as though he could stand to gain some weight.

"Why not?" the youngest one asked innocently.

He looked over at her. "Because, we don't take money from strangers."

"Well then." Grace drew in a quick breath. "My name is Grace Bidwell, so now we're not strangers. It's only a small gift for you to enjoy this sparkling, spring day. Tell your mama I meant no harm."

"We ain't got no mama," he huffed, casting his expressionless eyes away from Grace.

"I'm sorry." Grace nearly took it upon herself to correct the lad's grammar but thought better of it.

The clerk returned, handing them each a stick of candy. With a nod to Grace, he went back to his work.

Grace frowned, noticing the older girl watching her closely.

She was about to ask them their names when the lad turned to gather the girls and all three of them clomped down the steps in an obvious hurry, disappearing from Grace's view.

Grace stared after them, thinking.

Eli strode over, tapping her on the shoulder. "Is there anything wrong, Grace?"

Grace turned around and looked into Eli's kindly, older face. "Oh, no. Not at all. I was wondering about those children just now. I don't believe I've seen them around."

"Seems like I've seen the boy before, but then we have such an influx of folks in Bozeman, a man my age can barely keep up." He chuckled.

Grace waved a gloved hand. "Oh fiddlesticks! You're not old and still have plenty of vigor. I wish my father did." Tears misted her vision, but she took a shaky breath and tried to put the situation out of her mind.

"I'm really sorry about your father," Eli said, his face softening. "What can I help you with today? Did you get your field ready for planting?"

She shook her head. "I'm afraid I haven't, and that's exactly why I'm here." She handed him the piece of paper. "I've written a notice to hire a helper with the farm. It's just becoming too much for me." Grace thought about how her back ached from helping her father in and out of bed, and the thought of bending in the field all day made her wince. "Do you know of someone needing work, or could I post this on your bulletin board? I'd be glad to pay you a fee."

Eli slapped his thigh. "I don't charge a thing for my board. I consider it a service to the community until we get a newspaper going." He smiled, his hands on his hips. "I can't think of a soul at the moment, but let's go nail it up right now and see what happens. There's always drifters and the like passing through."

"Well, as long as they're reliable. I need someone who's not afraid to work."

"Or someone who *has* to work and will work hard." Eli grunted.

"That's true. You are so kind, Eli, to me and Pop. Please stop over to see him soon. He misses you but hasn't felt well enough to take the ride into town like he used to. It's not easy for him," she said, following him to where the bulletin board hung next to the service counter.

"I'll be sure and ride over with the missus soon." He pinned the paper at eye level where it was noticeable. "Is there anything else today?"

"No, Eli. I appreciate this, but I'd better be getting back to the farm."

"You can repay me with some of that delicious huckleberry pie you make when I stop over." He grinned down at her.

"I certainly shall. See you soon, and thanks again." Grace waved to the clerk as she left, hope springing in her heart.

Before returning to the farm, she decided to stop by and say hello to her friend Ginny. Avoiding the deep ruts in the road, she crossed the street in her buggy, took a left, and stopped. She hopped out and looped the horse's reins around the gatepost, stepped through the wrought-iron gate, and walked up to the sprawling porch to ring the bell. As she waited, Grace admired the potted plants and wicker furniture where she and Ginny had enjoyed much conversation and tea. Virginia, a Southern transplant after the Civil War, had married well. Frank was a successful attorney, but she was down-to-earth with all her Southern charm, and once she and Grace met at church, a fast friendship began. She insisted that Grace call her Ginny.

The door swung open and Ginny's smiling face greeted her. "Grace, I'm so glad to see you. Please come in," she said in her Southern drawl.

As Grace made her way through the door she said, "Are you sure? Is this a bad time?"

Ginny laughed. "It's never a bad time to see my friend." She led the way to the parlor, beautifully furnished in colorful tapestry with heavy Persian rugs and comfortable chairs flanking the fireplace.

Grace took a seat on the brocade settee and Ginny asked, "Shall I ask Nell to make us some tea?"

Grace shook her head. "I can't stay long. I just needed to see another human face besides my pop or I shall go mad! I get so lonely sometimes," she murmured while staring at the fire in the hearth.

"My dear friend, I wish you'd come to dinner soon and meet Warren, Frank's new business partner."

"I know you mean well, Ginny, but I've seen him at church. I don't believe he has any interest in knowing a widow."

Ginny nodded. "He does seem to have a flock of ladies around him, I'll agree, but he doesn't know what he's missing."

Grace tittered. "You are so biased, Ginny! But I love you for it. Now let's change the subject if you don't mind. What have you been doing since I last saw you?"

Ginny frowned at her. "I'm on to you, Grace. You must put the widow weeds behind you now. Life is too short to spend all your time only taking care of your father. He can stay alone for a few hours. You simply must find a way to do something for yourself, and that should include meeting eligible men. You *could* marry again."

Grace chewed her lip and looked into her friend's eyes filled with genuine concern. "Maybe . . . I'm not sure I could ever love again. Losing Victor was the hardest thing I've experienced in my life."

Ginny reached over, patting her hand briefly. "I know, and I'm very sorry. But trust me, you need to get out a bit more—"

The sound of voices in the hallway floated within hearing. Ginny turned in the direction of the doorway. "Looks like you'll get to meet Warren after all," she whispered.

Grace started to reply but Ginny put a finger to her lips. "Shh, here they come."

Grace's protest caught in her throat as the footsteps drew closer. She should've gone on home instead of stopping after leaving the mercantile. She wasn't in the mood to meet a man of Ginny's choosing—or anyone else's, for that matter. To be truthful, she wasn't sure what she wanted.

Ginny rose from her chair as her husband approached. "My dear Frank, you're home early. Hello, Warren," she said to the gentleman next to her husband. He nodded hello and gallantly bent to kiss her hand.

"You're spoiling my wife and she's going to come to expect more attention from me." Frank chuckled, then kissed his wife's brow. "Grace," he said, suddenly spotting her on the settee, "it's good to see you. You must meet Warren Sullivan, my new business partner." He turned to Warren. "This is *Miss* Grace Bidwell."

"It's very nice to meet you," he said and stepped over to where Grace stood, taking a brief bow. His dark hair, shiny from applied pomade, fell across his forehead as he bowed, and a whiff of spicy cologne hung in the air. His pin-striped suit was impeccable.

Grace murmured hello with a slight tilt of her head, mindful as his piercing dark eyes that held a promise of mystery swept over her. She wasn't sure if his was a look of appraisal or something else.

"I've heard lots about you—all good." He grinned.

"I was just telling her that we should all get together. How about dinner Saturday? Are you free?" Ginny asked.

"Great idea," Frank said, touching his wife's arm.

Warren turned to smile at Ginny. "Why, yes, I believe I am, but maybe you should ask Grace first."

Grace felt put on the spot. "Well, I'm not certain. I'll have to let you know, Ginny." She rose, clutching her reticule. "I really must be going now. I can't leave my father for too long."

"I'll walk you to the door," Ginny said, flashing her a conspiratorial smile.

2

Robert stared down at the two coins in his hands—the last of his money. He clenched his jaw in anger. How could Ada have done this to him? Bitterness stung his tongue, but he held his would-be outburst in check when he glanced over at the three children. He reasoned that it really wasn't their fault, but how in the world was he going to be able to feed and clothe his ready-made family? He watched Becky bending over the fire, stirring a pot of watered-down rabbit stew with a wooden spoon. He'd made camp this week outside of Bozeman since he couldn't afford a hotel room and no one would take his credit, but he didn't blame them really.

Becky glanced up and shot him a glare, so he looked away. The feeling of animosity was mutual. How could he feel any different when his wife of only two months sprang the surprise of three children right before she passed away? He needed a walk to clear his head. It was too much, just too much for him.

He headed away from camp and moved through the forest, feeling a heavy weight of responsibility and yet wanting to run as far in the opposite direction as he could. He was a complete failure. Losing his wheat farm and a wife simultaneously was too much for one man to bear. He'd begged and pleaded with God not to take Ada, and what had that gotten him? The surprise of three children!

He leaned against a large cottonwood, the bark scratching him through his thin shirt, and gazed out at the landscape. Spring breezes flittered through the tree's branches with a quiet whisper—the whisper of the Lord? *Be strong and of good courage . . .*

"I'm sorry, Lord, for my doubt and bitterness. I'm having a hard time seeing beyond today. Help me . . ." was all he could choke out, remembering the Holy Spirit utters petitions when he couldn't. He dragged his hand through his long hair with a sigh, then shoved his hands inside his pockets and started back to camp. He didn't want the children to feel abandoned, but how was he supposed to have emotions for them when they'd only met a few weeks ago, after burying his wife? They barely knew one another.

He knew he was going to have to try harder since he'd promised Ada on her deathbed. Now he was regretting that promise. They couldn't take care of themselves, and it was certain her sister who had them before wanted no part of more children to add to her burgeoning household of five. God forbid they would become indentured servants or forced into industrial labor as many orphaned children had been. If he could only find work, he could afford to rent a house, perhaps, and put a roof over their heads. Thankfully, it was still cold only after the sun set. Mornings, while chilly, were tolerable.

Tomorrow he'd go to town one more time and ask around before they moved on to the next place. With new resolve and determination, he *would* find something. Maybe he could get Becky to trim his hair so he'd look more presentable—*if* she decided not to stick him with the scissors! The thought gave him a chuckle when he entered the clearing, determined to make the best of his predicament.

Grace took care of the horse and buggy when she returned home, then hurried inside to fix supper. Her dad was sitting in the parlor reading and looked up when she entered, giving her a warm smile. How she loved him! A sweeter man never lived, she was certain.

"Pop, I'm sorry I'm running late," she said, and she leaned over to give him a peck on his wrinkled cheek. "I stopped by to see Ginny. Are you starved?"

He laughed. "Only a little. How was she faring?" He struggled against the arms of his chair to rise, but Grace instantly reached for him.

"Let me help you. Where are you heading?" Grace felt his thin shoulders beneath her hands as she half-lifted him. The doctor had told her he may have had a mild stroke that affected his legs, but Owen was able to walk, though somewhat unsteadily. Only time would tell if his strength would return.

"To the kitchen to help you." Owen smiled up at his daughter.

Once she got him steady on his feet he held on to her arm as they went toward the kitchen. "Ginny is her usual happy, matchmaker self."

"I see no harm in her trying, my dear. She wants to see you happy, you know."

"But I am happy." Grace steered him to a kitchen chair, then walked over to the stove to heat up supper for them.

Her father harrumphed. "Now, Grace. You can't be too happy taking care of me all the time and doing most of the chores here single-handedly."

"All right, have it your way," she replied. "Truth be told, that's exactly the reason I went to town today—to post a help wanted ad at the mercantile."

"You did? I'm glad to hear that. This farm work is too much for one person." He scratched the stubble on his chin. "It's been a while since I rode into town. I need to keep up better with what's happening."

"Next time, if you're feeling stronger, you can come with me. I hope I get a response soon."

"I have a feelin' you will, daughter—yes, you will."

Grace nodded, hoping he was right. Her back ached every morning from the previous day's work. Cutting wood, hauling water to the cow trough, feeding the chickens, and hoeing the garden took all her time and energy. She sighed and thought back to Warren—well dressed, handsome, with an air of confidence. He was only being polite. Grace knew she wasn't in his league. All she had to do was stare at her calloused hands and fingernails to confirm that she wasn't a genteel lady like Ginny, raised in the South with servants. She felt her father's eyes on her. "Why are you looking at me like that?"

He chuckled. "Wondering what was going through that pretty head of yours, that's all. Want to tell me before the dumplings boil over?"

Drat! She quickly turned back to the stove, reaching for the grate, then slid the pot half off, away from direct heat, and stirred the dumplings to keep them from sticking. Satisfied

18

they were fine, she looked at her father. "Ginny introduced me to Frank's new business partner."

"That's nice. Is he married?" Pop's watery gray eyes snapped to attention.

"No, but we're worlds apart, so don't go getting any ideas." Grace caught the twinkle in her father's eyes and shook her head.

3

"Now you kids stay close to camp and I won't be long." Robert tightened the cinch below the horse's belly, then mounted.

"Where ya going?" little Sarah asked innocently. "Can I go?"

"No, Sarah. I'm going to town, so you mind your sister," he answered. Then he turned to look directly at Tom. "You look after them while I'm gone."

"What'd you think? That I wouldn't look after my own sisters?"

Tom's sullen look grated on his nerves. "I never said you wouldn't. I'll be gone long enough to inquire about work, then I'll be back, unless I get hired on the spot. So don't go roaming off. I don't want you young'uns getting into anything while I'm gone."

Becky stepped up to the horse and looked up at him. "And if you can't find a job, will we be moving on *again*?"

"I reckon so. I have to feed us somehow." Robert pulled his hat snug against his head.

"If you leave that carbine, I can find us a rabbit or somethin' for supper." Tom stood with his hands crossed against his chest, chin firm.

"I don't need a kid running around with a shotgun trying to kill something. You leave that to me."

"I'm almost thirteen and not a kid anymore!" Tom shouted, stalking off.

Robert shook his head then gave his horse a slight kick with his heels, leaving the girls staring after him.

First, he checked at the mill on the outskirts of Bozeman, but they weren't currently hiring and told him to come back in a couple of weeks. He didn't have weeks. He rode into Main Street, a blur of ox trains, mule wagons, emigrant wagons, and cowboys. He tied up his horse at the mercantile store. *At least I know about farm implements*. Could be they needed another clerk with all this bustling activity in a growing town. He could only hope.

A sudden shout caused him to turn around to see a runaway horse and carriage barreling down on a woman about to cross the street. With surprising alacrity, he bounded to her side, pulling her to safety just as the horse and buggy passed. The driver was struggling to control the wild stallion that suddenly flew past them.

"Whew! That was close. Are you all right, ma'am?" He steadied the attractive woman who clutched her hand to her chest, her face blanching white.

"I suppose so," she answered while straightening her lopsided hat. "Thank you so much. I believe that was Darrell. He's always causing trouble. I'll wager he won't even come back to see if I'm all right." Then she stuck out her hand. "I'm Virginia Harrison—Ginny to my friends."

Her accent was sweet and smooth to his ears. "Robert

Frasier." He shook her hand, struck by her friendliness, and noticed the wedding band on her left hand. He wanted to run. *Can't trust a woman who's so friendly . . .*

"Are you new around these parts?"

"Yes, I am." But he offered her nothing else. Best not to say much or else someone might pry and find out he was living outdoors with three young children.

"Then welcome to Bozeman, Mr. Frasier. I hope you'll find our fair city a place to stay."

"That all depends on finding work or not, but thank you for the welcome." He felt her eyes sweep across him, not in a condescending way, but rather trying to appraise him—or so he thought. He could tell she was upper class by the fine clothing she wore. He needed to get away. "If you'll excuse me—"

"Forgive me if I was staring, Mr. Frasier, but I think I know of someone that might be able to help. Follow me into the mercantile?" She tilted her head to hear his response.

"Well, I . . . of course." Not knowing what else to say, he took a deep breath, said a brief prayer, then followed the lady up the mercantile steps. She sashayed past the busy shoppers and up to the counter where a kindly gentleman stood. As soon as he saw her, he greeted her.

"Mrs. Harrison. Nice to see you this morning so bright and early." Then he saw Robert slightly behind her. "What can I help you with?"

"Eli." She turned, indicating Robert. "I'd like you to meet Mr. Frasier, new in town and looking for work."

The store owner was a kindly older man with a road map of deep grooves imprinted on his smiling face. Eli stretched out his hand and gripped Robert's in a firm shake.

"I believe Grace posted a help wanted notice on your bulletin board yesterday. Do you know if anyone has responded yet?" Ginny asked.

"How 'do, Mr. Frasier. I don't rightly know, Ginny, but let's see if anyone removed the sign while I was busy earlier." He strode over to the bulletin board, gave it a swift glance, then pulled the paper away from the tack. "Looks like it's still here, Mr. Frasier. Grace Bidwell is looking for a hired hand to help on her potato farm. Think you can handle that?" Eli looked past Ginny's head to Robert.

"Sir, I feel confident that I can. I used to own a farm. Can you tell me where Grace Bidwell lives?" He twisted his hat in his hands, quietly thanking God for the near run-down of Miss Ginny. "I'd like to speak with her."

"Wonderful!" Ginny clapped her gloved hands together. "Grace is a good friend of mine, so I'll draw you a little map on the back of this paper."

Robert nodded. "I can't thank you enough, Mrs. Harrison."

Ginny's heart pinged with happiness. This could be the answer to Grace's predicament and free up a little time for her instead of tying herself to that farm. This man had a sincere face even in his frayed broadcloth coat and faded tweed trousers. There was a certain weariness about his countenance—perhaps from job hunting or lack of sleep? But no matter, Ginny looked beyond the outward and was able to see that underneath his haggard, thin face, was a good man, and she immediately trusted him for some reason. Normally, she was a good judge of character—she hoped so this time.

Grace settled her father in his easy chair and carried out the wash to hang in the stiff breeze. She loved the smell of sunshine on the sheets when she crawled into bed exhausted at night. Holding the wooden pins at the corner of her mouth, she bent down, lifting a sheet to pin on the clothesline. After she clipped one sheet in place, she looked beyond the clothesline, and saw a lone rider in the clearing walking his horse. *Maybe his horse has lost a shoe?*

She dropped her hands to her side as he stopped a few yards away, removed his hat, and waved.

"Begging your pardon, ma'am, but can I have a few minutes of your time?" He held out a piece of paper that she recognized as her ad.

She nodded. "Go ahead." While he spoke, she sized him up. He was about her age, she guessed, but rather gaunt for his height.

He nodded. "A friend of yours showed me this at the mercantile store, and I came to apply for the job. I'm a farmer by trade."

"Friend?" *How would he know any of my friends?* One had to be cautious. Just because he held the ad in his hand meant nothing. He could be a road agent, or worse.

"Yes. She said her name was Ginny and she introduced me to Eli."

"I see." He *did* seem sincere when she looked directly into his eyes the color of tempered steel. "Let's go inside to talk instead of underneath the sheets."

"Yes, ma'am," he said with reserve, but she noticed he squashed the quiver at the edge of his mouth at her comment.

24

She took him to the parlor, where her dad looked up from his place beside the window and put aside his book. "Pop, we have an interested person come to inquire about helping out around here." She did a half-turn and introduced them. "This is my father, Owen Miller. And you are?"

Robert stretched out his hand. "Oh, sorry. My name is Robert Frasier."

"Forgive me if I don't stand, young man," Owen answered. "Please have a seat and tell us about yourself."

"Yes, sir." He backed up and took a straight-back chair that creaked as he took a seat. Placing his hat on one knee, he began. "I'm a farmer by trade—wheat farmer, actually—and if it's a handyman you're needin' then I'm a jack-of-all-trades, so to speak."

"Wheat farmer, you say?"

Grace knew sometimes her pop was hard of hearing but also had a habit of repeating things anyway.

"Then what in tarnation brings you here?" Owen asked.

Grace watched as the man looked down at his hands briefly, then up again. "I need the money, and unfortunately my wheat crop wasn't enough to sustain the farm the last couple of years."

Owen rubbed his chin. "I think I see. You lose your farm?"

Mr. Frasier nodded sheepishly.

"Well, I'm sorry about that."

Standing next to her father's chair, her hand on his shoulder, Grace cleared her throat. "Please, Mr. Frasier, tell us if you'll be staying long or just passing through Bozeman."

"I have no immediate plans for the future except to find a decent job. If I work for you, then I'll be staying right here until you no longer have a need for me."

"We need help with planting the potatoes as soon as possible if we intend to harvest them by August. Sounds like you're used to hard work, so I shouldn't think that would be a problem. There's always something that needs to be repaired around here as well. My health is not what it used to be, but my daughter has been a big help." Owen smiled up at Grace, then after asking Robert a few more questions, they agreed on his salary. Owen squeezed Grace's hand in affirmation.

"Mr. Frasier, you're hired, and for now we can make a place for you in the barn if you'd like so you wouldn't have to travel from town each day . . . unless you have a family," Owen said.

"That won't be necessary." He glanced at Grace but didn't smile. "I'm an early riser by habit." He stood, twisting his hat in his hands nervously.

Owen shot a quick glance at her. "Suit yourself," he grunted. "Can you start tomorrow?"

"Indeed I can, sir," he answered, gripping his hat until his knuckles were white.

"Great! Then we'll see you bright and early in the morning." Owen grinned, shaking Robert's hand when he leaned over.

"I'll show you out," Grace said, quickly leading the way to the front door. She trusted her father's intuition and hoped the hired man would relieve some of her burden.

Owen sat quietly, ruminating over the young fella he'd just hired. He felt empathy for him but wasn't sure why, other than the fact that he'd lost his wheat farm. Maybe he simply reminded him of his youth. He wasn't the first one to go through hard times, Owen thought sadly. But he seemed decent enough. One plus was the fact that he wasn't too proud to admit his failure and look for work. That showed some ambition. However, there was a hollow look in his eyes. There was something about him that Owen couldn't figure out. Why on earth would a man not be able to find work in his hometown? Did he want a fresh start, or was he hiding something? Usually he considered himself a good judge of character, and he knew time would tell if he was correct in his thinking. Anything was better than no help for Grace if they were to make a go of it this year.

Sometimes he wished he'd entered the pearly gates when he'd gotten sick. Then he wouldn't be such a burden to Grace. If only Victor hadn't up and died suddenly, she'd be busy with a family instead of caring for him. She deserved better than working herself to death and seeing to all his needs. But that was too much wishful thinking, he surmised. That never got him anywhere, so he leaned his head back in his chair for a little snooze. Perhaps he'd dream of Margaret.

Robert followed Grace out to the porch. "I'm much obliged, ma'am." His lips formed a tight smile but his eyes spoke something different. Grace decided he was a troubled man.

"No need to thank me. We'll have to see how you work out, then I'll be thanking *you*." She smiled at him, then stood with her hands behind her back, waiting for him to leave so she could finish the wash. He seemed to want to say something.

"Pardon me, but if you don't mind me asking—what's wrong with your father? Is there any way I can help?"

His question surprised her. "I don't mind telling you. He had a spell with weakness in both legs and isn't strong.

Dr. Avery thinks it was a possible stroke. I can handle him okay, but having someone to help with the farm will ease my workload immensely."

A squirrel skittered across the yard between them, giving her a start. Robert made some sort of sound, but not laughter.

"I thought maybe that might be the problem for him," he said. "Anyway, my offer is open when or if you need assistance." He tipped his hat, then walked to his horse. After gathering the reins, he turned to face her. "See you bright and early then. And you can let me know what you need me to start first, which I suspect is the plowing." He mounted his horse and folded his arms across the saddle horn with ease, gazing down at her with his hazy gray eyes.

Grace shielded her eyes from the sun with her hand as a gentle breeze lifted her bangs. His gaze wasn't unfriendly. Instead, it seemed to hold no emotion. "You're right, Mr. Frasier. Have a good evening."

After he rode away, she went back inside and found her pop sound asleep in his chair—which was how she found him more often than not. His mouth was slack and his chin relaxed against his chest. She tiptoed to the kitchen, filled with thoughts of losing him too. She was already lonely enough.

4

On the ride back to camp, Robert wondered about Grace. Why was a comely woman like her living alone with her invalid father? Hard work could break a woman. He should know—his mother exemplified that, God rest her soul.

He found himself missing Ada even though their marriage had been brief. He shook his head. *Would I have married her if I'd known about the children?* Hard to say, but he rather doubted it. He wished she hadn't kept it a secret. That's the main reason he'd left when the wheat crop failed—he'd felt humiliated the day an attorney and Ada's sister had shown up with three children, only hours after her funeral. Humiliated and shocked, he'd been the laughingstock of his own community.

So here he was, trying to scrape out a living to support *her* children, and it angered him! Teach him to trust any woman again. He vowed to himself he'd never marry again. Someday, when the children were old enough to be on their own, he'd leave the country. 'Course he'd be so old by then, love would be the furthest thing from his mind.

He tried hard to change his attitude as he entered the clearing where he'd left the children. He knew in his heart they didn't deserve his anger. All three of them were sitting on rocks, leaning over and drawing in the dirt with a stick.

Sarah hopped up, running to him with a cheerful greeting. "We're playing a game," she shouted.

Robert dismounted. "Is that so? What kind of game?"

"We're making our dream home. Come see!" She took his hand and pulled him to where Becky and Tom sat.

With twigs and pine needles from the forest floor, they'd outlined a two-story house with shutters and flowers in the yard, a rough outline on the porch of a couple along with three children and a dog. Robert's heart lurched with a clear reminder—*all* children needed a real family. "Mighty nice, Sarah," he choked out. "How about we eat our supper and I'll tell you about my new job?"

"*Finally*," Tom said with a stern look at Robert. "Becky, dip soup for the honoree who's finally got a job."

Becky uncrossed her arms. "Maybe soon we'll have some *real* food."

Sarah slipped her soft, little hand into his, guiding him to have a seat by the campfire. "Everything's gonna work out just fine!"

"Yes, Sarah, but how do you know this?" Tom asked.

Sarah handed Robert a bowl of soup while Becky dipped the rest. "'Cause, I had a dream last night and an angel told me, silly. You just wait and see."

Robert watched the expressions between the two of them—Sarah giving an angelic smile, convinced by her dream of a family, and Tom who rolled his eyes.

Becky took her seat on a camp stool, steadying her bowl.

"You and your dreams! You know nothing about the future. If you did, you'd be more worried about living with a step-father who doesn't want us!"

Quick tears formed in Sarah's eyes. "He never said he didn't want us. Besides, with Mama gone, God will take care of us."

Robert's heart squeezed, and he tried to think of a reply. "I never once said to you that I didn't want you." He saw Becky's eyes lower, not wanting to look at him.

"Children, let's say a blessing for the soup that Becky made for us." He looked into the bowl at the thin watery stuff and pretended it was chicken 'n' dumplings, then blessed the food.

"So you were going to tell us about a job?" Tom stared at him.

"Yes I was. I'm going to work on a farm not far from here. But I want you all to stay out of sight for now. When I get enough saved, I'll rent us a couple rooms at the boarding-house in town."

"Can't we go tomorrow?" Becky pleaded. "I'd give any-thing to sleep in a real bed for a change."

Sarah echoed her plea. "Oh, yes, please?" Her eyes flashed in anticipation. "Becky and I can share a bed."

"I'm sorry. Not until I earn some money." Robert pretended he enjoyed Becky's soup, but soon set his bowl aside. He wasn't all that hungry anyway. "The wagon will have to do for you girls a little while longer, and Tom and I will sleep underneath as usual."

"I can hardly wait," Tom said sarcastically. "Just what are we supposed to do all day while you're gone?"

"Your aunt packed your school books, so you can read and do your arithmetic until I can get you settled. I'll ask about school tomorrow so you can finish out the school year."

"Just how I wanted to spend my spring—teaching my sisters." Tom stood, angrily slamming his bowl down. He picked up a stick and walked over to their straw design and savagely destroyed it, leaving a messy pile of straw. "See this? It's never gonna happen no matter what you dream, Sarah!" He stalked away from the camp.

Becky and Sarah were suddenly quiet, but Robert saw their tears. He sighed, not sure what to do next. He was weary and wished he could be alone with his thoughts.

Sarah reached over and patted his hand. "Don't fret none. He hates school, but I like it. Becky can be the teacher."

Becky made a face. "I can try, but Tom's a whole lot smarter than me."

Robert sighed. "I'd better go after Tom."

"I'll come with you," Sarah said, hopping up.

He looked down at her. "I'd rather you stay and help Becky clean up."

"I need to take the dishes to the creek and wash them, so come with me. I can use your help." Becky's voice was softened as she tried to pacify her younger sister.

He left them gathering the dishes and walked in the direction Tom had gone. He wasn't sure what he'd say to the boy. Having no experience with kids left him searching for answers.

The farther he walked into the woods, the cooler it became, as wind swayed the tall pines. A sound of rushing water in the distance led him to a waterfall that flowed into Bozeman Creek. He surmised the water fed the farmlands surrounding the adjacent area—maybe even the Bidwells' by way of Gallatin River.

When he drew closer, he saw Tom was standing on a boulder at the edge of the creek bed tossing pebbles into the rushing water. The roar of the water was so loud that Tom didn't hear him walk up until Robert was standing alongside him. Tom jumped and glared at him before going back to throwing rocks with force.

"Look, Tom—I know you don't like the situation we have any better than I, but we need to have a truce between us until we can get something worked out." Tom said nothing and looked straight ahead, so Robert continued. "I'm not your enemy, and I know you don't like me, but for starters we've got to work together for the sake of your sisters." The silence was heavy, but Robert waited, wishing he knew what Tom was thinking.

"All right then. If you don't want to talk about this, then I'll leave you alone." Robert started to leave, but Tom turned to look at him.

"Why didn't you just leave us with Aunt Mildred? At least she was family." Tom's eyes snapped angrily.

Robert shifted his weight and gazed at the boy. "You don't get it, do you? I hate to break it to you, but your *Aunt Mildred* didn't want y'all around." There. He'd finally told him.

Tom's face crumpled. "I thought she liked us."

Robert felt bad that he'd blurted out the truth. "Tom . . . it's not that she didn't like you. It's hard to take care of three more children when you already have four."

"But she was Mama's sister! Mama sent us off to stay with her because she was so sick—but I didn't know she'd die!"

"Tom—I know. I didn't know she would either. I never even knew that your mother had any children. I will do right by you and your sisters until you decide you're old enough to be on your own."

"I guess I should be grateful, but I don't know what I feel right now."

"That's understandable. You've had a great loss. Besides, I don't know how I feel about all of this myself. That's why we have to call a truce." Robert held out his hand. "Deal?"

Tom stared down at Robert's hand, hesitating. After a long minute, he finally shook Robert's offered hand. "Deal, for now."

Robert wasn't reassured by Tom's answer and tried to remember when he'd been Tom's age. "We'd better start back to camp. It's getting dark, and I don't want to leave the girls alone." He led the way until Tom fell into step with him, and both were silent on the walk back.

5

Grace was thankful for the display of pink clouds stretching across the sky in the evening dusk and pulled her shawl closer to her, folding her arms as she walked. She enjoyed taking walks after supper, listening to the sounds of the birds—which included an occasional eagle's screech. It was about the only time she seemed to relax and allow herself to be surrounded by Montana's beauty. Was it only last year she and her father took evening walks together after supper before retiring? Now walking had become difficult for him.

She squinted, scanning the sky for what appeared to be smoke in the distance. She couldn't tell whether it was at the Hedricks' farm or on her land, but she doubted it was hers. Her thoughts traveled back to earlier when they'd hired Mr. Frasier.

He looked muscular, from what she could tell, though he was trim. Most likely from the hard work of being a farmer. *I shouldn't be lingering on whether or not he looks masculine as long as he does his work here.*

It was time she headed back down the path to the farmhouse.

The light from the windows behind the curtains gave off an inviting, homey welcome along with the cottonwoods swaying nearby. She hoped when anyone neared her home, which wasn't very often, they felt comfortable. If God had blessed her with children, this would be the time of evening she'd be getting them ready for bed. But that hadn't happened, and she wondered if other women felt what she did—a deep desire for children to hold, sing to, nurture? Sighing, she wondered if Ginny's advice to get out more was advisable. These days, she spent most of her time taking care of Pop. She'd skipped invitations to sewing circles or picnics at church, believing the farm work and taking care of her dad was a priority. She loved her pop and was fiercely devoted to him. Too much, some might say. But he was the only family she had, and the thought of losing him . . . well, it was too much to bear. A hoot owl's call from a nearby pine tree echoed her sentiments.

Grace spied Robert Frasier walking up the lane to the house just as she reached for her bonnet before stepping outdoors to milk Bessie. He still had the same somber look on his face, and she couldn't help but wonder what he'd look like with a smile. He must have a lot on his mind.

"Good morning, Mr. Frasier," she said.

He tipped his hat. "Mornin'."

They met in the middle of the yard and once again Grace observed his deep-set steely eyes beneath his bushy dark brows. He didn't appear to have had much sleep. "Have you had breakfast?"

"Yes. What do you want me to start with first?"

"Well, I've been plowing the furrows to plant the potato

seeds but wasn't able to finish. If you'll follow me to the barn, we can hook Cinnamon up to the plow and get that completed."

"Yes, ma'am. Lead the way."

A blue-gray duck waddled over and followed next to Grace. "Mornin', Bluebelle," she said with a smile, and the duck quacked back a friendly greeting. "Meet Mr. Frasier." Grace paused to look over to Robert. "Bluebelle is a special type of duck—a Blue Swede—that my dear friend, Ginny, ordered especially for me on my birthday. We're hoping to get another duck to mate with her." Grace felt her face burn hot at mentioning mating to an almost complete stranger. *What must he think of me?*

"She's a beauty," he said.

But Grace was aware he couldn't care less about her Bluebelle. She hurried to open the large barn door, allowing bright morning sunlight to flood the dark interior. Cinnamon made a loud noise of hello when she saw them. Grace walked straight to her, pulling back the latch and entering the stall to lead her out. "Cinnamon, meet your new friend, Mr. Frasier."

Robert strode up to her and stroked her jaw. "Yep, we're going to get to know each other pretty well by day's end, Cinnamon."

His speaking to Cinnamon told Grace that he was kind to animals. He'd better be. Cinnamon had been her horse for a very long time. "If you'll get the harness off the wall there"—Grace pointed to the tack on the far wall—"we can go outside and get her behind the plow and in the field."

Grace paused with Cinnamon at the barn door, but when Robert came up from behind, the horse kicked him hard. He yelled, and a look of pain crossed his face. "What the—!"

He glared at the horse and the duck squawked away, fluttering her wings.

"Oh my goodness! I can't believe Cinnamon would do that!" Grace was shocked and rushed over to Robert, who was grimacing and leaning over to rub his calf. His straw hat fell off in the sawdust on the barn floor. "Are you all right? What can I do?" Grace snatched up his hat and handed it to him.

"I'll live, but that horse of yours is not as gentle as I perceived." Robert shook the sawdust from his hat with a tiny smile. "I reckon she's not used to anyone but you?"

"I suppose, and I'm really sorry. Want me to take a look at your leg?" She already knew the answer, but felt she had to ask anyway.

"Nope. It's just a bruise—I'm happy it wasn't my head she kicked."

"I don't know why she did that, and I'm very sorry. Shall we continue?" Grace chewed her bottom lip and caught him staring at her. *Probably wishes he'd never answered my ad.* She knew how painful a kick from a horse could be, and she felt awful about it. "Why don't you let me hook up the harness, and then you can plow? That way you won't be anywhere near Cinnamon's behind."

"Suit yourself," he answered.

When she was done, Robert nodded and reached for the plow handles, trying to hide the sharp pain in his calf. It wouldn't do to let on about it or Grace would consider him weak and not fit to work on their farm.

He limped along toward the open field. The day was showing signs of being perfect, and he liked nothing better than to be outdoors. Birds twittered, then flew up to the trees with a worm or two to feed their little ones. Fluffy clouds overhead would keep the plowing cool—and he was grateful for that—but it did seem a bit odd to work alongside a lady he barely knew, much less take orders from her. He couldn't help but wonder about her. Her voice nearby brought him back to the task at hand as she walked toward him.

"You can see where I started a few days ago, so you can pick up from where I left off." She pointed at two long furrows of rich soil. Long lashes framed honey-colored eyes peering at him from beneath her spoon bonnet. "Are you sure you're all right?" She seemed reluctant to move away.

"Yes, ma'am."

"Then I'll go get the seed potatoes I started last week from the cellar and start planting on the other two rows." She turned toward the duck. "Come along, Bluebelle."

He nodded and watched her walk away, Bluebelle's webbed feet pattering behind her in a scene that was almost comical. But Grace didn't seem to mind.

Robert was anxious to get started before the clouds parted and the sun beat down. He threw the leather straps across his shoulders and gave the reins a snap, saying, "Giddyup, Cinnamon." Cinnamon moved forward and Robert followed, allowing the plow to cut a straight row through the rich earth.

He continued for a while, sharply aware that Grace had returned, basket in hand, bending and dropping potato starters, eye pointing upward in the dirt, then returning with a hoe to cover the long trenches with the plowed dirt. Once he paused to rest and glanced her way. He saw her straighten, placing her hands in the middle of her back to give it a stretch. Planting *anything* was hard work, and somehow he felt sorry for her.

She caught his eye, lifting her hand with a small wave. He

smiled back, knowing she couldn't see that from where she was, then finished the row he was on. It was nearly lunchtime and his stomach was growling. The children would have bread and beans from a can just as he'd packed in his knapsack. He hoped they would stay out of trouble. Tonight he planned on moving the camp a little closer so he wouldn't have as far to walk the next morning. When he had enough money, he'd find a place in town. He hoped he could hold it all together until then.

Robert soon heard the dinner bell and looked up to see Grace at the back porch, tall and graceful, signaling it was lunchtime. He unhitched Cinnamon and turned her out to pasture before striding over to the house's porch. "I'll go retrieve my lunch and eat under a shade tree, ma'am," he told her.

"Why, there's really no need, Mr. Frasier. I've already made lunch. Pop said to invite you."

"Thank you, but I'll go rest under that big cottonwood," he answered.

Her face fell, but she quickly gave him a smile. "Perhaps another time then."

He tipped his hat to her, then walked in the direction where he'd left his knapsack. He had to admit, the smells from the kitchen were enticing.

6

By late afternoon, half the potatoes were planted. The rest would be completed the next day, so Robert headed back to his campsite, tired but with a sense of accomplishment. He always felt good after a day's work. He hadn't gone far when he heard a sound on the trail behind him and glanced around. That blasted duck was following him.

"Go away, Bluebelle!" He flailed his arm out and the duck backed away. "Go home and stay there." *Listen to me—talking to her*, he thought to himself. *I'm beginning to sound like Grace.* Finally the duck left and he walked on, anxious to see how the children had fared and get the camp moved before dark. It was probably best not to stay in one spot too long in the woods. Besides, he wasn't sure whose property it was— maybe the government's.

Sarah skipped toward him, curls bouncing and a big smile on her baby face. "You've been gone an awfully long time, Papa," she said, throwing her arms about his legs, which made him wince. "Is something wrong?"

He noticed her use of *Papa* and smiled down at her. She

was so sweet and innocent, how could he be annoyed at her? "No, I'm only a little sore. You see, I've not used a few of these muscles in a couple of months. What did you do today, and where's Tom?"

Becky walked up to them. "He's cleaning our supper by the creek. He caught some nice trout, but I don't know anything about frying them. Do you?" she asked, resting her hands on her skinny hips.

"Sure do. Let me wash up, and you can watch and learn." Robert tried to sound cheerful, but he was reminded how after a long day in the field, his mother's home-cooked meal would be waiting for him. It seemed like a lifetime since he'd had a good meal.

Tom entered the clearing with a string of fish, not saying much. "Here's supper." He handed them to Robert.

"Thank you, Tom. I'll get this cooking in a few minutes, but after we clean up I want to move the campsite a little closer to the farm I'm working on."

"Aw, again?" Tom folded his arms. "I'm sick and tired of moving and living outside."

So Tom's attitude hadn't changed much since their talk. "You know something, Tom? I'm tired of it too, but remember it won't be for long."

"Anything you say." Tom shuffled off to the nearest rock, propping his elbows on his knees, resting his chin in his hands.

"I'll wash my face and hands and be back in a moment. Becky, you can help by emptying some grease into the Dutch oven and putting it over the fire to melt. But not too much. Sarah, find the cornmeal and soon we'll have us a feast."

Over supper, Owen asked his daughter, "So what did you think of our Mr. Frasier?"

Grace eyed her pop. "The most I can say is that he's a hard worker and a man short on words."

Owen chuckled. "Grace, you know most men aren't talkers, especially when they're working." He spooned a pile of green beans on his plate. "By the way, I'm so glad you've been able to attend to the garden with everything else you've had to do. Wish I could be of more help."

"Pop, you'll get stronger every day, so don't worry."

"I'm not so sure of that. My energy is suffering for sure, but at least I can walk a little. That doggone left leg of mine drags a bit, but I'm grateful to the Lord that I'm not worse. As long as the new hired help works out to help take the load off you, then I'll be happy."

Grace reached over and took his hand. "Pop, please stop worrying about me. If things work out, I promise to join the ladies sewing circle or something."

"I'd like to see you get to know Frank's new partner." He grinned at her, giving her hand a squeeze.

She shook her head. "I don't know. He seems so . . . so sophisticated. What would he see in a farm girl?"

Owen jerked back in his chair. "Whatever do you mean? You're intelligent, hardworking, sweet, and not a kinder person lives in these parts—"

"And plain, not stylish, widowed with little means." She sighed.

"Widowed is true, but you're a nice-looking, Christian woman that any man would be proud to have as his wife. I don't know much about style, but you can learn anything you need to, I'll wager."

Grace had to laugh. "Oh, Pop, you're so biased."

"I only want what's best for my darling daughter before I'm six feet under." He winked at her.

"No more talk about that. How about another slice of bread?"

Grace stood combing her hair, wondering how much of what her pop said at dinner was true. She knew her looks were passable, and she did have nice hair and straight, even teeth. Even if she could afford it, the truth was she had no sense of style like her friend Ginny. She peered closer to the mirror, gazing at new lines forming around her eyes. Most of the time she wore a hat if she was outside for very long, but she had to admit—she was aging, and thirty was just around the bend, heaven forbid! Where had the years gone?

With a heavy heart, Grace settled in bed after saying her prayers, her mind wandering to everything that needed doing on the farm until sleep overtook her, giving her some peace.

She was awake before her dad and slipped quietly out with a basket to the chicken coop for fresh eggs to make breakfast. As she gathered the eggs she thanked God for the bounty of eggs and vegetables she and her pop enjoyed. The simple things in life always delighted her—the smoothness of warm brown eggs, the color of fresh green beans and bell peppers, or juicy red strawberries from the garden. Not to mention the fat red laying hens. "Yes, my ladies," she said gently to them, taking their prized eggs, "we are blessed beyond measure by your feeding us."

"Are you in the habit of talking to the chickens now as well as the duck?"

Grace swung around, startled, and saw Robert standing at the door of the chicken coop. She supposed he was trying to sound chipper, but there was no trace of a smile.

"Heavens! You startled me." She looked up at him with a smile, trying to pretend she wasn't standing in her robe. "Mmm, I suppose you're correct. I confess that when one spends so much time alone on a farm, talking to the animals comes naturally." She laughed. His lips almost curled into a smile, but instead he reached into her basket, picking up an egg.

"Ever cook a soufflé?" he asked.

"I hardly have time to do any fancy cooking, so the answer is no. Have you?"

His warm eyes held hers. "A time or two."

Grace waited. "And is there more to your story?"

"My mama used to instruct me in cooking, and I tried my hand at a soufflé—with her help of course. She was quite the cook."

"How'd it turn out?"

He gave her a lopsided smile for the first time. "Not half bad. It takes patience and practice." He put the egg back into her basket.

"Then perhaps one day you can make us one." Happy that he nearly smiled, she fiddled with the buttons at her throat. She should've dressed properly before going outside, but frankly she hadn't thought about the new hired help arriving early.

"I hung up my apron ages ago. Anyway, I couldn't sleep, so I came on over early."

"Then you can have breakfast with us." Grace started for the door to latch it.

"Thanks, but I'm going to have a look around at the out-buildings and see what needs repair before the milking, if that's okay with you."

"That's fine." She nodded. He tipped his hat and walked toward the smokehouse with a slight limp. He was a peculiar man to be sure. One who could cook a soufflé? Very odd indeed.

Robert looked for, and found, chinks in the logs of the smokehouse. It wouldn't take long to fill them and nail any loose logs in place. He made a mental note to get the materials he would need to do repairs. He left the smokehouse and crossed the open yard to the corral. It was in decent shape but the gate could use a new latch.

Strolling through the pasture in the tall grass with only the wind for companionship, he had a moment of peace. He already liked it here. He wouldn't be honest if he didn't admit to himself that he wished things could go back to before Ada's passing, when he hadn't felt so burdened. Would she have told him about her children eventually? He supposed so.

Grace was so different from Ada. Grace was more down to earth. He thought back to earlier at the chicken coop—Grace standing there in her robe, basket in hand, her face fresh from sleep and looking more relaxed than yesterday, giving her a girlish appearance.

He shook his head. Time to get to the milking. As he turned back, the delicious smells of frying bacon assaulted his nostrils and his mouth watered. At the end of the week when he got his pay, he planned on taking the children to town for a good meal. Wouldn't that be a nice surprise?

7

As Grace headed out to hang the wash, carrying a basket of laundry on her hip, she spied Robert near the well with his pants leg rolled up. She watched while he pumped the cold water, letting it run across an unsightly bruise on his leg. She drew in a sharp breath. *That's where Cinnamon kicked him!* She felt bad, knowing it must really hurt after seeing him limp this morning. Should she see if there was some way she could help? She felt funny approaching him about it.

Her dad caught her eye and motioned to her from the open window where he sat reading the newspaper. Grace dropped the clothespins into her pocket and hurried over.

"You need something, Pop?" she asked, leaning toward him. She thought she'd left him comfortable enough in the spot where he usually dozed off after dinnertime.

"I don't, but our hired man might. Why don't you stroll over there and see if you can give him some of that bear salve I made for sore muscles?"

"Well, I don't know that it's any business of mine to—"

Her pop waved his hand in the air in exasperation. "For

goodness' sake! The man was kicked by our horse. It's the least you can do. Who knows if he's got a woman at home lookin' after him."

Grace shook her head with a loud sigh. "All right. I'll do it, but only because you asked me to. I'll come get the salve."

"No need. I have it right here." He handed her the jar. "I keep it handy for when I'm hurting."

"Is that so? I never knew that," she said, an eyebrow raised. She turned and walked over to the well. Robert's boot and sock lay on the ground, and he bent over to retrieve them without hearing her come up.

"Uh, I don't mean to intrude, Mr. Frasier—"

"Miss Bidwell. I didn't see you." His face reddened as he held his boot and sock to his side, one bare leg exposed, and his pants rolled up to his knee.

Grace's eyes traveled down his leg to his foot, twice the size of hers, splayed out in the dirt. It'd been a long time since she'd seen a man's bare foot and she realized she was staring.

"Oh, sorry. I brought some salve for that bruise. I couldn't help but see it. It looks awful. It must really hurt."

"Aw, it's not too bad, but I'd be much obliged to give that salve a try." His gunmetal-gray eyes glinted at her until she turned her attention to the jar of salve.

"My pop made it from a bear he killed before he took ill. He swears by it. Now if you'll prop up your leg, I'll smear some on the bruise." She opened the jar, then used two fingers to lift out a gob of the thick goo.

Robert did as he was told, bracing himself on one leg while he hiked the other one on the rim of the well. He closed his eyes, murmuring as she spread the salve.

She wasn't expecting so much hair on his legs, which made

48

it a little difficult for her to rub the salve in. She lightly touched her fingertips against the purple bruise on his calf that was swollen. "From your sighs I'd have to say I must not be hurting you?" she asked after a few moments.

"No, ma'am, not one bit. Take as long as you want. Either the salve will heal me or your tender touch will." He opened his eyes to give her a frank gaze.

Grace jerked her hand back, surprised at his admission. "Well, I think that's quite enough for this time, Mr. Frasier."

"Thank you," he said, dropping his leg to the ground, and quickly rolling his pants leg down. He leaned against the well, quickly jerking on his sock and boot. "I'll get back to work now."

He limped off and Grace wiped her fingers on her apron before going back to hang the wash. She felt a little unsettled somehow.

Sarah wanted to explore, and Becky had told her she could, but not to wander off too far before supper. She headed in the direction of the path that Robert always took, taking note of the wildflowers—purple, pink, and white. She'd have to find out the names of them. Perhaps she should collect some to make Becky smile. She hardly ever smiled anymore. She gathered a bunch and skipped along the path, enjoying the sunlight that filtered through the trees for a good distance until she heard a rustle in the woods and paused. She hadn't meant to walk this far into the deep woods alone. Robert had warned them that Indians or road agents were always a possibility, but she wasn't sure what that meant. A sound in the underbrush from behind startled her, and she turned around. To her amazement, a blue-gray duck squawked at her and flapped its wings.

Sarah took a step back, unsure if the duck was going to pounce on her, but it soon folded its wings again and strutted in her direction. Curious, she bent down and held out her hand to the duck. To her surprise, the duck nibbled at her fingers, making her laugh from its tickle.

"What are you doing out in the woods all alone, my little friend?" she asked, as if expecting an answer. "I see. You don't want to tell me. That's perfectly fine, because you don't have to have a reason to take a walk on a gorgeous spring day, do you? My name's Sarah. What's yours?" But there was only silence as the duck blinked its eyes at her.

"See the pretty flowers I picked for my sister?" Sarah bent down, and to her surprise the duck allowed her to stroke its back until it closed its eyes. "I'd better be getting back to camp now. I hadn't meant to come this far and Becky will be worried." She began to skip back down the trail, but the duck followed.

Sarah stopped and wagged a finger. "Now, see here, Mr. Duck. You'd better go back home, 'cause if you come to our campground, you might wind up in a pot for stew!" But the duck continued nipping her ankles and she giggled, staring down at the fluff of blue.

"Oh, dear me. What to do?"

Robert entered the clearing as all three of the children's heads snapped up where they huddled, guilty looks written across their faces. They were up to something, but he was tired and didn't feel like an argument over supper. "What's going on here?"

"Oh, nothing," Tom said. "We were just sitting here planning a trip to town."

"Is that so? And when are you going to town?"

"As soon as you get your first pay. Remember? You promised us a good meal and a real bed to sleep in." Becky glared hard at him.

"I wouldn't get too excited. I won't get paid until the end of the week and it won't amount to much." He sat down on a folding camp stool and propped his elbows on his knees when he heard their grumbles. "We'll have to figure out and make do with what we can."

"Didn't you get any money for selling your farm?" Tom asked.

"I'm sorry to say that it went back to the bank. I thought I told you that before. Let's not talk about the past, but start thinking about the future, which *will* include school."

Tom thrust his chin up, folding his arms. "What good is school? Didn't seem to help you any."

"Now let's be fair—you don't have all the facts, Tom, so let it drop," Robert reminded him. "I promised to do good by you all and I meant it."

Sarah came up to Robert, leaning over to wrap her small arms about his neck. "We know you did, Papa."

The smell of her warm face touching his cheek made him musky inside, and she'd called him Papa again. He smiled up at her, wondering how she could.

After the children went to bed, he sat alone watching the dying embers of the campfire. His soul felt restless. It was hard to admit that he was depressed. He felt like a stranger in this land, without a place to lay his head or call his own. Would he ever be able to own a home or land again?

His mother had once told him, after his favorite school-teacher had suddenly been dismissed, that there were no surprises to God—only to us. Everything was part of His plan. If we trusted Him for our future when He said, "This is the way, walk in it," everything would turn out right in the end.

But that was so hard to do—trust. He'd trusted Ada and where did that get him? Strapped with an instant family he hadn't wanted and without a wife! He was thirty and had a dusting of gray at his temples—and what woman in her right mind would want to marry a man with three children? Women wanted to have their own little ones to cherish.

He stood and fiercely kicked the dirt to cover over the fire, deciding it was time for bed. *Wonder if Grace is in bed?* She impressed him with her quiet ways and how she tended for her father and put him first above her own needs. Perhaps that was why she hadn't married. "But what difference does it make to me?" he grumbled aloud. She meant nothing to him except that she employed him—or was that her father? He really wasn't sure. An owl hooted from the pine above him and he looked up to watch the big eyes of the owl blink. "What do you say, ol' wise owl? Agreeing with me?" He chuckled, making his way to his bedroll under the wagon.

8

Grace had been so busy with chores that a couple of days passed before she realized that she hadn't seen or heard a peep out of Bluebelle. Donning her hat, she set out to go look for her. *How does one call out to a duck?* she wondered. Stepping outside, she saw her father and Robert chatting, but they paused when they saw her coming.

"You've got that troubled look on your face, daughter. Somethin' wrong?" Owen asked.

"I hope not," she said, tying the strings of her bonnet. "Either of you seen Bluebelle lately?"

"Can't say I have. Have you, Robert?" Owen glanced over at him.

"No, I haven't. Want me to help you look for her? I was taking a short break, if that's all right with you," Robert answered.

Grace waved a hand. "Oh no, no, you go right ahead. I'm sure Pop will enjoy some company. If Pop forgot to tell you, work is only half a day on Saturdays and you're off on Sundays. It's the Lord's Day and we like to honor it," she said, noting his broad grin and thanks with a smile. She gave a brief wave, then strolled down the lane and away from the house, calling out Bluebelle's name.

A balmy breeze kissed the cottonwood's tender new leaves while the sun warmed the pathway beneath them. Now, where had that silly duck gone? Ginny had ordered the duck from Sweden, and Grace was sure that it hadn't been cheap. But that was like her friend to do something nice to surprise her.

Grace continued to walk farther, calling out Bluebelle's name until she came to the creek, surprised to find three children wading in the water. She made her way down the slope to the creek bed below. The three children turned from the creek bed to watch as she made her way toward them, and to her surprise, there was Bluebelle floating around in the creek.

"Bluebelle!" Grace cried. "You naughty girl, running away from home!"

The duck waddled to the edge of the bank at the sound of her mistress's voice while the children stood gazing at the duck and her. Grace paused, looking at the faces that seemed so familiar. Where had she seen them? "How did you get my duck?"

The boy shrugged, but the smallest girl answered, "She followed me home one day. Does she belong to you?" Her sweet voice was music to Grace's ears.

"I know you—you're that nice lady from the mercantile store," an older girl said.

Now Grace did remember them. "Yes, you're right on both counts. What are you doing way out here? Do you live nearby?"

"Well, sort of," the older girl replied.

"Sort of? What does that mean?" Grace wondered if they

were runaways, trying to escape being forced into the working mills.

"Our papa is at work and returns at suppertime. Are you gonna take the duck? She sure seems to know your voice," the boy replied.

"I certainly am. But you can always come visit her. I live a couple miles just up that path. You can't miss it." Grace smiled down at the little girl. "We'd welcome some company. I'm sure we could find some cookies for you," she added.

"I'd like that." The little girl smiled up at her, and Grace was struck anew by her beauty.

"I must go now. You children be careful around the creek now." Grace scooped up Bluebelle and tucked her under her arm. "This creek is on my land and I would feel responsible if you fell in. The water is icy this time of year."

The boy shot his sister a look of surprise. "Uh, we'll be going home too now." He nodded at the two girls.

Grace waved goodbye, reluctant to leave them. It surprised her that any parent would let their children explore this far from their house, she thought as she walked back to the farm. Now she wished she'd taken the time to ask more questions. What had happened to their mother? She should have asked. From their appearances, she'd have to say they were poor. If they were *her* children, she'd somehow see to it that they had adequate shoes and clothing. She sighed. Maybe that was all the children's parents could afford. She made a mental note to ask around and find out about their parents.

Turning her thoughts back to Bluebelle's escapade, she fussed at her the rest of the way home. Still, she was grateful that she'd found her. "Bluebelle, what should I wear to Ginny's supper party tonight?"

Bluebelle fidgeted under her arms, so Grace decided to put her down and follow her the rest of the way home. "I know what you need—a companion." *Just like me.*

Grace was the last to arrive for dinner at Ginny's when Nell greeted her and took her wrap. "They're waiting for you in the parlor, Miss Grace," she said while waiting for Grace's bonnet.

"Thank you, Nell." Grace smoothed her hair into place, then walked into the parlor.

Warren rose from his chair as she entered. Tall and dashingly handsome in his three-piece suit and clean-shaven face, he nodded and said, "Nice to see you, Miss Bidwell."

"And you as well," she replied.

Ginny came forward, taking Grace's hands. "I'm so glad you could make it. I wasn't sure you'd come. I should have told you to bring your father." Ginny's face grew serious for a brief moment.

"He sends his best to all of you, but he's pretty comfortable by the fireplace with his books."

Frank walked over to give her a peck on the cheek. "Always a delight to have you, Grace. Won't you have a seat?" He directed her to a chair.

Grace felt Warren's stare as she found a chair, so she tried to avert her eyes and focus on her friend's sweet face.

"We'll be dining in a few moments. I believe Nell outdoes herself when we have company. We never eat as well when it's only the two of us," Frank teased.

Ginny tapped him on the arm. "Pshaw! You know that's not true, Frank."

"I have a hard time believing that you are starved for a good meal, Frank." Grace laughed as Frank patted his stomach beneath his vest.

"I'm sure you ladies are correct."

Nell stood at the doorway. "Supper's ready now, Mrs. Virginia."

Ginny turned toward the doorway. "Thank you, Nell." Turning to her guests she said, "Shall we?"

Throughout the meal, the conversation flowed amicably about current events and the thriving but new community of Bozeman. Warren caught Grace's eye once or twice and she wondered what he might be thinking. She struggled to find something sensible to add to the conversation, having little time for more than the farm and her father.

Frank looked at his guests. "Did you hear we are going to have a church erected? The church will allow visiting ministers of other churches courtesies in the use of the building."

"It'll be nice to not have to meet in the Masonic Lodge," Ginny added.

"I'm sure Pastor Alderson is very happy about that," Grace commented, then took a bite of her food. There was a slight pause as everyone continued with their meal.

"Changing the subject, what is it you like to do for enjoyment, Miss Bidwell?" Warren asked from across the table.

Grace laid her fork down. "Well, to be honest with you, Mr. Sullivan, I have little time to engage with what's happening around town. The closest I've come to having a bit of free time is a walk along the Gallatin River that runs through the valley."

"Well, that's too bad. Perhaps we can change that. I'm new

to this area, so perhaps you could ride with me sometime and we'll both discover the points of interest." He grinned at her and she swallowed.

"I—I—don't know. I haven't much time to myself." *Is he asking to come courting?*

Ginny laughed softly. "I'll bet you can find an hour out of your day now that you have hired help on the farm. It'd be good for you for a change."

Grace stared at her friend, whose eyes twinkled back. *Just wait until I get her alone!* She directed her gaze back to War-ren. "I'll have to let you know."

Frank cleared his throat. "Grace takes care of her father who's been sick recently, and we are praying for his improve-ment. Aren't we, dear?" He looked at Ginny.

"Of course we are! But Grace could enjoy a break now and then."

"Then it's settled! I can come to call for you tomorrow afternoon. What do you say?" Warren pleaded.

"Well," she said, finally giving in. "I suppose I could. But only for an hour."

"You have my promise." He gazed at her from over the rim of his glass until she looked back at her plate, pretending interest in her peas. She wondered about his background. Did he have siblings? How did he decide to become an attorney? His eyes held something mysterious behind them . . . or was it just his way of flirting?

Nell entered with a dessert of apple strudel and served it along with piping hot coffee. They sat around the table talk-ing until much later than Grace had intended. She backed her chair out from the table. "I've so enjoyed the supper from my lovely hosts, but I must be going now."

Everyone else stood as well, commenting on the lateness of the hour, then made their way out of the dining room.

Warren approached Grace. "May I please walk you to your carriage, Miss Bidwell?"

More like a buggy. A nice carriage hadn't been within her budget. "That won't be necessary," she answered, walking to the door to retrieve her bonnet and wrap. "I don't live very far. Just on the outskirts of town."

"No harm in an escort, especially with a dashing young man offering," Ginny teased.

Grace almost rolled her eyes at her friend but knew that was not lady-like. "Well, if you insist," she said, turning to Warren.

"I do." Warren took a step forward and settled her wrap across her shoulders. The dominance of his height and masculinity felt strangely pleasant beside her. No man had been in her life—other than her father—since Victor's untimely passing. And she hadn't given thought to anyone until now.

After her father was asleep, Grace slipped out onto the front porch, took a seat on the steps, and wrapped her arms about her legs. The multitude of stars made a brilliant display against the dark night sky, making her catch her breath. It was one of the things that she loved about this land—the wide-open spaces with the never-ending sky. She was reminded of the Psalms, that God counted the stars and called them by name. *How, Lord, with too many to count, can You do that?* It was all too unfathomable for her to take in.

Feeling small and insignificant—yet amazed that she was able to talk to the Creator of the universe—Grace bowed her head asking for His guidance in her life. She prayed for the children she'd encountered and for her father's health. Afterward, she sat quietly, allowing the peace of the night sounds—a hoot owl, the gentle whisper of the quaking ash, and the flowing creek in the distance, to envelop her with its embrace.

9

The following Saturday afternoon, Robert drove the children to town. "We're going to have lunch after I get you all enrolled for what's left of the school year."

Tom rolled his eyes and muttered something about how he hated school, while the girls chattered away about making new friends.

Once they parked outside the general store, Robert told Tom to keep an eye on the girls in the mercantile while they all looked around. He found Eli and asked about school.

"You'll need to see Sam," Eli responded. "Samuel Anderson. He's the teacher. They meet in the back room of a log store on the edge of town. But you won't find him there today."

"So where *do* I find him, then?"

"I don't rightly know, but if you show up Monday morning before eight o'clock, he'll get them enrolled for certain."

Robert shook his hand and murmured, "Thanks. I need to go round up the kids."

"By the way, how's the new job working out?" Eli's bushy eyebrows knitted together with his question.

"I think it's going good. Grace and her father are nice folks to work for."

"Yes, they are. None better. What does Grace think about your children?"

Robert shifted on his boot heels, staring back at the older man who seemed to be prying into his affairs. "What do you mean? She hasn't met them."

"Oh, but she *has*. You haven't told her you have a family then?" Eli looked shocked.

"I didn't see that there was any need to. What does that have to do with my working for them?"

Eli removed his wire spectacles, wiping them on the edge of his apron. "I suppose it doesn't, but news travels around here. I'm sure Grace would enjoy meeting their mother since she met the children right here in the mercantile one day."

Robert sighed. "My wife passed, unfortunately."

Eli glanced back to Robert with a frown. "I'm very sorry, I wasn't meaning to sound nosy. Is there anything I can do for you?"

Robert answered in a low but steady tone, "Yes. You can stop prying." He spun around, leaving Eli sputtering.

She's met the children! But she didn't know whom they belonged to. Robert hadn't wanted to let anyone know that they were homeless, fearing someone might take the kids away from him. Soon he'd have enough saved to reserve a place at the boardinghouse. He'd never been so strapped for cash in all his life, and he had too much pride to let on to anyone, especially Grace. But he knew he shouldn't have spoken to Eli that way either. Come Monday, he'd apologize.

"Let's go, kids," Robert called out, sounding gruffer than he meant to. "We are going to the Timberline to enjoy a home-cooked meal tonight. Not that Becky's cooking isn't good, but it'll be a nice change."

"But what will we do about school? Don't you want us to go to school?" Becky whined.

"Oh stop being such a worrywart, Becky. You already know how to read and write," Tom grumbled.

Robert stopped on the sidewalk outside the café. "I'll take you Monday, so quit your worrying, Becky."

Sarah smiled up sweetly at him through her enormous innocent eyes. "Will I be able to go too?"

"Probably, but we'll see. Now let's go find something good to eat."

"That'll be a welcome change from Becky's tough rabbit stew," Tom said.

Becky shoved him hard, then followed Tom inside the Timberline Café, where delicious smells welcomed the hungry group.

Once they were seated and ordered, Robert immediately saw Mrs. Harrison walking in their direction. He hoped she wouldn't see him, but much to his dismay, she caught his eye with a broad smile, sashaying straight up to his table.

He rose from his chair when she stopped. "Mr. Frasier. We meet again." Her head bobbed and her enormous hat tilted to one side as she glanced at the children with a furrowed brow. "I didn't know you had any children."

"Good evening, Mrs. Harrison," he choked out. He hoped she wouldn't mention the encounter to Grace but wasn't sure how close their friendship was. He only knew she had suggested he apply to Bidwell Farms as hired help, and that she'd given Grace a duck. "Nice to see you again," he responded, ignoring her question and avoiding eye contact. She leaned toward the children who sat quietly watching, and for once Robert was glad they had clammed up.

––––––––

Ginny smiled at the children. "You three have that hungry look written on your faces." She laughed softly. "In case you're wondering what to order, they make the best pot roast in these parts and their yeast rolls are simply divine!"

"We've already ordered fried chicken," the youngest said loudly, rubbing her small hands together. "It's my favorite."

"I'm Mrs. Harrison, children. What are your names?" They were a grubby little band who looked as though they had just been outside playing and hadn't washed up.

The oldest glanced over at Robert, who nodded his head in approval, before speaking. "I'm Tom and these are my sisters, Sarah and Becky."

Becky was openly staring at her, and Ginny felt a twinge of sympathy, noting that the young girl wore a plain, faded dress with a stain or two. "I'm very happy to meet you all, and I hope you'll be happy in our little town." Ginny turned to Robert, still feeling the children's eyes on her. "Do sit down, Mr. Frasier. Are you waiting for your wife?"

He shifted on his feet, yet continued to stand like a gentleman would. But his face darkened with a scowl. "Uh, no. Sorry to say."

Nothing further was elicited from him, and Ginny instinctively knew he was uncomfortable. "Well, I'm meeting my husband, Frank, for lunch, so I must be going. I hope the job is working out for you?" This was only the second time they'd met, and while she waited for an answer, Ginny held his deep, slate eyes—eyes that displayed distrust. She wondered why. Something in his past?

He nodded. "Yes, it's good. Thank you again for the tip."

"I'm glad to hear that. Well, I must be getting along before Frank comes after me." Glancing at the children, she added, "If you need anything—anything at all—please let me know."

He nodded and Ginny waved to Frank, sitting near the back of the room. *I'm pretty sure Grace didn't mention that the hired help had a family. Come to think of it, he didn't say they were his children.*

Owen watched his hardworking daughter weed the flower bed, taking time to straighten and stretch her back. She loved flowers and he wished he could be of more help to her. Maybe one day. Secretly, when he was alone, he tried walking without assistance, but he couldn't walk for very long. Sometimes his legs tingled more than at other times and he felt stronger, but he still tired easily. He hated more than anything this feeling of being useless. It stripped him of his dignity, what was left of it. Without Margaret it was hard to go on living. She'd been his partner, friend, and lover. Now she walked with the angels. No sweeter woman ever walked the earth than his Margaret. Well, maybe Grace, but she wasn't his wife.

Since he didn't know how long he'd live, Owen wanted Grace to get on with her life—before she regretted being a woman of "a certain age." Since Victor died, Grace was a changed woman—more serious. He prayed every day for someone to steal her heart so she could have a real family with kids. He'd seen the longing in her eyes at church when she'd admired Luella's newest baby. A pretty woman like his daughter should have more in life to anticipate on a Saturday afternoon than weeding a flower bed.

Owen distinctly remembered the day he was mucking out the barn and suddenly felt an overwhelming tiredness sweep over him. Unsteady, he'd taken a step forward to sit on a bale of hay but fell over instead. Grace had found him, and somehow, after what seemed like hours, the two of them managed to get him up on his feet and inside the house. He hadn't told Grace that his legs began feeling funny months before.

That'd been four months ago. The doctor, when he was finally able to see one, wasn't hopeful that he would recover the use of his legs but also wasn't sure what was wrong with him. Possibly a stroke. Regardless, Owen wasn't one to give up easily. He couldn't, in fact—until he knew Grace would be all right.

Grace waved to him, then wiped her hands on her apron, signaling the end of her weeding. As she took a seat next to him on the porch, she sighed with relief. "It looks better without the weeds, doesn't it?" she asked, looking down at her dirty nails.

Owen smiled. "Yes, dear, and the flowers thank you, I'm sure. I'll try to help you rustle up some leftovers so you don't have to wear yourself out cooking tonight."

She reached over and patted his hand. "Sounds good to me, Pop, but you don't need to help. Just keep me company."

Owen saw weariness in her eyes and felt sorry for her. Trying to make her smile he said, "How about a game of checkers after supper? It's your turn to *try* and beat me." He chuckled.

"*Try?* Have you forgotten that I beat you three other times before last night?" She laughed heartily.

He chuckled. "I call it beginner's luck. That's all." He winked at her and Grace just shook her head.

10

"It's going to be a spectacular spring day, Pop." Grace had just returned from gathering eggs. She removed her bonnet and shawl, hanging them on a peg by the back door before refreshing his cup of coffee.

"Is that so? You're in a great mood this morning."

"Why shouldn't I be? Spring always invigorates me. I think I'll work on cleaning my wardrobe after we decide what Mr. Frasier needs to tackle this week." She glanced down at the watch fob attached to her blouse with a frown. "It's well past breakfast and he's late this morning."

"Mmm . . . He could start by replacing some of the chicken wire on the coop. I heard a coyote last night, and it'll only be a matter of time before one ventures closer to the chicken coop for his dinner."

"Then I'll tell him to start there this morning," she said, pouring herself a cup of coffee. "I hope he hasn't quit."

"Don't be silly—" A sharp rap at the back door interrupted Owen.

Grace set her cup on the table and hurried over to open the door. Robert stood there, twirling his hat in his hands.

"Sorry I'm late. I had a personal thing to take care of this morning."

Grace stared into his serious face but didn't ask questions. If it was personal, then it was up to him to share. "And here I was worried that you had quit." She gave a gentle laugh and he quirked a brow.

"I wouldn't do that to you. Besides, I'm enjoying it here. I thought I'd better find out what assignment you had in store for me this morning."

"I was just telling Grace that we have a coyote on the prowl, and we need to secure the chicken coop better," Owen said, leaning aside to see Robert at the door.

"Mornin', Mr. Miller. I'll get right on that."

"Want to join us for a cup of coffee? We had our breakfast an hour ago," Owen said.

"Uh, I guess I don't have time," he answered with a sheepish look at Grace.

Was he waiting for her approval? As an answer she reached over to the stove for the pot then took a cup from the cupboard. "You do now."

Robert placed his hat on the table, then took a seat in a straight-back chair. "Thanks, Miss Bidwell."

Grace took her seat again. "Please. Why don't you call me Grace? Miss Bidwell sounds so formal and old."

He was mildly surprised but replied, "Yes, ma'am. Please call me Robert. I haven't been called Mr. Frasier since the bank foreclosed on me."

She nodded her pretty head at him. "All right. I meant to invite you to our church that meets in town."

"I'm not much of a churchgoer lately."

"Oh." Grace took a sip of coffee and gazed back at him over the rim of her cup.

Robert didn't feel like explaining why and was glad she hadn't pressed him further. He couldn't imagine dragging the children to church until they were settled in a boardinghouse. They needed a real bath and clean clothes—Tom needed a haircut and so did he. "I'll need some lumber and a roll of wire to get started on that coop."

"I could ride into town with you, son, to buy a few supplies you might need—that is, if you would like some company," Owen offered.

"That would be just fine with me. But are you feeling up to it?"

"I am if you can assist me into the buckboard. I can always wait in the wagon while you get the supplies. I want to take a ride on this beautiful day God has given me."

"Of course I'll help you. It'd be nice to have someone to talk to." Robert glanced over at Grace, whose face held clear surprise.

"Pop, you surprise me, but I'm glad you feel like getting out of the house today. I think it'll be good for you to be outdoors in the fresh air."

Robert downed the rest of his coffee. "Thanks for the coffee." He turned to the older man. "I'll hitch up the buckboard. Think you'll be ready by then?"

"Absolutely. We'll meet you on the front porch. I'll just go grab my coat and hat." Owen struggled to stand and Robert was instantly at his side with a helping hand until Grace came to his aid.

"I've got him. Go on ahead and bring the wagon around," she said, then leaned closer and whispered, "Thank you." He could feel her breath lightly on his ear and it tickled, making him feel uncomfortable. He took a step back and nodded okay.

Once in the barn, he hurriedly hitched the horse to the wagon and brought it around to the house before hopping down to assist Owen. "There you go," Robert said with encouragement as Owen lifted his good leg onto the step and pulled with his arms. He landed in the seat, smiling broadly down at Robert.

"That's good, Pop." Grace was beaming at both of them. Robert was surprised at how her countenance had changed. She appeared so pleased that her father had decided on a trip to town, and his heart warmed watching the two of them interact.

Grace stood watching as they rumbled down the lane toward town, when an overwhelming feeling of loneliness swept through her, making her wish she'd invited herself along. Might as well go feed Bluebelle then start the laundry. Grace sighed. Nothing would get done standing here. *Besides, it's a good thing for the men to have some time without a woman hanging around all the time.*

It felt good to be going somewhere. Owen sat back, watching Robert guide the horses toward Bozeman. A perfect spring day, and he had nothing to complain about—other than his limitations with his legs. But at least today, he would set aside his weakness and try to enjoy the ride. He looked over at Robert, who stared intently ahead, and wanted to know more about this quiet man who had stepped into the role of running the farm.

They rumbled along in quiet. Owen took in the bunchgrass and wildflowers blooming profusely and the birds twittering about. He'd forgotten how much he loved this valley. Finally, breaking the morning silence, Owen said, "Son, I appreciate you allowing me to come along today. It's about the first time I've felt like getting out, to tell you the truth."

"I can understand that. Glad you came along. As I said before, I don't mind the company. I'm glad that the drive is just a few miles. Makes it real convenient to the farm."

"That it does. Grace works herself to death most of the time, so I'm glad you came when you did. You were a mighty big help getting those potatoes in."

"Speaking of your daughter—I couldn't help but notice the farm is called Bidwell Farms and not Miller Farms. I guess I thought it was your place, not hers."

"It's her farm, but I came to live with her and her husband, Victor, after my wife died. Unfortunately, Victor died suddenly three years ago." Owen paused, a lump in his throat from thinking about his son-in-law. He cleared his throat and continued, "Victor was a good man and a hard worker. Once he was gone, I was able to help out, but then I started having trouble with my legs, unfortunately for Grace."

Robert turned, looking at him with a flash of surprise. "And for you as well. I had no idea she was widowed."

"She doesn't like to talk about it, and I can't blame her. How about yourself? Young man like you should be married with a family by now." The question seemed to unnerve Robert, and he fidgeted on the seat of the buckboard.

After a moment of silence, Robert answered, "To tell you the truth, I don't like to talk about it much either. I was married briefly."

Owen noticed his clenched jaw and the tenseness in his shoulders. "Oh, sorry. I didn't mean to pry—"

Robert chuckled, looking at him through steely eyes. "Well, I figure you did but I may as well tell you. My wife died suddenly as well. She was very sick."

"Chalk it up to bad manners on my part then, but I'm truly sorry."

"No hard feelings. Don't worry none."

"It's so hard to lose someone you love." He heard Robert harrumph. *Maybe an arranged marriage?* "Is that why you left your farm?"

"Partly. My wheat crop failed soon after she died, so no, not exactly. But I did lose the farm to the bank and had to find something fast."

"I see." Owen could tell that was about all Robert was willing to divulge. "Then I'm glad you showed up at Bidwell Farms."

"Me too, Owen. Me too."

The rest of the drive they were both lost in their own reverie. It was the second time Robert had been to town today. The first time was to take the children to school. Even though they had just a few weeks left of the school year, he knew it would give them something to do until he was established. Tom hadn't wanted to go and only reluctantly gave in, but Becky and Sarah were eager to be with other children. He wished he'd been able to outfit them properly, but maybe by the next school year he could manage that.

He'd watched as Becky tried to comb through Sarah's tight curly hair, finally giving up. He knew nothing of hairstyles, but he thought she looked rather cute with the ringlets falling about her shoulders. Too bad they didn't have pretty bows for their hair.

Wait . . . Was he starting to get sappy about the kids? Surely not! He mustn't let himself get that close to anyone again. He reminded himself that he was only looking out for their welfare and that's where it stopped. Period.

When he'd inquired where the school was while they were leaving the café on Saturday, Robert was told to go to the log store of Squire Fitz. It was easy to locate this morning, and he soon found Samuel Anderson, the schoolteacher, who greeted them warmly. A tall, fastidious man, Samuel shook Robert's hand with a firm grip, welcoming him to the community.

"I apologize for the lack of our town's school facility herein, but hopefully the citizens will see the benefit of having a better location and perhaps pay for a school for the children to meet in someday," he said, showing them to the back room of the log store.

"This is Tom, Becky, and Sarah," Robert said. The children stood rigidly, feet planted to the floor, but the teacher quickly ushered them to a rough-hewn log seat with a table in the middle of the small classroom. The other children chattered when they walked by, but Mr. Anderson quickly restored order.

Robert started for the door. "I really must be going. I'm already late for work. Thank you, Mr. Anderson." He shifted his gaze to Tom. "Tom, you know the way home. See you all back there later." With that, he turned back toward the front of the store—and felt the burden of responsibility leave his shoulders for the time being.

Robert hoped they'd fit right in with the other children. It was about time they were doing something productive with their hours. He turned his thoughts back to Owen, who was talking as they drove into town and rumbled down Main Street.

11

Owen was happy to see his old friend Eli, who clapped him heartily on the back.

"What a great surprise to see you in town, old man!" Eli grinned.

Owen chuckled. "Who you calling old? We did grow up together, and if memory serves me right, you're nearly a year older than me."

Eli scratched the scruff of his beard, gazing at him through bushy, overhanging eyebrows. "Yeah, but I was always better lookin'! Seriously, me and the missus have been meaning to get out to see you, but what with running the shop and our daughter Matilda about to have a baby, we never seem to have enough time in the day."

"I understand. I hear you've already met Robert." Owen indicated Robert standing next to him.

Eli nodded. "Yes, we have." He looked at Robert. "A time or two." He glanced back to Owen. "Say, you seem to be walking pretty steadily."

"Today, I reckon so, but other times . . . well, it's up and down—depends on how tired I get as to how good I'm able to shuffle around. I'm slow, but I'll take any kind of walking I can get. It beats the alternative."

"That's for sure. Now what can I help you out with today?" Eli placed his hands on his hips, waiting.

Robert handed him a slip of paper. "Need two-by-fours for the henhouse. Owen says we have a coyote."

"Well, if there's one—there's another. Owen, you have a seat over here next to the stove, while we gather the lumber and nails. Need any chicken wire too?"

Owen let Robert guide him over to a chair. "Ask Robert. I'm only here for the ride."

"Then I'll pour you up a cup of fresh coffee," Eli said. "Be back in a jiffy." He and Robert walked away, leaving Owen to enjoy the sights and smells of the general store. He'd forgotten how much he enjoyed the trips to town to get supplies or see his friends. Now that he was a little stronger, he determined the trips should become more frequent—even if he wasn't able to go alone. He missed the bustle of the small town, vibrant with folks pursuing whatever venture had brought them this far out West.

Eli returned within a few moments and handed him a steaming cup of coffee. "Here you go. Anything else I can get for you while you wait?"

"Thank you, friend. But I'm happy as a fat cat just enjoying the warmth of the sun through the window."

"Then I'm going out to the lumberyard to help Robert find what he needs. Won't take us long." He scooted out the back door, and Owen felt envy that his older friend was more agile that he was.

He turned his head to see a tall woman briskly enter

the store. Her silver-streaked brown hair peeped out from a drover's hat, and she sported men's pants stuffed into sturdy boots and a drab woolen duster. As she removed her gloves, her eyes immediately swept over the store. She momentarily glanced his way over her round spectacles, then quickly engaged the store clerk with her shopping needs in a no-nonsense manner.

Owen quietly watched her over the rim of his cup. *Now that is a woman who knows what she wants.* He tried not to stare. The clerk seemed to diminish under her gaze, nervously responding, although she wasn't being unkind—just direct. Owen didn't remember ever seeing her before. The clerk hurried off to get whatever it was she'd asked for, but Owen hadn't heard exactly what that was. Suddenly, he found her eyes on him while she leaned against the counter, waiting. He managed to give her a brief smile, and to his surprise, she lifted her hand in a brief wave.

Mmm . . . a widow woman? He'd ask Eli. Eli knew all the gossip even though there were two other mercantile stores in town. The woman appeared to be about his age. Nothing wrong with looking and wondering, he surmised. Something that had never crossed his mind, not since Margaret's passing. Sometimes he longed to have someone—a companion—that he could relate to. Not that he couldn't talk with his daughter—but it *was* different.

He watched through the window as Eli and Robert loaded timber and a roll of chicken wire into the wagon before walking back into the store.

Robert hurried over to him. "Do you have any other business in town, Owen? If not, I'm loaded and ready to go."

"I reckon not, son." Owen looked over at Eli. "Eli, who's

that lady standing over there in the duster? I don't remember seeing her around here before."

Eli turned to look. "Oh, that's Stella Whitfield. Folks call her an old maid. She's opened a boardinghouse down the street but keeps to herself."

Owen scratched his chin thoughtfully. "And here I thought I knew everyone around the valley."

Eli shot Owen a lopsided grin. "You interested in meeting her?" he asked loud enough for only Owen to hear.

Owen's head shot up. "Me? 'Course not." He chuckled. "Who'd want an old widow man with bad legs? No one."

"That's not true. She's a nice lady, but I've always thought she's either lonely or odd—not sure which." Eli scratched his head.

"We need to get going, Owen, if you intend for me to get repairs done today." Robert reached out to offer support, which Owen gratefully accepted. Sometimes, rising from a seated position was more difficult than walking.

Once he was on his feet, wobbly but steady enough to walk, they started for the door. "Thanks for the coffee, my friend. Come out and see us, you hear?"

"We sure will. Take care of yourself."

"Thanks for your help loading the wagon, Eli," Robert said.

Owen noticed Stella discreetly observing them out of the corner of her eye. A comely woman, but years of hard outdoor work and possibly worry etched her face. The clerk returned and she focused her attention on him, and Owen wondered what she thought of a man like him needing help. He wasn't what a body would consider an advanced age. Did it matter anyway? He told himself it didn't, but somehow his ego suffered.

Grace was in the kitchen when she heard a loud squawking from the direction of the henhouse. She threw the dish towel down, stopping only to snatch the Henry leaning on the wall nearby, then ran out the back door and looked out. It took only a moment to spot the slinking coyote as he stole away from the henhouse, his prize held tightly between his jaws. She lifted the gun, took aim, and fired but missed him. *Drat!* She fumed. The gunshot only caused the chickens to squawk louder.

She leaned the gun against the henhouse wall then hurried back outside to calm the chickens down. Repair of the henhouse was one day late.

Grace was sitting on the porch, resting from hoeing the vegetable garden, when she heard the men's voices drifting up the lane to the house. She had to smile when she saw both of them talking and her pop's smiling face more relaxed than she'd seen it in a long time. She rose from her rocking chair, greeting them with a warm hello. Robert helped Owen out of the wagon and up onto the porch, both of them still laughing and talking.

Grace helped to settle Owen into the rocking chair, then stood back observing him.

"I so enjoyed getting away from the house, and Robert was most kind with his assistance." Owen grinned up at Robert, who gave him a nod.

"Anytime you want to take a ride anyplace at all, you let me know." Robert started for the steps. "I better get to working on the chicken coop now."

Grace laughed. "You're a little late for that. A coyote took off with one of my prized laying hens while you were gone." Robert stared at her, disbelieving.

"What?" Her father sat straight up in his chair.

"You heard me right, Pop." Grace turned to Robert, but he was bounding down the steps two at time toward the wagon. "Let me help you, Robert," she said, following him to the wagon loaded with wire and lumber.

He climbed back up into the wagon and picked up the reins. "No need, I can handle it. You go take care of Owen before supper. He's probably tired after our trip to town."

Grace backed away as Robert turned the wagon around. She'd check on him later, but she supposed her pop came first. She was mighty glad that she could count on Robert now—she was beginning to like having him here all day. Maybe someday he'd stay for dinner . . . and she could talk him into making that soufflé he'd talked about. The thought made her smile, and Owen gave her a curious look.

Once she had her father settled nicely by the window with his copy of *Moby-Dick*, she asked him about everyone in town. "Was Eli surprised to see you?"

"He was, and he told me he and the missus didn't ride out to see us because Matilda was about to have a baby. Did you know about that?"

A sudden pang squeezed her chest, and she drew in a deep breath. "No, I did not."

Owen must have sensed the change in her tone. "I'm sorry that you never had children, I really am. But we truly can't know God's plan in all that. I wish I did know."

"I'm okay, Pop. I'm happy for Matilda. I'll have to knit her a blanket or something."

"You know, I really like that new fella," Owen said.

"What fella?"

"Like you don't know. Robert, of course. Now, don't go taking this the wrong way, but it's almost like having the son I never had all these years. Nice to have someone to have 'men talk' with."

"Is that right? Well, I won't take it personally. I need my friend time with Ginny, so I suppose it's much the same thing." She adjusted a light coverlet across his legs.

"He told me he was married before. Wife died after an illness."

A long silence filled the room before Grace spoke. "Is that so?" It made no difference to her. Did it? *Who? How long?* But she didn't dare ask. It really made no difference, she told herself again.

"Now you sound like Robert. He wanted to know why the farm was named Bidwell instead of Miller—so I told him."

"I'm not sure he needed to know that. He is only our hired help, after all."

"Give him a chance, Grace. He seems like a good man to me. I'm usually not far off the mark when it comes to what people are really like."

Grace changed the subject. "I'll go see if he needs any help holding the wire or nails. We don't want those varmints coming back tonight. I'll be back soon and we'll have supper."

"Why don't you ask him to stay?"

"Maybe. I'll see." She slipped out the door.

12

"I thought I'd see if I could be of some help," Grace said, nearing the makeshift sawhorse where Robert was bent over measuring the length of a piece of wood. He glanced up, pencil between his teeth, pausing as she approached. The blue color in his flannel shirt turned his steely eyes into a cool shade of blue.

He removed the pencil, lifted the board to feel its smooth edges where he'd sawed the length. "You might help by lifting the edge of that chicken wire I've already nailed while I push this board underneath."

She moved quickly to assist him, while the chickens walked about picking at the ground and, occasionally, her boot tops. "I sure hope that coyote won't come slinking around again."

"Guess you aren't good with a gun or you'd have put a bullet through him," Robert said matter-of-factly.

Grace felt her face flush. "That's not entirely true. I do know how to use a gun, but he was already nearing the woods by the time I ran outside."

He moved to stand next to her, sliding the wood beneath

the wire. "Let me get a couple nails to hold it in place. Then we can place the wire back across."

Grace nodded, noting the outdoorsy smell of him and the very nearness of his shoulder close to hers. He'd rolled back his shirtsleeves, and she caught a glimpse of dark hair curling against tanned forearms.

He reached inside his shirt pocket for a nail and began hammering the wood in place. Once it was secure, he reached over to grasp the wire she was holding back. His fingers brushed the knuckles of her hand, and she felt something in the pit of her stomach. Grace glanced at him, and he stiffened, moving aside. "Sorry," he muttered, then continued nailing the wire in place.

They worked in rhythm for a few minutes when she ventured another conversation. "Pop tells me you were married before."

Robert quirked an eye at her. "I was."

Seeing that he wasn't about to say another word, Grace quietly said, "You didn't tell us when you came for the job."

"Would it have mattered?" He didn't look at her when he spoke, just picked up another piece of wood to cut.

"Well, I guess not, but I thought it was curious. That's all."

"I'm not in the habit of sharing my personal affairs with my employer." His jaw set like hard steel as he lifted the saw. "Can you hold that end while I saw this piece?" He motioned to the sawhorse.

She held the board steady as he sawed the wood. He was downright peculiar. "I know Pop told you that I'm a widow."

"Yes, he did, and I'm sorry." Robert sliced through the wood with a smooth, steady back-and-forth motion.

"I guess that makes us kindred spirits in a way. We've both

been widowed." She blew away a lock of hair that fell across her lip as she held on to the wood.

"I reckon. You can let go now. I can take care of the rest." He paused, squinting at her in the sunlight.

"Why don't you have supper with us? I have plenty." Grace stood holding her breath while clasping her hands in front of her.

"Maybe another time." He turned back to the henhouse and started nailing the board in place.

That was it? No excuse—just no? "And here I was hoping you'd show me how to make that special soufflé of yours," she prodded.

"Not today, but thanks for the invite." He turned to face her, gazing through cool, narrowed eyes.

Grace stood with her arms folded and said with a teasing grin, "I don't believe you can really cook." She saw his lips part with a half-smile at her teasing. *Watch out—you may actually give me a heartwarming smile any minute.* But he didn't.

"You might be surprised at the many talents I have—"

"Such as?"

"Well, I don't like to brag, but I can sew a straight line and once helped piece a quilt top—or part of it—with my grandmother. So don't underestimate me."

She laughed. "Then I suppose you like to keep your talents well hidden?"

He moved to lift another board in place, then said over his shoulder, "Maybe so. I share them only with special people."

"Then I must be one, since you told me you'd whip up a soufflé one day." She dropped her arms to her side.

He looked at her in surprise. "I did?"

"Not exactly, but you brought it up."

He finally smiled enough that she could see that he had nice teeth. "You don't give up, do you?"

"Pop said I could be a nagger until I got what I wanted."

"I agree. I meant to tell you to keep your eye on Bluebelle or put her in the barn at night."

Conversation over. Just like that! He started nailing the last board as if she were already gone. Her disappointment stung and her throat tightened. "I will. Goodbye then."

She whirled around and stepped away, somehow feeling foolish. *If Pop hadn't pushed me, I wouldn't have asked at all—and I won't again.* She was irritated at herself. She didn't want to seem like she was flirting with him. He seemed reserved around her but was talkative with her pop. *Why?*

Robert watched Grace walk back to the house, pausing to scoop up Bluebelle. There was no need for him to entertain the idea of getting to know her better. He didn't trust women. All they seemed to want was a ring on their finger. Images of his first wife swam before him. He'd done that and wasn't about to make that mistake again. But she sure was pleasant to look at, and if he didn't know better, he'd say she was flirting with him. Well, looking didn't cost a thing.

He finished up, knowing the chicken coop was secure. He needed to get all his tools put away and try to get back to the children to see how school had gone. At least they weren't aimlessly looking for something to do while he was away at work. Kids could get into a heap of trouble with time on their hands—he should know.

13

When Wednesday rolled around, Tom waited until the class had their first lesson in spelling at the schoolhouse, then raised his hand to use the outhouse. The teacher nodded and told him not to dawdle. Tom didn't intend to—he had better things to do. And school wasn't one of them.

He made a pretense of walking in the direction of the outhouse once he was outside, but he kept walking up the lane to town. He was through with education. He had it in his mind to find a job in town, and that was right where he was headed.

He didn't take time to enjoy the cacophony of nature sounds or the fine spring day, as was his normal habit. Before long he'd reached town and strode up the street until he found the mercantile store. Mr. Eli seemed like a nice enough man. He'd start there since he'd at least met him.

Tom spied Eli opening a box, and wasting no time, Tom walked straight over to him. "Mr. Eli, you got a minute?"

Eli paused, still holding a bag of dried beans, and looked

at him with surprise. "How 'do, Tom? What brings you to town? I thought you and your sisters would be in school."

"They are, but I'm not. Could you use some help around here? I need a job."

"Is your father okay with you not going to school?" Eli asked.

"He doesn't care, but you won't tell him about me, will you?"

"Now listen here, Tom. I can't make that promise. Besides, if you don't show up at school, he'll eventually find out."

"But don't you have some work for me to do around here? I'm a quick learner. I'll work for anything—you decide. We could use the money." Tom held his breath while the store owner gazed down at him with a doubtful look in his eye. Eli would either tell Robert or help him out.

"To be honest, my clerk quit just yesterday, so I could use the help—at least until I can hire a grown man."

They shook hands and Tom breathed a happy sigh. "You won't be sorry, Mr. Eli. Just tell me what you want me to start with. Oh, and let me be the one to tell Rob—I mean, my papa."

Eli nodded, then led him over to where he stocked supplies.

By the end of the afternoon, Tom surprised himself at how fast he could work. He'd unpacked four boxes of shotgun shells, three of tobacco, and a large box of longhandles. Much better than being in that dumb school. He whistled while he worked and the time passed quickly by. At lunchtime, he sat on the back porch and ate the meager sandwich Becky had packed, with his stomach growling for more, but he wouldn't complain. He felt a certain freedom away from his sisters for a change, but he sure missed his mama. He sniffed and wiped his nose on his shirtsleeve. He'd have to make sure he got home before Robert. There was no need to tell him he wasn't at school if the girls kept quiet.

Grace had begun spending a little more time on her appearance in the mornings than she used to. She told herself it was just that she should always look presentable in case Warren dropped by, but really she wanted Robert to quit thinking of her as just a widow. Ginny was right. She should try to get out more and be with other people. After all, she'd grieved a long time for her husband, and no matter how she cried, that wouldn't bring him back. Maybe it was time to look to the future—if she was to have one at all. She pulled her hair into a smooth chignon and donned a homespun dress with a stiff white apron, then she headed in the direction of the kitchen to whip up a batch of bread to rise. She passed the door to her father's bedroom—open as usual in case he needed her help. Hearing him talking to himself, she stopped just outside the door to listen.

"—Lord, You have been so gracious to me all these years and blessed me with a sweet daughter and wonderful wife— God rest her soul—and I try not to ask too much for me but for many others who are worse off. But if You have an inclination to hear an old man's plea, would You consider healing me of my affliction? Maybe give me energy and strength in my legs to do things as I used to on my own? I ask for healing, Lord, if it's part of the plan You have for me. If not, then I'll continue to make the best of what time I have left on this earth. I thought I'd take a moment to ask because I reckon I only want Grace to have another chance at life without being saddled with me. I'm grateful for the wonderful years I've had and hope I have a few more. Thank You for hearing my prayer."

Grace held her fist up to her mouth to keep from crying out to him, then slipped away from the door. It wasn't the first time she'd heard her father pray, but never a prayer asking for healing. Hot tears flooded her face, so she turned around and went back to her room. Seeing her cry would only upset him. She'd prayed God would heal him, but she was wise enough to know that healing was not always His answer. It was a while before she could put on a bright face to go help her father with his morning ablutions.

"How's the new schoolin' going?" Robert asked while he and the children were sitting around the fire. They'd eaten a meager supper consisting of potato soup and day-old bread that he quickly put together when he got back from the Bidwell farm. He waited as each one of them clammed up, then glanced over at Tom before answering.

"It's okay," Becky finally offered. "Mr. Anderson is strict, but today he helped me understand my math equations."

Robert nodded. "That's good, Becky." Then turning to Sarah, he asked, "And what do you think about your new school, little lady?" She was usually the first one to offer up an answer, but he noticed Sarah wasn't her gregarious self tonight.

Sarah's eyes widened. "I like it just fine. Some of the girls stared at my clothes." She threw a look over at Tom.

"What? Why you lookin' at me? It's just an ordinary school." Tom looked at the wood in his hand that he was whittling.

Robert glanced in Tom's direction. "I thought you might have a little more to say." Robert felt something was amiss in Tom's demeanor. "We'll have to do something about your clothes, Sarah. I'm afraid you've outgrown the dress you're wearing. By the way, kids, I should have enough money saved soon to get us a place at the boardinghouse in town. Won't that be nice?"

They all began to speak at once. Robert held up his hand. "Hold on, I can't hear a thing you're all saying."

Sarah got up and sat next to him. "Papa, will me and Becky have a room together?"

Robert was startled for a moment to hear her call him Papa again, but it pleased him. Being called anything but Robert might take some getting used to. "We'll see. We can string up a curtain and divide the room if I can't afford an adjoining one."

Becky clapped her hands together. "Oh, I can hardly wait. A real honest-to-goodness bed! Anything is better than sleeping outside."

"Humph! Soon as I'm old enough you can all have the place to yourself." Tom scraped the wood a little too hard and nicked his finger. He sucked the droplet of blood away.

Robert threw him a questioning look. Was he really such a bad father to him? He thought they'd come to some sort of understanding and even a bit of friendship. "Is that so? Where are you aiming to go? And just how old do you think you need to be to go off on your own?"

"About thirteen and that's not too far away," he answered. "I think I'll know all I need to know by then."

Sarah giggled, swinging her legs back and forth. "Mama always said you were a smart one, Tom."

"Yeah, he's smart all right," Becky retorted, and Tom glared back at her.

"You have a lot more to learn, son, I'm afraid. It's time we all went to bed so you won't be late for school tomorrow." Robert rose, trying to push thoughts of Ada out of his memory and all the trouble her death had caused. Sarah held on to his hand but got up and followed him to the wagon.

———

"Thanks for keeping my secret, Becky. I was afraid for a minute that Sarah was going to give me away."

Becky sighed heavily and folded her arms. "I don't know if I can continue to lie, Tom. You know mama didn't teach us that way."

"Maybe not, but look who lied about having children. Just let me figure this out for myself. I feel like we are nothing but a big burden for Robert."

"*Papa*," she reminded him. "You wouldn't actually leave me and Sarah, would you?"

Tom shrugged. "I don't know. But I do know one thing—I don't want to live like this."

14

Grace enjoyed working in her vegetable garden, knowing it promised the bounty of a good harvest that would soon come. Bluebelle quacked and waddled around with interest at her every move, making her laugh aloud, but Grace worked around her. Time spent outdoors on such a gorgeous spring day gave her time alone to think. Uppermost in her mind was the potato crop. Her father had walked with her to the field to inspect it, which took all his strength, but he'd declared that it looked good and healthy.

Pausing a moment, she glanced up, shielding her eyes to see Robert walking about the field and checking it out as well. In the weeks since he'd come to work for them, she'd noticed the paleness of his skin tanned to a warm brown, and his hands took on the look of a farmer—broken, ragged nails and calluses. There was something altogether pleasing about this image and his presence. She was beginning to become familiar with the way he stood, one hand resting on his hip, slightly bent shoulders that pulled tight against the suspenders he wore with his faded brown work pants. Most times his broad hat hid his eyes from view, which he seemed to prefer, but she could still guess his mood by the firm set of his jaw or his tight-lipped way of speaking. A few times she'd caught him smiling—slightly—but she didn't remember ever hearing him laugh.

She created a well with a mound of dirt around the tomato plants, listening to the cacophony of birds in the blueberry bushes, until she heard a rider coming up the lane. It was Warren. She straightened and shook the dirt from her skirt, then smoothed her apron. He was supposed to have come before now. She guessed he'd finally found time. She would've expected him to drive a buggy dressed as nicely as he was in a dashing pin-striped suit and vest. He drew his horse up near her and dismounted with a broad grin, showing a dimpled cheek and a charming glint in his deep-set eyes.

"I'm sorry to drop in unannounced, but work has kept me slaving away."

She withheld a smile since he hadn't showed up when he'd said he would, but said, "I understand."

He removed his gloves. "Do you have a moment?"

"Yes, I can use the break from weeding. Why don't we have a seat on the porch? Can I get you something to drink?" He followed her toward the house, and she saw Robert turn from the potato field to glance at them.

"No, but thank you. I can only stay a short time. Frank will be expecting me."

They took a seat in the rockers on the porch. "Oh, are you working on a big case together?" Grace asked.

"Not really, just general law stuff. Nothing that would interest you, I'm sure."

She leaned over her rocker's arm to ask, "So tell me—do you like working with Frank? Ginny and I are very good friends."

"So she tells me. You must get very lonely out here away from town."

"Oh, town's not that far, and there's plenty here to keep me busy."

"I'm sure, but you're isolated from people. When's the last time you've been out to a restaurant?"

Grace narrowed her gaze in thought for a moment. She really couldn't remember, but it had been a very long time.

"See what I mean? How about I come for you Saturday night for a nice dinner in town?" He flashed her a charming smile.

"Well . . ." She hesitated. "I don't see why not. I'd like to get my pop settled before I leave. He's been having some health issues."

"That's no problem. I'll pick you up—say, about six o'clock?"

When she nodded he grinned. "Perfect!" he said, rising from the chair. "I must hurry along for now, but I shall be looking forward to spending an evening with you."

"I'm flattered." Grace felt her face flush, then followed him down the porch steps.

"Not at all. A pretty lady like you needs the attention of an eligible man, and I'm just the one to see to it." He lifted her hand to kiss the top—much to her surprise. "See you soon, Grace."

Quickly he was off and galloping out of the front yard, leaving behind a trail of dust. Grace couldn't help but turn in the direction of Robert, who was now walking over.

"Is there trouble or something you need help with?" he asked when he drew near.

"Oh, no! Not at all. Warren works for Ginny's husband, Frank. He's asked me out to supper Saturday night."

He stared openly at her and her heart pinged under the scrutiny of his pensive eyes. "I see. I didn't mean to pry."

"I didn't think you were, only looking out for us out here. Excuse me, but I must finish the weeding before I start supper."

He started to walk away but paused, then asked, "You said yes, didn't you?"

"Not that it's your concern, but yes I did, and I'm looking forward to getting out for a change." Was it possible that he looked at her a little longer than ordinary? Or was she imagining it? If so, it was the first time two men had ever been interested in her at the same time. Maybe they were just being nice. *Don't let your heart rule your head.* But she smiled as she returned to the garden, taking note of the thoughtful expression on Robert's handsome face.

Tom set off down the road away from town, taking his sweet time and pausing to watch a herd of antelope in the lush valley. They sure were a pretty sight, but he knew Indians and most folks hunted them for food. It was hard enough for him to kill a rabbit for stew.

He heard animated voices ahead and slowed his steps. He normally passed a farmer or two on their way to town and back. He hoped there weren't Indians nearby. He'd seen them once, far away, close to the foothills. They'd seemed peaceful and ignored him for the most part. Still, he needed to be cautious. Before rounding the curve in the dirt-packed road, he walked quietly along the edge to creep behind the brush—just in case.

It wasn't Indians or a farmer. To his surprise, a well-dressed man stood with his thumbs in his pockets talking to the driver of a wagon. Then he walked to the back of the wagon, lifted the tarp, and seemed to be counting cartons. Tom wondered what was in them.

The businessman circled back around to the man in the wagon. "Okay. Looks good." Tom couldn't hear much of what they said. The man on the wagon seat leaned down to hand the businessman an envelope while chewing on a wad of tobacco in his mouth, then finally landed a spit some yards away. *Amazing*, Tom thought, *to be able to spit that far.* He'd like to try that sometime, but he knew Robert wouldn't allow it, and without a friend to challenge, there wouldn't be much fun in it.

The two men shook hands and the businessman got back on his horse, giving it a swift kick in the ribs before heading back in the direction of town. The other man took the fork in the road after a crack of his whip across the two horses' backs.

Tom pushed through the brush and back onto the road, thinking it seemed a mighty odd meeting to him. He was glad they hadn't seen him in case they were up to no good. He had to hurry home to beat Robert back from work before supper. His stomach growled, reminding him he was fiercely hungry.

Grace saddled Cinnamon, determined not to let the day pass before enjoying a ride in the country. Her pop was napping and Robert had already left for the day. She had to admit, she was more than a little curious about how he spent his time. Maybe he had someone he regularly saw in town. Once she'd been tempted to follow him, but she decided that was out of the question.

The breeze lifted the sash on her bonnet, but the wind and air felt fresh on her face so she let her bonnet hang down her back. She hadn't ridden this far or as fast in quite some time, and it was obvious that Cinnamon needed the workout as well.

Columbines and asters dotted the Gallatin Valley, while the tender pale-green leaves of the cottonwoods were beginning to unfurl. She felt alive and exhilarated with the adventure of being one with nature and totally alone for the ride . . . or at least she thought she was.

There was something in the distance in the clearing between a stand of pines trees that caught her eye. As she slowed Cinnamon to a trot, it became apparent that it was a campsite—on *her* property. What in the world? She drew closer but continued with caution.

"Hello there!" she said, drawing the horse up and dismounting. To her surprise, the three grubby children she'd met twice before rose from the campfire with shocked looks on their faces, as if they'd been caught red-handed. "Where are your parents? I must speak with them." Grace fought to control her irritation and waited for an answer.

The boy—Tom, she remembered—stepped up closer. "I remember you—you're the lady with the funny duck!"

"And so I am, but can I please speak to your mother? Or is she not around?"

The little one grasped her older sister's hand. "Tell her, Becky, that we don't have a mama."

"Shh, Sarah." Becky frowned down at the little girl and Tom shifted in his boots.

"What do you mean? Are you children here all alone?" This was getting more confusing than the first time Grace saw them at the mercantile. That would explain why the children looked unkempt.

"No, they're not alone. They're with me," a familiar voice behind her said.

Grace turned around. "Robert? What are you doing here? I don't understand—"

"I'll explain everything." Robert walked from behind the wagon parked just out of view of the campfire.

Her mind was whirling. Whatever was going on here—right under her nose? "Yes, indeed you will. Did you know that this is my property? How long have you been camping here?"

"Long enough to know we hate living outside," Becky offered, and Robert threw her a look to silence her.

"Children. I need to speak with Grace. I mean, Mrs. Bidwell."

"Got yourself in hot water now, Papa, haven't you," Tom jeered, then disappeared from the clearing.

"Tom—" Robert's voice was stern.

"I want to stay right here and look at the pretty lady," Sarah said, smiling up at Grace.

Grace almost forgot her fury with the child's remark. Sarah allowed Becky to pull her back to the pot over the campfire to help peel potatoes, although they were still within earshot.

Robert strode over to her and motioned for them to walk away from the children. "Grace, I was trying to be out of here before you ever found out we were staying here."

"I don't understand any of this. Why have you all been living in a wagon outdoors in the first place? This is not the

Dark Ages, in case you hadn't noticed." She stared into his eyes, hoping for some easy answer to explain this dubious predicament. "And with children, no less!" If he only knew the soft spot she had for children, he would've understood her anger. She felt the girls' eyes on them, but when she looked over at them, they pretended to busy themselves with supper.

"I know that it's none of my business what my hired help does outside of his work, but don't you think you could have enlightened me when there were children involved—"

"Please, Grace. Take a deep breath, and I'll do my best to explain as much as I can."

"You mean as much as you care to!" Really! She had a good mind to turn him in to the authorities. Her heart twisted in her chest. They needed a mother. One hard look at them told her that. "You better have a clear explanation why you've been living in the woods of all places, on *my* property, alone with three children!"

15

Robert had never seen Grace like this in the short time he'd known her. She was angry, but other than the fact they'd camped on her land, he wasn't sure why she was so riled up. Her eyes snapped with annoyance and her cheeks flushed a bright pink.

As far as an explanation, he only owed her the fact that he'd trespassed, which was true.

"If you're finished railing at me, I'll try to explain this to you." He directed her toward the path in the woods. "Let's walk and talk for a moment."

She allowed him to lead her into the wooded stand of pines out of earshot of the children. It was cooler under the trees and the fresh scent of pine and evergreen enveloped them.

"I'm listening, Robert."

"Truth is, I'd planned on getting rooms at the boarding-house as soon as I could save enough money. I really had no idea this was part of Bidwell Farms or I might've asked you if we could pitch camp. We weren't bothering anyone, and there didn't seem to be anyone else nearby. Besides, it was close enough for the children to walk to school."

Her eyes narrowed with concern in them. "I'm a bit surprised."

"Unfortunately, yes, they are my children," he admitted reluctantly.

As soon as he said the words, he saw his mistake. Grace stopped walking and looked at him as her mouth flew open, then she clamped it shut just as fast. "I'm sorry," he said. "That was a bad choice of words."

Her lips formed a tight line of disgust. "Indeed."

They continued walking. "Look, Grace, I know now that I was trespassing, and I'm begging your forgiveness. I was really pinched for money after my wife died and I lost the farm. Since their aunt brought the children to me to raise, we've been on the road trying to find a place to settle." He sighed, realizing he was telling her more than he intended.

"Why was their aunt bringing them to you? That makes no sense at all to me, Robert."

Robert swallowed. His tongue felt thick and his mouth dry. "They're not my children—what I mean to say is I never knew Ada had any children. It was hard for me to accept." He couldn't look at Grace but continued to slowly walk, head down, as he observed the crushed clover beneath his feet.

Grace's voice softened. "I can only imagine."

"Please, I don't want to discuss this anymore. You needn't worry about my affairs."

"As long as you and the children will come back with me to the farm and stay," Grace said matter-of-factly.

Robert paused in their walking to face her directly. Was she serious? "This is not your burden. We can't do that—"

"I insist. You and Tom can sleep in the barn and the girls can sleep in the extra bedroom until you find an adequate place to live."

"But—"

Grace squared her shoulders, then pulled her bonnet back upon her head. "It's settled. I want to help as much as I can, Robert. I can't have an employee of mine with children running loose and uncared for. It isn't right. What would people say if they knew?"

She's mighty smug, but pretty when she's rattled. "I've done the best I could by them. They were dumped on me, and I can't do the same to you, Grace."

Her hand rested lightly on his forearm. "You won't be. Trust me on this. I do want to help. Don't you think it'd be good for the children?"

He scratched his chin, thinking. "I suppose we could give this arrangement a try, if the children agree."

Her lips broke into a bright smile. "Then let's go ask them now."

The last thing Tom wanted was to share a small space in the loft of the barn with Robert at a place where he was working. Now, his every move would be watched by Robert or *that* lady, although she *seemed* nice enough. But could she be trusted?

He slipped on his overalls while Robert was still sleeping and hurried down the ladder. Outside, the sun was already up and Mrs. Bidwell was crossing the yard. When she saw him she paused.

"Good morning, Tom. Are you hungry? I'm getting breakfast ready and I'm about to wake your sisters."

"I reckon." She was awfully cheerful for this early in the morning, unlike his mama. But looking back now, Tom knew the reason for her lack of energy was because she was very sick. He wished he'd known then. Maybe he could've been more of a help and a better son to her. He knew he was hardheaded most of the time. Hadn't Robert said as much? He blinked back the tears. He was nearly a man now, so he would try not to dwell on it, try to make his mama proud.

"Great! Follow me and we'll see if I can fill you up." She gave him a tender smile.

"Want me to go get Robert—I mean, Papa?"

"No need. I'm sure he'll be along soon. Do you like hot-cakes and bacon?"

Tom's mouth watered. "Oh, yes, ma'am, I do."

"Then you're in for a treat, because I have blueberry syrup that I made myself for the topping." She opened the back door and they stepped inside the kitchen.

Tom almost cried when he entered the homey kitchen that held the heavenly smell of frying bacon. He was sure he must be dreaming. A fat cat was curled up on a rug by the hearth that had a low-burning fire, and the table was set with real Blue Willow dishes just waiting for guests.

"I'm Owen. You must be Tom," said a man who stood by the stove, frying thick slices of bacon. "Have a seat. I'll be done with breakfast in a jiffy."

"Yes, sir." Tom pulled out a chair and his stomach growled loud enough for anyone to hear. The man walked slowly but not well. Strange, because he didn't look very old to him.

The kitchen door opened and his sisters came in, smiles mirrored in their faces.

Sarah ran over to him and hugged his neck. "Oh Tom! We slept in a real bed last night."

He extracted her arms. "I'm glad, Sarah."

"Yes, it was heavenly," Becky echoed. "Can I help you, Mrs. Bidwell? I'm used to cooking."

"Thank you, but Pop and I have it almost ready. Why don't you two have a seat?" Mrs. Bidwell said.

"Tom, where's Papa?" Becky asked, pulling out chairs for her and Sarah.

"I see him coming now," Mrs. Bidwell said as she looked out the window. She turned back to flip the pancakes onto a large platter and carried them to the table.

Robert tapped on the back door, and Mrs. Bidwell stepped over to the door to greet him. "Do come in and join us for breakfast."

Tom thought she seemed excited to see him, and he wondered about that. It was curious to him. Did she actually *like* him?

Robert peered past her into the kitchen, and Tom nodded at him. "Grace, you didn't have to do this. I . . . didn't expect all this." He waved his hand over the table laden with food.

Mrs. Bidwell waved the spatula. "What? Did you think I'd have my guests scrounge for their own food?" She chuckled. "Please, come on in or the children will be late for school."

"Sit by me," Sarah pleaded.

Robert pulled out a chair next to her and sat down, glancing at Tom and Becky. "I'm glad to see you all up and dressed before me for a change." Then he turned to Mrs. Bidwell and said, "We can't thank you enough for your generosity, but we didn't expect you to wait on us."

Owen shuffled over to the table with the bacon in hand and set it down. "Morning, Robert. I'm sure Grace is more than happy to cook for someone besides her complaining father," he said with a smile. "Let me offer the blessing so we can eat."

This way of living was foreign to Tom, but he could get used to a warm house and food on the table. Would their life ever be like this? He vowed right then that when he grew up, he would have a home with children, and they would never want for anything.

16

After everyone had left and the dishes were done, Grace was in the parlor at her desk writing a list of items she needed from town. The first thing on her list was new frocks for the girls and pants for Tom. She realized that the condition of their clothing wasn't neglect from Robert as much as it was a lack of cash flow. Three children had been thrust upon him right after he'd lost his own livelihood. She hoped to remedy that or at the very least outfit the children for the last couple of weeks of school before summer break. She hoped Robert wouldn't mind. She decided she should ask first.

Grace heard the sounds of a carriage enter the yard and she moved the lace curtain aside to see it was Ginny. She hurried to the door just as Ginny was stepping down out of the carriage.

"I hope you don't mind an impromptu visit from a friend," Ginny called.

Grace was quickly by her side and taking her arm. "Never! I'm always happy to see you. You're out early this morning. Let's go inside and catch up."

Settled in the parlor with fresh coffee and gingersnaps, Grace noticed the soft mint-green gown her friend wore reflected her green eyes. "You look marvelous, as usual, Ginny."

"Thank you, Grace, but you have a spark in your eye as well. Could it be that Warren has been courting?"

"Ha! He never kept his promise to come that Sunday, but he did drop by yesterday. I had all but given up."

"Then what's the new bounce in your step that I detect?" Ginny scrutinized her face for a clue.

"I didn't realize I had a bounce." She chuckled. "Maybe it's because of new developments around here."

Ginny cocked an eyebrow. "And that would be?"

"Uh . . . a few extra guests in the home."

"Really? I didn't see anyone but your father."

"Let me tell you about it." Within a quarter hour, Grace had explained about Robert and the children and how she'd convinced him to bring the children to her farm temporarily. Then she sat back, feeling tired from the telling of it all.

"Whew! Grace, that's quite a lot for you to take on, considering your dad and running the farm."

"True, but it's only for a while, and you know how I've always wanted children."

Ginny's face paled, and she stared past Grace and out the window.

"Ginny, what's wrong?"

"That's just it. Nothing's wrong, but knowing that you wanted children makes this all the harder for me to tell you." She gazed back at Grace.

"Me? What are you talking about? Are you—?"

Ginny's head bobbed up and down. "Yes, yes I am!"

They both burst out with laughter, and Grace squealed

with delight, clasping Ginny's hands with her own. "Oh, my dear friend, that's so wonderful! And I'm extremely happy for you and Frank. I mean that."

"Thank you. I was worried that you'd be upset."

"Heavens! Never with you, Ginny. Do I wish I had children? Yes, I do, but that doesn't diminish my happiness for you and Frank."

Tears sprang into her friend's eyes and Grace handed her a handkerchief.

Ginny sniffed into it. "It must be the pregnancy making me cry at the least little thing."

Grace giggled. "I've heard that can happen. But let's talk about a baby shower for you. Oh, and did you hear that Matilda is going to have a baby as well?"

Ginny clapped her hands. "That's wonderful news. No, I hadn't heard. I'm afraid that I've been a little distracted," she said with a smile.

"Perfectly understandable, my friend. Are you feeling well? You look wonderful!" Grace eyed her.

Ginny nodded. "I am. I had a few mornings when I couldn't face breakfast, but that seems to be over for now."

"I'm really very thrilled for you and Frank. How is he taking the news?"

Ginny grinned. "My goodness, he's as proud as can be! And very attentive, as though I'm all of a sudden fragile."

Both of them giggled.

"I would expect as much from him. He's a good man, and you're lucky to have him for your husband."

Ginny looked at her friend's sweet, genuine face. She had prayed that someone would come into Grace's life again. A wonderful person like Grace deserved love and happiness, because she had so much to offer.

A call from Owen interrupted their schoolgirl chatting, and Grace excused herself to go check on him.

Grace returned a moment later, Owen on her arm, and Ginny smiled when she saw him. "My, but it's good to see you up and walking. I heard you were in town for a change of scenery." She rose and walked over to give him a peck on the cheek. Upon closer inspection she noticed his eyes were brighter than the last time she saw him, and the dark circles had all but disappeared.

He gave her a brief hug. "It's always good to see you. I think I've improved a little, thanks to my daughter and Robert, but I can't walk as fast as I used to."

"Robert?" Ginny glanced at Grace. "You mean the hired hand?"

Grace flushed and answered, "Yes. He has great patience with Pop." She guided Owen to a chair and he sat down.

"Grace tells me that you have good news. I'm happy for you, Ginny. There's nothing like having a child."

"Thank you. We're very excited, and I want you two involved in the baby's life as much as possible." Ginny could feel her eyes misting over. Her emotions seemed to be all over the place, and when she looked at Owen, she was reminded her baby wouldn't have a grandfather or grandmother.

"We'd be honored," Owen replied. "Wouldn't we, Grace?"

"You know that we would. Why don't I make us some more tea?"

There was a small feeling of unsettledness in her tummy, so she said, "Tea would suit me well, thank you."

"I'll be back in a few minutes. You rest right there and chat with Pop." Grace scooted out of the room.

"Owen, do you mind if I ask you something?" Ginny whispered.

"Of course not. Ask away." He leaned forward to hear.

"Has Ginny said anything to you about Warren? Do you think she's interested in him?"

"She's not said much at all, other than he's taking her to dinner on Saturday. Why?"

"Just wondering. Frank seems to like him a lot, but I'm not around him much. I only want my friend to find happiness—with the right person. I'm worried about her."

Owen lightly chuckled. "Grace can take care of herself. She's a strong woman." He sat back in his chair.

"You're right, I'm sure, and I'll bet we both want the same thing for her."

"I know exactly what you're thinking, Ginny. I'm a burden for her, by no fault of my own, but she needs to be reminded that I don't want to be the center of her life. I want her to feel free to leave the house or go be with other ladies and hopefully find love. I'm worried she'll have even more to do now with Robert's children."

"Then we are in agreement." She smiled at the old man. "She has such a generous spirit that she forgets to take care of herself."

Owen leaned forward again and said under his breath, "To tell the truth, I've noticed that she seems different whenever Robert is around—happier somehow."

"Really? Well, that could be because she has a strong man to help out now."

Owen shook his head. "I don't think so."

Grace entered with a tray, so Ginny motioned to him with her eyes that the subject was closed for now. It'd be nice for Grace to have two men courting her, Ginny thought. She turned her attention to the tea Grace was pouring and changed the subject.

Ginny was about to leave when Robert walked up to the house, bare arms exposed and tanned, shirt opened at the throat. Ginny watched Grace's expression change to a splendid warmth and her eyes became soft when he said hello. Was there something between them? *Well, I'll be! My suggestion he apply for the job may have amounted to a whole lot more.*

"Nice to see you again, ma'am," he said with a tilt of his hat, and to Grace, "I don't mean to interrupt." He propped his leg on the step and leaned on it.

Grace flashed him a wide smile that made Ginny think, *Uh-huh . . . I knew it!*

"Hello, Robert. You're not interrupting, since I was about to take my leave." Ginny started for her carriage, and Robert stepped quickly to her side.

"Here, let me help," he said, and she allowed him to assist her to her seat in the carriage.

"Your manners are a plus for you. Coming from the South, I can tell you that women want to be considered strong but love chivalry at its best from a gentleman," Ginny commented, pouring on her Southern drawl a little thicker for emphasis.

Grace giggled. "Ginny, sometimes you're so funny."

Robert stood back with his hands on his hips. "I'll take that as a nice compliment coming from a Southern belle then," he answered seriously but void of a smile.

Dear me, it's hard to penetrate his protective shield. "Well, I must be going now. Hope to see you in town soon."

Grace waved goodbye as Ginny hurried down the lane. She turned to ask Robert about buying the children a set of clothes. If she could only drag her eyes away from his muscular, tanned arms . . .

"Robert, was there something you came to speak to me about?"

"I only wanted to let you know that I'll be up on your roof for a little while. I saw a few shingles that need nailing down until I can buy some replacements." He turned and pointed up at the roof over the kitchen, and as she moved back around to look up to see, her side brushed his shoulder.

He moved away as though she'd bit him and gazed at her through cool, gunmetal-gray eyes. "I hope that my pounding on the roof won't be a problem for you or your pop. I know he likes to take afternoon naps."

He has the most intriguing eyes, but he acts like I'm a threat instead of a friend. She centered her thoughts and replied, "Don't worry about him. Pop can sleep through most anything."

"That's all I need to hear." He started to walk away, but her hand on his arm held him.

"Robert, I was wondering . . . Would you mind if I bought the children a change of clothing? I realize that school will be over soon, but they really need clothes that fit. Don't you agree?"

He seemed surprised as he considered her offer, rubbing

his chin with his thumb. "Okay, but only if you take it out of my pay. I don't take charity," he said firmly.

"I understand, but I could give the children a few chores after school to do as payment. What do you think of that idea?"

He chuckled softly. "If you can get much out of them, then have at it. But remember, I warned you."

"Perfect!" She lifted her skirts and hurried up the stairs. She wanted to write up a list of items they could help with. At the top of the steps, she stopped and turned to him. "Would you object to me taking them to town for shopping?"

"My goodness, when you get an idea, you really get fired up, don't you?" He shrugged. "Sure, it's okay with me."

"I'll talk to them after school, then." Grace was excited to be able to do something for the children, and she couldn't wait to get started.

17

With the sun's rays warming his back, Robert had a great view from the top of the roof. Since he was already up here, he'd decided to check out the back part of the roof that wasn't clearly visible from the ground and found many places wanting. He hoped a new roof was in Grace's budget. Now he wished he hadn't told her to go ahead and buy those new clothes. Better to get down and give her the bad news before she did anything.

He carefully climbed back over the rooftop toward the front of the house, and hearing voices below, he realized he was already too late with his advice. In her apparent eagerness, she was waiting for the children when they returned, and the animation in their voices told him she'd already given them the news.

He heard Tom say something about needing shoes more than he needed pants before pulling up his leg to expose the holes in the bottom of his shoe. Grace gasped and he heard her confirm that Tom was right, then they all followed her inside, where she most likely had some sort of cookie waiting for them.

Grace acted like they were *her* children, and that baffled him. Why in the world would she care about them? He didn't get it. It was almost as if she'd decided they were her charges instead of his. *Be grateful in all things*, he heard from a voice in his head. *I am, Lord, I am*. He wasn't used to such kindness and it felt nice. He also liked the way she'd looked at him earlier with her honey-brown eyes. *Stop it and get back to work before you land in trouble*, he told himself.

He reached for his hammer and nails from his leather work apron and started repairing the roof. Once he paused to enjoy the cooling wind against his face and watched an eagle soar. He'd much rather be the eagle—free, with no responsibilities, riding a tailwind that blew over the Gallatin Range.

There were times at night he asked God where his future was going. Since Ada's death, he'd lost perspective. There was no one to build a life with. He admitted that even though she'd deceived him, he still missed Ada and reckoned he would always have a place in his heart for her.

Maybe he should consider moving on after the potato crop was in. No woman was going to want to marry a man with a ready-made family. Especially when the kids weren't babies. Most young women wanted children of their own flesh and blood. *Might as well face the facts, Robert, you're not young yourself anymore.*

It wasn't long before Becky came out and called him in to supper. He needed to let go of his foolish notions of ever finding happiness. Besides, the smell of supper was at least something he could look forward to. He started down the ladder to go wash up.

The spring weather couldn't have been more perfect the Saturday Grace took the children to town. Owen decided he'd go along too, and Tom offered to help him getting in and out of the wagon. She left the farm in the capable hands of Robert, who admitted he hated shopping and trusted Grace to do the buying.

While Eli fitted Tom with a good sturdy pair of boots, Grace and the girls wandered over to the ready-made frocks looking for something to fit them. Once, when she glanced back to Eli and Tom, their heads were down and they were speaking in whispers.

Sarah found a simple dress with tiny blue flowers. "What about this one, Miss Grace?"

Grace held the dress up to Sarah's shoulders. "I think it will work nicely, especially because it will complement your pretty blue eyes," she confirmed. Sarah's sweet smile was thanks enough for Grace as she watched her staring at the dress.

"I think we should also look for some new underwear," Grace suggested.

Becky looked at her with a furrowed brow. "Are you sure you can afford that? Robert, I mean our papa, said until the potato crop comes in you might be having a hard time making a go of it like us."

"Did he now? Don't you worry about that, Becky. I wouldn't have brought you shopping if I couldn't pay for it. I believe we'll have a good crop this year because of your papa's help."

Becky paused from looking through the clothes and peered shyly at Grace. "You like him, don't you?"

Grace felt her face go pink. "Of course I do. He's a hard

worker and has taken a huge load off me," she answered, then went back to picking through the ready-made frocks. *Whatever possessed that child to say that?*

"I don't mean like that." Becky said nothing more, and Grace was glad that she let the subject drop.

Owen shuffled slowly around the large mercantile, checking out the saddles and tack. He had a hankering to go riding. Must be typical spring fever. He'd been avoiding the back of a horse because he was worried about his balance lately. Every so often, he would have sharp, stabbing pains in his hips, but he refrained from telling Grace. She had enough on her mind, especially having three children in the house. Maybe it was time for him to see the doctor again.

He made his way through the store out to the sidewalk, but he hadn't gone far before he was shaky. Plopping down on a bench, he watched the town traffic. Directly across the street in his view was the bank, and he watched a woman walk out with a few other patrons. Was that Stella? Hard to say beneath the leather cowboy hat. It looked like her—she had no visible femininity in her manner of walking, which was a stride full of strong purpose. A book was tucked under her arm and spectacles framed her face. He wished she'd decide to come his way. Suddenly, she did, almost like an afterthought. She crossed the street, making her way in his direction. Had she seen him? *Don't be silly!* Even if she had, she wouldn't be crossing to talk to him.

Owen sat up straighter, just in case she walked by. She stepped over deep ruts in the street and came near. He pulled himself up and greeted her with a tip of his hat. "Excuse me. I saw you the last time I was in town." Owen saw her stiffen and draw back, shoving her spectacles back up her thin nose to give him a strange look.

"Excuse me." She started to move past.

Where he got the nerve, he couldn't say, but he heard himself speaking again. "Eli told me your name was Stella. I'm Owen Miller. I thought I'd just introduce myself to you."

She stood perfectly straight and prim, gazing at him from behind her spectacles with keen eyes. "I hardly know why, but Eli's a good man and I know he wouldn't have told you about me unless he trusted you. Well, nice to meet you. Good day."

"Stella," he said, "how about a cup of coffee before you finish your errands?" He was close enough to consider her green eyes behind her spectacles. For all her standoffish attitude, he found warmth there.

"Well, I'm not sure. I don't know you—"

"You said you trusted Eli's judgment. That must mean something—and I'm harmless enough over a cup of coffee." He flashed her a broad smile, hoping to soften her. He even surprised himself. Maybe he was lonelier than he thought.

She stared openly at him. "My, but you are persistent, aren't you? I suppose one cup would be harmless." She looked down at his hand holding on to the chair's arm. "Is the Timberline Café too far for you to walk?"

He quickly pulled his hand off the chair. She didn't miss much. "It's only a couple doors down, so I believe I can make it."

To his surprise, she offered her arm after moving her book to her other side, and he took it. They quietly moved between the Saturday shoppers to make their way to the café.

Fortunately, there was one table for two left close to the window, which Owen preferred in case his daughter came looking for him. He pulled out a chair for Stella and noticed as she took her seat that she laid her book on the table and placed her spectacles on top, which he thought was odd. Perhaps she didn't need them all the time but only for reading—but that made no sense, because she wore them while walking. He sat down carefully and smiled across the table at her.

"We are here for a quick cup of coffee and perhaps a slice of pie," Owen told the waitress. It was too early for lunch, and he intended to save that time for Grace and the children. "That okay with you, Stella?"

She turned to the waitress. "Please bring me a cup of your best hot tea."

The waitress giggled. "Ma'am, we've only got one kind and it is the best!"

Owen nearly laughed until he caught the abashed look on Stella's face. He suddenly felt sorry for her.

"That will do," Stella answered. "And a bit of lemon."

Owen gave her a level stare. "I thought everyone drank coffee. My mistake."

"I like coffee okay, but I prefer hot tea. I guess the habit came as a result of my father and mother. She always made delicious hot tea served in pretty china cups."

"How nice for you."

Stella leaned forward a bit to ask, "I know you didn't ask me for a cup of coffee only. So what was your reason?"

Owen chuckled. "Reason? I merely want to get to know you after seeing you in the mercantile. I've never seen you here before. To be truthful, I'm a widower living with my daughter at Bidwell Farms. What about you?"

She fingered the gold watch fob on her blouse. "I . . . The truth is, running the boardinghouse keeps me so busy seeing to the needs of others that I rarely have a lot of free time. When I do, I enjoy my books, my cats, and long walks."

"I see. So do you enjoy being around people who come and go at the boardinghouse?"

"Yes. But I have to admit that my pets and books are far superior to some of the folks who rent a room from me," she said, laughing. "Oh, don't look so serious. I was only joking."

He laughed then. "Thank goodness. I was beginning to think you were from royalty." He decided he liked her green eyes with lines around them when she smiled. Her skin told him that she hadn't protected her face from the elements like most women, so it was hard to judge her age. He thought it might be close to his own.

She squirmed in her chair. "Tell me about yourself."

"Not a lot to tell. My wife, Margaret, died a long time ago, so I came to live with my daughter, Grace. She was married to a potato farmer who died three years ago. Then my health became an issue, and the doctor thinks I may have had a stroke. It's affected my legs somewhat."

"I'm sorry. Health is more valuable than wealth in my opinion, especially now that I'm older."

The tea and coffee were served, and Owen watched as she added a squeeze of lemon and a teaspoon of sugar. There was no mark on her otherwise tan hands where a wedding band would have been.

"If you don't mind me asking, are you a widow?"

She gave a small laugh. "No. I've never married. Never felt the need to."

"What about having a friendship? I'm in need of company other than my daughter occasionally."

Stella tilted her head, openly sizing him up. "What makes

you think I need any companionship?" she asked with a twinkle in her eye.

He felt his shoulder muscles relax. "Maybe a lucky guess, but seeing as you and I are close in age. I thought maybe . . ."

Their eyes locked above the rims of their cups, and they burst out laughing together.

The two of them continued talking about their interests, the weather, and things going on in town. Then Stella sipped her tea and Owen enjoyed his strong cup of coffee in amicable silence while they watched passersby going to and fro on the Saturday afternoon.

Finally, she looked at her watch fob. "I must be going now. It was quite the morning getting to know you. Perhaps we could do this again, and if there's no pie, I make tasty donuts," she said, retrieving her book and glasses.

Owen pushed his chair back. She'd said *perhaps* as though there would be another time, and he suddenly felt joyful—a feeling he hadn't experienced in a long time. "I would look forward to that, Stella. I need to get back before Grace sends the sheriff after me."

Without mentioning it, she placed her arm to offer him support as they strolled outside. Owen felt almost giddy.

18

By the time they'd wrapped up their shopping with much laughter and chatter, Grace felt she'd known the children a long time. Sarah complained of hunger pains, which was no surprise since the shopping had taken a while.

"Let's find my pop and scurry on down to the café for lunch before we head back home. I think you children deserve it for humoring me with the shopping."

"I don't see him, Mrs. Bidwell," Tom said.

"I saw him go outside a while ago," Becky mentioned.

"Maybe he wanted some fresh air. He loves watching the Saturday crowd in the streets. We'll find him," Grace said confidently.

They gathered up their purchases but hadn't gone far when they noticed Pop walking toward them with a woman. Grace was surprised. A timid look splattered across Owen's face when he noticed Grace, as if he'd been caught stealing one of her hot biscuits before supper was on the table.

They stopped in the middle of the sidewalk. "Pop, we were just looking for you."

"Well, here I am, then," he stammered. "Uh . . . this is Stella Whitfield. We were sharing stories over a cup of coffee while you shopped. Stella, this is my daughter, Grace, and her newly acquired charges."

Grace was mystified. Where had he met this woman? Why was Stella holding her father's arm? "Hello, Mrs. Whitfield."

Stella nodded to the children with a tiny smile, her hat brim bobbing. "It's *Miss* Whitfield," she emphasized without blinking an eye. "But please call me Stella."

The children murmured a greeting and it was obvious they wanted to hurry along. Sarah and Tom were poking each other, and Becky was staring across the street at another young girl who had caught her eye.

"All right. I will, but you must call me Grace." She turned to her father. "I thought I'd take us all to lunch at the Timberline today."

Stella started to move away. "If you'll excuse me, I must get home and back to my novel. I can't wait to see how the story ends."

"Please stay and dine with us," Grace offered out of politeness, and her pop said, "Yes, why don't you?"

Stella took two more steps, backing away. "No, thank you, though I appreciate the invitation."

"Then perhaps you can come to the farm for lunch some time." Owen shoved his hands in his pockets.

In spite of herself, Grace heard herself agreeing with him. "Yes, anytime."

"Goodbye, children." Stella beamed down at them.

"I hope to see you around soon," Owen said.

"Me too. Bye now." With a curt nod and her determined way of walking, she darted off.

Immediately, Grace looked at her father. "You've never mentioned Stella, Pop." Grace knew she must sound annoyed, so she tried to speak low enough so the children walking behind them couldn't hear.

"There's not much to tell. I just met her on the street today."

"Pop! You can't be serious," Grace sputtered as she stopped at the door of the café.

He screwed his mouth to one side, then finally said, "Close to it. I first saw her in the mercantile when I came in with Robert for the chicken coop supplies. Eli told me who she was."

"Can we please eat now? I'm starving," Sarah pleaded, tugging on Grace's skirt.

"Yes, yes of course. Let's go inside." Tom, Becky, and Sarah filed past her, and Grace paused, looking at her father again. "I want to know more about Stella when we get home."

Owen chuckled. "Don't fret, daughter—you're not responsible for me entirely."

Robert shoved his hat back, wiping his brow with his large handkerchief. He glanced again up the road from where he was working on the fence railing for the third time. Grace had only been gone about three hours, but it seemed like all day. He was used to having her come to wherever he was working and either give him advice about the chore at hand—which he didn't need—or spend her time with mindless chatter. But for some reason, he was missing that today.

It was hard to believe how quickly the children had taken to her and her to them. Almost like they belonged to her. She was what they needed—a motherly influence. While he should be grateful, he was concerned that the kids would get too used to her and then he'd be leaving. Lately, he'd given leaving a lot of thought. He wouldn't leave right away, but after the potato crop was in and to the market. He couldn't stay here forever, and from the looks of the visit from that businessman who was courting her, he wouldn't be needed here at all in the very near future.

Then why was Grace always in his thoughts when she wasn't around? Hadn't he been burned by Ada? Though he'd fallen head over heels in love with her, in his heart, he thought she'd used him—knowing she was dying and needing to find someone to take her children. He'd been duped. Just like that. *Women! Can't trust them.*

He muttered under his breath, and because he wasn't watching what he was doing, he cut his hand on a nail that he was pulling off the fence. Yanking his handkerchief from his back pocket, he mopped away at the blood dripping down his hand. He heard the children's voices before they appeared up the lane, so he quickly wrapped his hand tightly and hid it from view.

Grace stopped the wagon before driving past him to the house. "Did you miss us?" she cheerfully called out to him.

I certainly did! But Robert didn't say it. "I've been too busy to notice your absence."

His remark didn't seem to faze her. "Why don't you take a break and we'll show you our purchases?"

"Me and Becky are gonna look so pretty on Monday!" Sarah said in excitement.

"All right, if you insist." Robert laid aside his hammer.

Owen motioned for him to hop into the wagon. "May as well ride rather than walk."

"If you insist," Robert replied again. He reached up to grab the side of the wagon but forgot his injured hand and winced in pain.

"Son, what's wrong?" Owen eyed him, while Grace's head jerked around to see him step into the back of the wagon to sit with the children.

Robert shook his head. "Only a minor cut. It's nothing to worry about."

When they arrived at the house, everyone piled out of the wagon, and Tom assisted Owen to the front porch while Robert reached up and took Grace's hands. She alighted in one swift motion, his hands holding her in his steady grasp. Her hair held the scent of fresh lilacs, and he found himself wanting to reach up and touch her honey-colored tresses. Instead, he took a step back.

Her eyes held his and in them he found warmth and concern.

"Are you certain your hand is okay? Do you want me to take a look at it?" she asked.

He suddenly had a hard time breathing and realized he was holding his breath. "I'm sure it's okay. I nicked it on a nail while repairing the fence. That's all."

The children were eager to show him what Grace had purchased and interrupted, all trying to show him their new things at once.

"Look at my new boots. I had to put them on since Miss Grace made me throw my old ones out." Tom grinned and stuck his foot out in front so Robert could admire them. He was standing up taller than before and clutched a brown parcel in his hands.

"Very nice, Tom." Robert looked down at his brogans. *My,*

the boy's feet have grown. Why haven't I noticed? "Looks like some sturdy boots that will last a while." Robert eyed the package. "What's that under your arm?"

"It's new pants and a shirt. Miss Grace picked them out. Want me to open it up to show you?"

"No need. I'm sure they're nice, and when you get a bath, you can put those on." Robert looked over at Becky and Sarah, who were eager to show him their new dresses next. While he watched them take their dresses out of the brown paper wrapping, he realized that they were nothing more than little children, happy to have something new to wear and to have Grace and Owen looking on them fondly. It occurred to him that they'd all been lonely since they'd lost Ada. He'd been so busy thinking only of how Ada had deceived him, and taking it out on the children who were basically floundering as they coped with the loss of their mother. He suddenly felt like a huge disappointment to the children . . . *his* children.

Sarah tugged on his sleeve. "Aren't they pretty, Papa?"

Robert came back to the present. "Yes, sweet Sarah. Both you and Becky have chosen pretty dresses. Since I know nothing of that sort of shopping, I'm glad Grace took you under her wing. I hope there will be more dresses in the near future."

Owen cleared his throat, and Robert thought he saw tears in Grace's eyes. "Why don't we all go have a glass of cold milk? I bet you Grace has something sweet to go with it." He motioned from his chair on the porch.

Grace piped up, "We could have the sugar cookies I saved if you haven't already discovered them, Pop."

Owen looked sheepishly at his daughter, and Robert

wanted to laugh. "I found them all right, but I only took one. Honest."

They all laughed and trooped inside for refreshments, and Robert felt at home for the first time in a long while. His day was ending on a positive note, but he still needed to tell Grace she'd need a new roof soon.

19

Grace stood before the cheval mirror with the girls looking on, admiring the dress she'd donned for her dinner date with Warren. She'd decided on one of the dresses that she normally wore to church, a frock of simple linen-colored broadcloth trimmed with black buttons on the matching bolero jacket. Although it wasn't new, it had a certain fetching look for spring.

"You are very beautiful," Becky cooed, and Sarah bobbed her head happily and said, "Yes. Almost as pretty as mama."

Grace twirled around to gaze at their sweet faces. "I take that as a very high compliment coming from you two."

"What's *com-pli-ment* mean?" Sarah asked.

"It means you've given me your personal very high approval if you've compared me to your mother." Grace smiled down at Sarah's serious face. "I couldn't ask for more."

"Oh, I hope that Mr. Warren knows how pretty and sweet you are," Sarah commented seriously.

"We'll have to see about that. I think I'd better go downstairs. He'll be here any moment. Thank you for helping me to decide on something to wear tonight, girls," Grace said as she walked to the door. "Good night, dears," she called over her shoulder.

She heard Becky say quietly to her sister, "I wish she were going with Papa instead."

Whatever gave Becky the notion Robert would want that? *Well, they'd better not get their hopes up.* It was quite clear that Robert was keeping his distance when it came to her.

When Grace got to the bottom of the stairs, Robert was just coming through the front door, but when he saw her, he paused with one hand on the doorknob and the other one on his hip. "My, but you look nice." His jaw twitched and he said, "I'm here to play chess with your father."

She walked over to him. "Thank you, Robert." His eyes briefly swept over her, then he moved to close the door.

"I think Warren is driving up now."

"Well, at least he's on time," she said, reaching for her wrap that hung by the door. "I'm glad you are willing to sit a while with my pop while I'm out. The girls are upstairs. I'm not sure where Tom is."

"He's around somewhere." Robert shifted from one boot heel to the other. "I appreciate the early supper you made for us. Your kindness is proving to lift the kids' mood somehow, and I'm grateful." He chuckled, and his eyes shone with pleasure.

"Do you think so?" Grace looked directly into his eyes, excited that he was smiling after mentioning the kids. It was one of the few times he'd smiled at her, and if she was responsible for the comment, then she was more than thrilled. She wanted to help the children in any way she could.

"I wouldn't say it if I didn't mean it." His deep-gray eyes

focused on hers briefly. Then he reached out, and she thought he was going to touch her arm, but instead he took the wrap from her to gently cover her shoulders while her insides quivered. She drew herself up with reproof. How foolish she was thinking he would intentionally touch her, and she was glad that he couldn't know her thoughts.

Warren parked the carriage and walked up the steps, looking spiffy and smelling of cologne. Robert excused himself to the parlor.

"Are you ready, Grace?" he asked as he stepped inside. "You seem eager—you are waiting by the door." He was smiling, but his eyes weren't reflecting joy.

Grace bristled at the way he greeted her. She'd taken the time to look her best, and that's all he could say? She thought back to Robert's admiring look. Was the handsome Warren used to receiving plenty of attention from the ladies? If so, he was courting the wrong person.

"I'm sorry if you thought that, but I was chatting with Robert, my hired man. He's come to play chess with my father."

Warren waved his hand. "Oh, that's good." Then he quickly added, "We must be going. I've made a reservation for us."

"I'm sure my father would like to meet you."

"Oh? I suppose we have a few minutes to spare." Though he'd acquiesced, Grace could tell he didn't like interruptions in his plans.

She closed the front door and walked him to the parlor where her father and Robert sat hunched over a chessboard. They looked up as she walked in.

"Pop, and Robert, I'd like both of you to meet Warren Sullivan."

Owen said, "Hello there. Mighty fine to meet you, Warren. Forgive me if I don't stand."

"Hello." Robert stood, offering his handshake.

Warren took the extended hand. "Glad to meet you."

"Grace says you are working with Frank as his partner." Owen leaned back in his chair and scrutinized him.

"Yes, sir, I'm working with him, but we aren't formally in partnership as of now. It's best to see how things go first between us."

Owen scratched his beard. "I see. Frank's a good, solid man. You can't go wrong partnering with him."

"I'll keep that in mind," Warren replied, glancing over to Robert. "I'm glad to hear you're working for Grace because I intend to get her out more. A pretty woman like her needn't be locked away all the time."

Robert agreed, and Grace noticed his intense stare at Warren. "True, but I believe Grace can do as she pleases and I see no rope around her neck."

Warren laughed heartily. "Touché. Nevertheless, I'm sure she feels an obligation to keep the farm from going under." He turned toward her and extended his hand. "Shall we go have that dinner, now?"

Why did he mention the farm going under? Had Frank spoken to him about it? It really wasn't any of his concern. Grace looked at Robert before taking Warren's arm. "I don't need defending, but thank you all the same."

He gave her a genuine smile and said, "Enjoy your night out."

Warren and Grace were on their way out when Tom clambered up the front steps and murmured hello. He paused a moment to look again at Warren, but said nothing else and went on inside.

❧

"Checkmate," Owen said just as Tom burst into the room. "Hi, Tom. I just beat your papa at chess."

Robert grinned. "Pure luck."

"I've seen that man before," Tom remarked.

"Who are you talking about?" Owen asked.

"The man leaving outside with Miss Grace."

Now Robert was interested. "Now where would that be, Tom?"

"Uh . . . on the road to town after work . . . I mean after school one day." Tom chewed his bottom lip.

"Work? You mean the work at school?"

"Never mind. Just thought I'd seen him before." Tom suddenly grew calmer and Robert suspected he might be hiding something.

Becky and Sarah waltzed in. "You didn't see him after school because you haven't been going to school," Becky blurted out.

Robert stood, hands on his hips. "What are you saying, Becky?"

Becky's lip trembled and Tom glared at her. "Shut up, smarty-pants!"

"What are you not telling me?" Robert looked from Becky to Tom.

"Just what Becky said," Sarah added. She went to lean against Owen's shoulder, and he slipped his arm about her, not commenting.

Tom shrugged his shoulder and gave Robert a defiant stare. "I don't need schoolin', and we need the money, so I got a job working for Eli at the general store."

Robert took a deep breath to control his anger. He didn't want to say something he might regret. "Becky and Sarah, I think it's time you got ready for bed," he ordered firmly.

Becky cast a glance at Tom, and when he nodded his agreement, the two girls scurried out of the room and up the stairs.

"Tom, why have you been lying to me and skipping school?" Robert demanded. "As long as you're in my custody, then you have to abide by my rules."

"I figured that I'd be thirteen soon and can earn my own way. I wasn't planning on staying with you."

"Do you want me to leave so you two can talk privately?" Owen asked.

"No, Owen. You're fine right where you are."

"Tom, where do you think you'd go?" Robert watched Tom's face for clues. Was he still angry? Would he really leave his sisters behind?

"I haven't thought about it."

"I thought we had an understanding. I'm doing the best that I can to provide for you and the girls."

"I reckon you are, but you'll never be my father," Tom retorted.

"And I don't want to take his place, but maybe sometime you can tell me more about him."

"I never met him—" Tom's expression was sullen and he looked away, avoiding Robert's eyes.

Robert's heart began softening. No father? *Shame on me for never asking.* "Tom, I'm asking you agreeably to go back to school because you're my charge until you're old enough to make decisions on your own. Do you understand?"

"Yes, sir," he mumbled.

"Who else knows besides your sisters?"

"Only Eli and the teacher. Can I go now?" Tom fidgeted with a piece of carving wood that he still held in his hand.

"As long as we understand each other and come Monday morning you're back in school where you belong. Is that understood?"

Tom nodded. "All right," he said, finally giving in. "I understand."

"Trust me a little while longer and everything is going to work out," Robert assured him.

But would it?

20

Throughout supper at the Stafford Hotel, Grace discovered that Warren was a voracious talker, and she was amused that much of his conversation centered on himself. She barely got a chance to speak unless he asked her a direct question, but that was all right with her since it gave her a chance to get to know him better. One thing about him, he was energetic and entertaining. He made her laugh a lot.

"My family is back East, but once I received my law degree, I was ready for adventure, and what better place to explore than the West? I'm so glad that I did now that I've met you." He rested his brown eyes on hers with open admiration. "I'm glad that you decided to get away from the farm for a night out. It must be very difficult taking care of your father without help."

Grace dabbed her mouth with her napkin. "I manage. He's not totally helpless, and Robert has recently been a very big help to me in keeping the farm going." At the mention of Robert's name, Warren visibly stiffened.

"You know you could sell the farm now and live in town and be free of worry."

"That may be so, but what would I do to occupy my time?" she replied.

"I would assume a husband and children would keep you busy." He gave her a boyish grin.

"I'd have to *have* a husband for that to happen, and if I did, I'd be just as happy being outdoors in my garden and walking the land. There's peace that only living on the land can afford," Grace explained, which was true.

"Oh, I'd see to it that you'd have lots to do. There's travel, community projects, caring for the house, or volunteering—but I'm not too fond of children."

She laughed. "But you're not my husband, and I'm simply more suited to living in the country. I long for children. I'm not accustomed to the lifestyle you speak about."

"You could be . . . and I might be just the man to change your mind, if given a chance."

"I would never leave my father alone."

"He wouldn't have to be alone. You could hire someone to keep him company."

"Mmm . . . You have it all worked out, don't you? Are you proposing?" She stared directly at him over the rim of her coffee cup.

He roared with laughter. "Not yet, but I was giving you options to think about. You needn't pine away forever." He leaned forward across the table and took her hand, his dark eyes appearing even darker. "Besides, I see loneliness in your eyes. I'd like to help you with that."

"I'm not sure what you mean."

"Surely you don't deny that you're lonely. I believe you have a lot to offer a man and you're pleasant to be around."

She stammered. "I'm not denying the fact that I do get

136

lonely from time to time, but presently that has changed, at least for the time being. I have three children under my roof until Robert can get them settled."

"And what does he give you in return for that?"

She withdrew her hand from his. "Are you insinuating—"

"Now, don't get all riled up. I know kids can be a handful. But Robert may be expecting more of your generosity."

Her coffee cup rattled as she set it down, much like her mind did. "I don't believe I like the way this conversation is going, so if you don't mind, we need to change the subject."

"I'm sorry, Grace. I didn't mean anything by it. Truly. Now that we're through eating, why don't we go enjoy a beautiful evening ride?" Warren said, pushing back his chair.

"That might be best, but don't you need to pay the bill first?"

He smiled as he took her wrap and laid it across her shoulders with a gentle touch. "I took care of that in advance." He had a way of making her feel pretty, feminine, and special—looked after. She had to admit, she craved the touch of a man, but she needed to go slow.

As they were leaving, they ran into Frank and Ginny making their way to a table.

"Grace, it's nice to run into you," Frank said. Then, indicating Warren and chuckling, he added, "Him, I see almost every day."

"Hello," Grace said, then briefly hugged Ginny. "Are you here for supper? Ours was delicious."

Ginny looked a little peaked. "Yes, a bit later than we normally go out. I had a little tummy trouble earlier but now I'm ravenous!" She laughed.

"You're eating for two, so I'm not surprised."

"If you'll excuse us, Grace and I were about to leave while we still have time to enjoy this nice evening weather we're having." Warren gently nudged Grace.

"By all means, we don't want to hold you two up." Frank moved aside for them to pass. "We'll talk later, Warren."

"Enjoy!" Ginny called. "Perhaps I'll see you at church if I'm up to it, Grace."

"I hope you will. Bye now." Grace allowed Warren to place his hand at her back, guiding her through the tables. The pressure of his hand felt strange. She hadn't been touched in a long while, and it was comforting.

When they arrived back at her house, the earlier conversation was forgotten and she'd enjoyed his funny tales of growing up with two sisters. He never again mentioned anything disconcerting, so she thought it must have been her imagination. She could see by the lantern's light on the porch that her father and Robert were sitting on the front porch.

"I see Robert is waiting around for you to return. I don't think he trusts me," Warren complained.

Grace giggled. "Don't flatter yourself. I'm sure he hasn't given much thought to you. He and my Pop like to sit and chat after a long day."

"Are you telling me he lives here with you?" He frowned.

"He sleeps in the barn with his son for now. He wouldn't hear of staying in my house."

"I see. Very discreet of him, I'm sure. Then I guess I'll say good night to you in front of an audience."

She took his hand and he assisted her out of the carriage. "That's the proper thing to do." *Heaven forbid! Was he planning on stealing a kiss?*

"Thank you for the lovely company. We'll have to do this

again soon." He took her hand in full view of her father and Robert and leaned down to touch his lips briefly to the back of it.

"Good night, Warren, and thank you for dinner." She withdrew her hand, blushing beneath his penetrating stare, which she could see from the light of the full moon.

He nodded, then got back in the carriage and left. Grace joined her father and Robert on the porch. "Pop, you didn't have to wait up for me."

"I wasn't spying on you, if that's what you think, daughter. Me and Robert were discussing a situation."

"Oh?" she asked, plopping down in a rocker. "I've only been gone a few hours and there was a problem? The children?"

Robert stood up and leaned against the porch railing, crossing his arms. "I'm not good at discipline because I've never had to do it. This parenting is new to me and not an easy thing."

"But what was the problem?" she pressed, pulling her wrap tighter around her against the night's chill. A hoot owl sounded in the distance, reminding her that it was late for all of them.

"Tom has been skipping school and has a job at the mercantile," Robert told her. "Things have been a little strained between us, but I thought we'd worked through all that. Guess I was wrong."

"Don't be too hard on yourself, Robert. Did Sarah and Becky know?" Grace asked.

"Yes, so tomorrow I'll have to have a word with them about keeping his secret." He let his arms drop. "I'm not sure why they would."

"I do. They're trying to take care of each other and you're

not their real father. You can count on it—they'll push you on everything," Owen advised.

"Maybe I can speak to them," Grace commented. "Tom just wants to be valued, and they've had a hard time losing their mother."

"Thanks, but I need to do this. I can't thank you both enough for treating them like part of your family."

"I have a suggestion. Why not see if Eli will keep him on once school is out for summer? That'll give him a little independence—which he's reaching for," Owen said.

"I like that idea, Owen. I'll talk to Eli about it. I just wish he'd told me about Tom working for him." He sighed. "I'd better get to bed now. Good night."

Grace watched him walk in the direction of the barn, shoulders slumped and his head down. She wished there was a way to help him, but they were his children, whether from birth or adoption. She felt sorry for him, but most of all she felt sorry for the children.

When Robert climbed the ladder to the loft, he saw Tom's slim form in the makeshift straw bed. He removed his boots and wondered if Tom was asleep. He doubted it.

"In case you're still awake, Tom, I'm not mad at you, only disappointed. I'm going to ask Eli if you can work for him during the summer, or at least until the potato crop needs harvesting. And you can keep the money you earn."

Tom never answered, but he shifted his body, making the straw crunch. Maybe the idea had at least made him smile.

21

Several days later, Grace stared at her reflection in her bedroom mirror. She was too thin and her muslin nightgown was loose. Too much work and not enough rest the last couple of years. Her wedding band slid down on her finger as proof, and she feared she might lose it. She fingered the thin gold band, deciding she ought to remove it. It had been three years. She'd kept it on mainly as a sweet reminder of Victor and to ward off the men in town when she had no desire at all for another relationship.

Am I ready now? Should she take it off? Was it time to leave the past behind her? She knew she'd never stop loving Victor. Never. Nothing could erase what they'd had together with its sweet memories, but wasn't God about a future and a hope for her life? He'd said so in Jeremiah. She wished she knew what that would be.

She sighed heavily, then slid the wedding band off and placed it in a carved wooden jewelry box her father had made for her as a young girl. Her hand felt naked without it.

It felt freeing to remove it, but at the same time, she felt a little guilty. Would Victor want her to move forward with her life? She would want him to if she had preceded him. Probably he would want the same.

Robert helped Owen out of the wagon, which he'd parked near the mercantile. Earlier he'd asked Owen if he wanted to take a short ride into town with him. Owen had quickly agreed and seemed eager about it.

When they got to the porch in front of the store, Owen said, "I'd like to sit out here while you go speak to Eli about Tom. You don't need me for that."

"It's up to you." Robert led him to one of the rocking chairs and Owen took a seat. "Want me to bring you some of that stuff Eli calls coffee?" He chuckled.

"Naw, I'll pass for now. I'm content to sit here and watch the goings-on."

"This won't take long." Robert strode away, looking for Eli.

Inside the store, Eli was busy with customers, so Robert strolled about the store waiting for a chance to speak to him. He paused, looking through the stack of shirts. Picking up a deep-blue flannel one, he fingered its softness but saw the price tag and put it back. He looked over at the stacks of fabric where two ladies were discussing the different designs. One of them held up a pretty green that would look wonderful on Grace. It was a mighty sweet thing she did, buying the children an outfit when she probably hadn't bought a new dress since her husband died.

Why he was thinking more about Grace lately, he couldn't grasp.

Finally, Eli approached him. "Sorry to keep you waiting,

Robert. It's hard to find good help and I've been a little short-handed."

"No problem, Eli. I wanted to talk to you without an audience if I could."

Eli's heavy brows formed a straight line above his eyes. "Oh. Well, we're alone now. What's on your mind, son? Everything okay at Bidwell Farms?"

Robert waved his hand. "Yes it is. I wanted to talk to you about Tom." Robert watched as the older man took a deep breath and realized what this was about.

"He finally told you?" Eli asked.

"Not exactly, but I won't allow him to skip school, and he knows that now. I wish you had told me."

Eli scratched his beard. "I considered it, but the boy was adamant that I not tell you, and I figured he'd get found out sooner or later. I think I understood the struggle he felt—wanting to grow up, but not quite there. Don't we all feel that at some time? Why didn't the teacher tell you?"

"Good question. I figure a lot of kids his age stay home to work the family farms. I wondered if you might consider letting him work here once school is out—that is, if you're still in need of help around here."

Eli grinned at him. "I might be able to do that, even if I have help by then. I'm busier than ever, and our town is growing faster than I can keep up, it seems. I'm missing a large order that should've been here a week ago—when it does arrive, I'll need a stock boy. After school is out, send him over."

"I appreciate that. I'm trying to do the best I can with him and his sisters, but it's hard."

"Ginny stopped by yesterday and mentioned that Grace had taken you all in."

"Word gets around fast, doesn't it? Yes, Grace has been very generous. The girls live at the house and me and Tom in the barn, but I'm going to move us to the boardinghouse soon."

"I see. Well, I'm happy for Grace. Owen told me she's always wanted children."

"I didn't know that, but I'm not surprised. She's very good with them and can get them to listen to her when I can't."

"Now, don't go getting discouraged. Life's too short for that, son. You let the Lord lead and you'll see that things always work out for the best."

"Ha-ha! I never would have thought that could happen."

"Just goes to show you, no one can really know another's heart." Eli stared into Robert's eyes. "Know what I mean?"

"I'm not sure, but I might have an idea. I'd better be off now. I left Owen outside."

"And he didn't come in to say hello?"

"I have a feelin' he was hoping Stella might be walking around town today. He saw her at church, and I think they have a mutual understanding." Robert chuckled.

When both of them stepped outside, Owen was nowhere to be found. "Perhaps he ran into Stella and they took a walk or something," Robert said, looking up and down the street but seeing no sign of him.

"Could be. It's like I said before—the heart can make one do funny things."

Robert nodded in agreement. "Don't I know it."

Owen wasn't searching for Stella. He'd decided to pay the doctor a brief visit to ease his mind.

Dr. Avery listened to Owen's heart and then stepped back

thoughtfully. "Friend, everything sounds good, and I'm glad to see you walk to my office alone. I'm very surprised." Earlier the doctor had checked Owen's reflexes in his hands and legs but said nothing.

"That's what I wanted to talk to you about. The feeling in my legs comes and goes—sometimes they tingle, sometimes they feel so weak that I can barely stand. Other times my feet feel like they're on fire."

The doctor narrowed his eyes. "How's your energy level been?"

"That's the strange thing, Doc. Sometimes I go for days and I only want to sit and read. Other times I have energy and help Grace with chores, but I don't usually last for too long. Then my back aches a lot and my arms feel weak. Oh, and another thing—I sometimes have deep pains in my thighs."

"Owen, I'm not sure what to think now. Some symptoms you exhibit are signs of stroke, but others are not. Do you mind if I share your condition with a colleague of mine back East?"

Owen's heart sped up. "Am I dying?"

"No, it's nothing like that, but I hate to admit I'm stumped by your illness. It's almost as if it waxes and wanes."

"Yes! That's exactly what I meant to say. I think if I knew what ails me, I'd be better able to deal with it. I don't mind if you talk with your doctor friend. Unless I'm about to have another stroke or heart attack—if you think that's what it is."

Owen watched the doctor take notes on his pad, then look up at him with a serious gaze. "I don't believe that'll happen, but I too would like to understand more of what's happening with your health."

Owen hopped down off the examining table and buttoned his shirt.

Dr. Avery gave him a reassuring smile. "I'd say you're in much better shape than when I last saw you."

"That's what I wanted to hear." Owen stuck his hand out and shook the doctor's hand. "Thank you for seeing me on such short notice."

"Any time at all, and let me know if anything changes."

Owen left and slowly made his way back to the general store. From where he was he could see Robert on the boardwalk, and he waved. Robert waved back and started in his direction. That boy warmed his heart. He was always trying to help him and encourage him to use his legs as often as Owen felt able. Owen was just happy to know that his ol' ticker was as sound as ever. Maybe he'd have a few more years left to explore new possibilities, and that had him smiling when Robert walked up and took his arm.

22

Days slid into weeks, and farm life evolved into a smooth, daily rhythm for Grace. She loved taking care of Robert's children—getting them off to school on time, then anxiously waiting for them to return at the end of the day. Her chores and time, which used to drag, simply flew. Most of all, she realized the void they filled in her life, and she loved the sound of their voices echoing through her home and the country-side. Her spirit felt lighter than it had since Victor's passing.

"You certainly are smiling a whole lot lately," Owen said.

"I am?" Grace answered as she set the table for supper. "I hadn't noticed."

Owen winked at her. "I doubt it has anything to do with Warren, even after you went sightseeing in the countryside and had dinner with him. Let me guess—you enjoy having those kids under our roof."

Grace bent over the table to set out the forks and knives. "Warren seems nice enough, but I don't know him very well yet. I suppose it's true that I'm happier with the children living here. They're so energetic and fun to talk with, and I can't help but notice Tom has taken a special interest in you, Pop."

"You think so? I like the kid too. Want me to call them to come eat now?"

"Yes. Everything is ready. I need to set the platter of ham on the table, and the bread is cool enough for me to slice now."

Moments later, everyone was enjoying a generous portion of baked potatoes and ham and bread dripping with butter. Above the chatter, Robert glanced across the table to engage Grace with a frank look.

Grace took notice and held her fork steady, wondering why he was staring.

The next moment she found out why.

"I wanted to let you know that I have booked me and the children rooms at the boardinghouse on Main Street. We'll be going tomorrow."

Grace's heart stilled and she cast a look at her father, who glanced at her with sympathy. "So soon, Robert? We don't mind having you here. I wish you would reconsider. I know sleeping in the barn is getting old, but don't forget we do have an extra room right here that the two of you can share." She was sure disappointment showed in her face despite her attempt to hide it.

"That's right. You could, Robert. With me living here you needn't worry—you know—that it wouldn't be proper," Owen added.

"Please, Papa, can't we stay?" Becky implored.

Robert turned to look at Becky, who was sitting next to Owen. "Becky, you were dying to get to town, remember?"

Becky grinned and tossed a look at Grace. "That was before I met Miss Grace."

"Yes. She's our angel." Sarah nodded, licking the juice of the ham from her fingers. "We can't leave. They might get lonely."

"Besides, who's going to help them with all the farm chores?" Tom wanted to know.

"I'm sorry, but I have already placed a tidy amount to hold us two rooms. It's money that I can't get back, so I'm afraid we are still going tomorrow. As to chores, I'm certain Grace would love for you to come help out any time you want."

"But Bluebelle will miss me," Sarah whined.

Grace listened to their exchange and sadness flooded over her. Of course she'd known they would leave eventually, but it somehow caught her off guard when he said it would be tomorrow. She had no ties to Robert or his children, and her mind couldn't think of any reason they should stay, but her heart was telling her differently.

She rose, stepping over to Sarah, and slipped her arms about her small shoulders. "You are always welcome in my home anytime." Sarah leaned out of her chair, grabbing on to Grace's waist, and sniffed, blinking back her tears.

Grace turned to Tom and Becky. "That goes for all of you."

Owen cleared his throat. "Why don't we finish our meal while we can enjoy having you here with us?"

Robert nodded. "I'll miss Grace's cooking, even if it was for a short time," he said, flashing her a genuine smile, and the children echoed his appraisal.

Grace felt her cheeks burn and took her seat. "Thank you all for the compliment." She picked at the food on her plate. She had convinced herself that the children had been a gift of God to fill her lonely heart for now. It didn't matter that it had only been a short time. People could form attachments quickly.

Just look at Sarah. Once or twice, Robert caught her eye with a pensive glance, but she wasn't sure what to make of it.

Robert lifted the carpetbags out of the wagon and directed the children to follow. They scrambled down, looking wide-eyed about and watching the crowded street. He knew they hadn't explored any further than the general store, and like all children, they were curious about the new surroundings that would become their home for the time being.

The four entered the foyer of the Whitfield Boarding House, which was not fancy, but homey. Robert tapped the bell on the counter and waited for assistance. From her perch on a nearby chair, a tortoiseshell cat lifted an eyelid, while another yellow tabby waltzed right up to Sarah and Becky, rubbing against their legs with a loud meow.

"Ooh, sweet kitty. Look, Papa, she likes us," Becky squealed.

Robert stared down at the cat as Sarah squatted down to pet it. "It seems that way."

"I'd rather have a dog," Tom commented, drily.

"That's not likely to happen while we live here—"

Heavy footsteps sounded from the hallway and a tall older lady appeared. "I'm sorry to keep you waiting. I was upstairs," she said, a little breathless. "Let me guess—you are Robert. I've met your children." She shoved her glasses farther up her nose. She had a pleasant smile and was soft-spoken.

"Yes, you are correct. I reserved two rooms for a few weeks."

"Yes, of course. I'm glad to have you." She turned her gaze to the girls. "I see you've met KatyKat. The one sleeping is Amelia, but it looks as though KatyKat has taken to both of you."

"I like cats," Sarah said.

"Me too—our mama would never let us have one," Becky said with a sigh.

"I'm glad you do, because these cats enjoy children." Stella turned to Robert. "If you'll sign the register right here"—she indicated a bound notebook with guest signatures—"I'll have you settled in no time. I believe my clerk has already collected your deposit?"

Robert scrawled his name on the ledger, then looked up. "Yes, that's right."

She stretched out her hand to him. "I don't believe I introduced myself. I'm Stella Whitfield."

"I've heard Owen speak of you," he said and noticed a flush to her cheeks.

Stella's handshake was firm, unlike most women he knew, but he wasn't surprised. She was a large-boned woman, almost mannish, but her eyes reflected kindness, especially when she looked down at the children. "Come, children, I'll take you upstairs to your room. We have a dining room where we serve breakfast, lunch, and dinner—which I'm sorry to say, you've missed tonight. Now, tell me all your names."

She chattered on as the girls followed her up the stairs. Robert shrugged at Tom and picked up the bags and followed.

Robert was glad to see the girls were thrilled with their room, which had two single beds and lacy curtains on the windows. Stella impressed him with the way she spoke to them, making them feel comfortable. He looked about the room he shared with Tom and determined the accommodations were adequate. Tom immediately dropped down onto the bed and, without pulling back the covers, released a loud sigh and in only moments was fast asleep. It was no wonder,

Robert thought. They had been on the road before he worked for Grace, and while the girls had shared a bed at Grace's house, he and Tom had slept on a bed of straw. Robert was tempted to crawl into bed, clothes and all, but his boots must come off.

He opened a window partway to get some fresh air, pulled back the bed covers, slipped off everything but his longhandles, and scooted between the covers. It was hard to relax enough to close his eyes, so he lay there listening to the street noise. His mind wandered back to Grace, remembering the sad look on her face when they'd left, and he felt sorry for her. It surprised him that she didn't want them to leave. He thought she'd be glad to be rid of all the extra work, but before they left, Owen had taken him aside.

"Please, let the children come to work with you from time to time. Grace has grown real fond of them," he'd told Robert. Robert noted that Owen hadn't included him in that fondness. *But what did I expect? I made certain that she didn't get too close.* Just as well. He wouldn't be good for her with all his doubts and his ready-made family, because he didn't know if he could trust anyone again. Women could be fickle. Besides, she'd seen Warren twice that he knew of.

Robert had made sure the fertilizer was spread on the potatoes during the week, and now his back was killing him. What he wouldn't give for the tender touch of a woman to rub his sore muscles after a long day of work. Finally, his eyelids grew heavy and he gave in to his fatigue.

Rain beating against the window near his bed woke Robert. He got up and stumbled to look out through sleepy eyes. The rain was steady, making the street a muddy mess with folks going to work and preparing for whatever the day held. The rain was exactly what they needed at the farm.

He glanced over at Tom still fast asleep, and he decided not to disturb him yet since it was Saturday. Grace had told him to go ahead and take his Saturday morning off this time while he got squared away in town with the children.

The smell of coffee brewing assailed his nostrils, so he slipped on his clothes, ran a comb through his hair, and went in search of breakfast.

23

Ginny could hardly keep her eyes open after lunch. Nausea every morning had confined her to the house, which was normal. But she'd recently read that sleepiness also accompanied pregnancy, so instead of fighting it, she gave in, enjoying the rain's pleasant pinging against the porch steps. She'd made a habit of enjoying her wicker chaise lounge on the wide, expansive front porch now that cold weather was behind them. The spring rains would make her flower beds lovely.

Her mind filled with thoughts of how life would be with a baby, and she could hardly wait to hold this little one in her arms. Soon she would consult with Grace on ideas for a nursery.

Grace. It made her sad that the one thing her friend had always desired was a family with children, which brought to mind those three children of Robert's. She wondered how that was working out, and decided to pay Grace a visit soon.

She dozed until she sensed Frank's presence hovering above her. When she opened her eyes, she was greeted by his smiling face—his deep devotion evident. It made her feel warm and feminine. In his hand, he held a fragrant bouquet of flowers.

"Darling, am I disturbing your beauty nap?" Frank teased, and handed her the flowers.

Ginny sat up and held the flowers to her nose, taking a deep breath. "Frank, they're lovely. Is your work over for the day? Aren't you home early?" Ginny was used to Frank dropping in for lunch since it was just a short walk from his office. But normally he worked until five o'clock.

Frank straightened, removing his coat and loosening his tie, and took a chair next to hers. "Only a little early today." He sighed.

"Frank, what is it? Difficult case?"

"If you want to call Warren a difficult case—then I suppose so." He scowled.

"Warren? Your own partner?" Ginny was surprised at his admission. They'd seemed to work well together these past few weeks.

"I haven't formalized the partnership yet. We had words today, so instead of getting angrier, I decided to come home."

Ginny took her husband's hand. "What about?" Frank was rarely upset about anything. Her husband was someone who always looked on the sunny side of life, and people enjoyed being around him. It was disconcerting to see him like this.

"Lately, he's been coming into the office whenever he chooses or going out for lunch and not returning in a reasonable time, so I called him on it. Glad I haven't signed legal documents adding him to the firm. I won't, anyway, until he pays for his share of the business."

"Oh, my. Did you ask him where he'd been at those times?"

"Yes, but his answer was vague—'with a client.'" Frank

waved his hand. "It may be nothing at all to get worried about."

"Well, you are a hard worker. I think you expect everyone to start with the same work ethic as you."

"Hmm . . . I suppose you're right. I'll give him more time to adjust to my way of doing business, then we'll see."

"Good idea." She squeezed his hand. "How about some tea or coffee before we have supper, although I think I could eat a side of beef all by myself." She giggled.

Frank laughed. "That's because you're eating for two!" He got up and kissed her slowly, his eyes misting. "Have I told you how much I love you, Virginia?"

She grabbed him by his coat collar and pulled him to her. "Yes, and I never tire of you telling me," she answered, then kissed him back.

The soggy weather was gloomy and depressing for Grace. It had rained all day—and the fields needed the rain, but the day seemed long and dark. She insisted on lighting every lantern downstairs to try to lift her mood.

"Want to play another round of checkers or chess?" Owen inquired.

"Pop, you know I'm no good at chess, and I'm tired of checkers." She walked about the parlor feeling restless. She missed the children . . . and Robert. The house seemed rather like a dead, empty cavern.

"I'm sorry that I'm not enough company for you," Owen said.

She walked over to him, planting a kiss on his head. "Oh, it's not you. I hate to admit it, but I got used to the children rather quickly, I guess, even though Tom was a little more than a handful."

He looked at her with sympathy. "I figured as much. I'll bet they'll be over next week."

"I don't know. There's more to do in town than come out here and do chores that I can't pay them for."

"Then we'll have to figure something out, won't we?" Owen gave her a conspiratorial wink. "Since we'll be in town for church tomorrow, maybe we'll see them."

"Did you enjoy your breakfast, children?" Stella asked as she removed the plates from the table.

"Yes, we did," Becky answered since Tom had snatched one more biscuit and his mouth was packed like a chipmunk.

"Miss Stella, it was wonderful. You have to remember I was the main cook, and not a good one at that." Robert pushed back his chair, then assisted Sarah with hers.

Sarah gazed up at him. "You weren't the only one, Papa. Becky helped too, and Mrs. Bidwell cooked delicious meals for us."

Becky beamed at her young sister.

"Right you are, Sarah. I didn't forget." Robert squeezed her hand gently.

Stella paused and looked straight at him. "Mrs. Bidwell. Would she be Owen Miller's daughter, Grace?"

"Yes, ma'am," Robert answered. "Do you know her?"

Stella wiped her hands on her apron. "Not really. I met her, though, the other day after I'd had coffee with her father. She seemed pleasant enough, but overly concerned with her father, I thought."

Robert thought that was a perceptive assumption but quickly made. "That may be true." He turned to the children. "We're going to church this morning so make sure you're all in the foyer and ready by ten thirty. We don't want to be late. Then you can have the entire afternoon to do as you'd like."

Tom licked the butter off his fingers, then asked, "Think we'll see Miss Grace at church?"

"I'm not sure, but if I had to wager on it, I bet even this light rain wouldn't stop her."

"I'm glad to hear you say you take them to church. It's mighty important to have God in your life and the sooner the better. That's all I have, God, my cats, and my books." Stella pushed the door to the kitchen open.

"Miss Stella, do you think I could borrow one of your books to read this afternoon after church?" Becky implored. "I couldn't help but notice that you have a lot of them in the parlor."

"Dear Becky, of course you may. I'll be happy to lend you something to read. But don't you have homework or something?"

Becky shook her head. "No, school is out now."

"Perfect, I wouldn't want it to get in the way of that," she remarked with a grin.

Grace stored her umbrella by the door and hurried inside with Owen. Eli and Dorothy, who'd just arrived and were on their way to find a seat, greeted them.

"It's so good to see you, Dorothy. You must tell me about Matilda," Grace said.

"We can catch up after church," Dorothy suggested with a smile as they walked to the meeting room.

Quiet chatter could be heard from the small faithful group inside who never let weather keep them from church on the Lord's Day. Grace looked forward to hearing the message from Pastor Alderson, a staunch citizen of the community and lay preacher. Folks said he was responsible for naming Bozeman. Grace knew him to be a man of many interests, but most evident was his love of the Lord.

A wave of hands from across the room caught her attention. Grace was mildly surprised to see it was Robert and his children. She waved back. "Pop, shall we go sit with them?"

"You go right ahead, Grace. I just spotted Stella sitting alone, and I think I'll join her."

Grace nodded to him. "All right. I'll see you after the service is over." She watched him wobble over, feeling a bit sad. A sudden and instinctive feeling punctured her heart as she pictured a gloomy future alone. *Is everyone leaving me?* She watched as Stella lifted her head to her father and gave him a reserved smile.

Grace dragged her eyes away as Sarah rushed over to her. "Will you please sit with us?"

Grace reached down to give her a hug. "I'd be happy to, Sarah."

Pastor Alderson stood by the door vigorously shaking hands with everyone as they left the service. "Pastor, I'd like to introduce you to Robert Frasier and his children," Grace said when it was their turn. "This is Tom, Becky, and Sarah."

The pastor smiled down at them and then shook Robert's hand. "I'm so glad you and your family came, Mr. Frasier. If there's any way I can be of service to you, please don't hesitate to seek me out."

"Thank you, sir," Robert replied. "I enjoyed the service."

"Then I hope you'll come back again. We are planning on building a real church for the town, and would appreciate you all being a part of that. I'll be speaking more about that in a future sermon."

"Then I look forward to hearing about it." Robert nodded at him and moved forward.

They all continued onto the porch where everyone was retrieving their umbrellas and stood about talking. Tom sat on the porch railing to wait, and the girls began talking to another girl about Becky's age. Eli and Robert huddled in conversation nearby.

"Dorothy, how is Matilda doing?" Grace asked.

"She's doing well, but the doctor thinks she's carrying twins so he's ordered her to rest. Otherwise, she would be at church today. How are you and your father doing? He seems a bit more cheerful than the last time I saw him."

They both turned to watch Stella and Owen talking to the pastor. "Mmm . . . I think you may be right, Dorothy." Grace folded her arms across her chest.

"I think it's wonderful that he's found a companion. Everybody needs someone, especially when you start getting old. I should know," Dorothy commented with a lighthearted laugh. "I don't know Stella well. Only speak to her when I run into her if she's at the store. A little eccentric, but I think she's an agreeable person. I tell you this because I can see the concern in your face."

"Really? I didn't know it showed. He is my father and very vulnerable since his health issue, you know," Grace explained.

Dorothy laughed. "Yes, but I have a hunch your father can take care of himself. Are you sure you're just not happy seeing him with someone other than your mother?"

Grace stiffened, and she turned back to look Dorothy straight in the eye. "I don't know, Dorothy. I really don't understand what I'm feeling."

Dorothy patted her arm. "Allow things to happen naturally . . . and then remember what your dear mother would want for Owen." Then, excusing herself to retrieve Eli, she left Grace to consider what she'd said.

Grace saw her father and Stella slowly making their way toward her and she tensed. Stella was holding on to his arm protectively.

"Are you about ready to go, Pop?" Grace asked as Robert walked over to join them.

"I was just asking your father to join us at the boardinghouse for a lunch of cold cuts and fruits." Stella stared at her above her spectacles.

"Stella owns the boardinghouse where I rented rooms," Robert inserted.

"Oh, we couldn't impose," Grace murmured.

"Yes, we could," Owen added with a chuckle.

"Please say yes, or I know Owen will just go home," Stella said. "Perhaps by then the rain will have stopped and you won't have a wet drive home. I'm just down the street."

The kids crowded around, waiting expectantly for her answer. "Say yes," Robert urged.

"Enough arm-twisting. Okay." Becky and Sarah clapped

with joy, which did her heart good. "Pop, let's get you in the buggy so you don't have to walk far."

But Stella held on firmly to his arm. "It's just at the end of this block. The walk will do him good," she insisted and pointed to her sign just down the street.

"I'll be fine, daughter. Why don't you let the children ride with you and we'll meet you there?" Owen's look was more a direct order, and Grace took the hint.

24

Lunch at Stella's was informal but delicious. Almost like a family affair, since most of the other boarders were either sleeping the day away or were out pursuing their own adventures.

"Did everyone get enough to eat?" Stella asked. A chorus of comments affirmed her question. "If you'd like to stay for coffee or tea, I'll see if I have any pie left."

"That sounds right fine, Stella." Owen nodded at her with a big smile from his end of the table.

"If you don't mind, Pop, I'd like to go check on Ginny while I'm in town. I'm guessing she's had morning sickness, or she and Frank would have been at church this morning."

"Good idea. Go ahead. I don't think Stella will mind if I hang around here a little more." Owen shot her a glance.

"I'd enjoy that," Stella said, gathering the dishes.

"I can stay and help clean up," Grace offered.

Stella shook her head. "Thank you, but there's not much to do. Please take your time."

Robert was suddenly at her side. "Mind if I tag along to

walk with you? Tom's off exploring and the girls are looking through Miss Stella's book collection."

"If you'd like to," Grace answered. "I won't be long, Pop."

"Take all the time you need. I'll be right here waiting for you." He looked pleased that Robert would go with her, and yet happy to be alone with Stella. *I guess I'll have to get used to this new side of him.*

Grace took her umbrella, although it appeared to have finally stopped raining. They walked a moment or two in silence until Grace finally broke the quiet. "Do you think you and the children will enjoy staying at Stella's?"

"I think so. 'Course, she can't make biscuits and gravy like you."

"Well, thank you for saying *that*. I hope that means I've been missed." *How did I let that slip?*

"Of course we miss you and Owen, but I did feel it was time to get out of your way. You have enough on you without the four of us."

"But I enjoyed the children so much." *And you.*

He paused on the sidewalk. "Look, before we get to Ginny's . . . I wanted to tell you that I've accepted a job with Eli at the mercantile."

Grace stood looking into his ruggedly handsome face. "You did?" Then she realized what his quitting meant to her and her potato crop. She was miffed. "Suit yourself. I ran Bidwell Farms before you came, and I'm capable of doing so without your help," she snapped, marching on ahead of him. It meant that she probably wouldn't get to see the children either.

He caught up with her and touched her elbow. "Grace, wait a minute. Let me explain."

"There's nothing to explain." She glared at him, removing his hand from her arm.

"Yes, there is, so don't get your petticoats in a tangle!"

She felt her face turn pink. "What is there to explain? You'd rather work for Eli than me. Sounds very clear to me." She felt her heart hammering against her ribs.

Robert cocked a hip and rested his hand on it. "Don't get so fired up! This is the second time I've seen you so angry—and both times directed at me. At least I'm getting your attention." A smile twitched at the edge of his mouth.

Grace folded her arms, but he quickly pulled her out of the walk to the edge of the drugstore building. His face was close to hers, making her heart pound harder. She couldn't take her eyes off his.

Still holding on to her hands, his eyes latched on to hers. "Now listen to me. I like working with you—I mean, for you—and I plan on continuing to do that. But I need to earn more in order to take better care of Sarah, Becky, and Tom. This morning after church, Eli asked if I'd like to work part-time for him. He's been looking for someone since his clerk left right before he hired Tom. We worked out a plan that I can work for you in the mornings on the farm, then afternoons and Saturday, I'll work for him."

"I see."

"Do you? The kids need a home and can't live in a boardinghouse for long. I promise to be there the entire time for the potato harvest. I won't let you down," he said.

She yanked her gaze away. "The least you could have done was talk to me about it first. Maybe I don't want you part-time."

"I'm talking to you now."

She shrugged. "Maybe Warren was right—I ought to

consider selling the farm." She knew in her heart that she'd never do that, but she felt sorry for herself.

"He's wrong, unless you figure on marrying him." He held her eyes with a steady gaze. "Funny, I didn't see him at church this morning."

Why did he care one way or another? Grace drew back. "Marry him? Ha! He hasn't even asked. If you must know, Warren is out of town. I must get going since I've left Pop waiting."

She began to move past him, but he suddenly pulled her to him, giving her a brief kiss on the mouth. Shocked, she pulled back and covered her mouth with her gloved hand. He'd kissed her right there, in full view of the town, and his lips felt full and warm . . . delicious. She felt her face and neck flame. With heat or embarrassment?

He dropped his hands with awkwardness. "I'm sorry. I don't know what came over me, except when you pout like that, your lips beg to be kissed." He guided her back to the sidewalk, looking straight ahead.

Grace wasn't sure she could speak and if she could, didn't know how to respond. Her hand shook as she patted her hair in place, then tightened her grip on the reticule she held in front of her, trying to act respectable.

"I think you'd better walk the rest of the way to Ginny's without me," he choked out.

She nodded and locked eyes with him, still tongue-tied, while he spun on his boot heel back in the direction of the boardinghouse. Grace squared her shoulders, took a deep breath, and hurried away. She tried to calm the thump in her heart before she saw Ginny, who'd be full of questions if she thought something was awry.

Frank answered the door when she arrived. "What a nice surprise," he said. "Ginny will be so glad to see you. The morning sickness is taking its toll, I'm afraid."

"I figured as much," she answered, following him to the parlor.

"Honey, look who's here to see you."

Ginny was lying on the chaise by an open window whose voile white curtains fluttered in a gentle breeze above her. She stretched out her arms to Grace in a friendly embrace when she entered. Ginny's hair was slightly disheveled and her face paler than normal. On the table next to her were crackers and a cup of tea.

Poor thing! Grace thought, feeling instant sympathy for her friend. "What can I do for you, Ginny? Anything at all. Please tell me."

Ginny smiled faintly. "You can help the time pass a little more quickly. I'm afraid that's all anyone can do." She pressed a delicate handkerchief against her upper lip. "I believe Frank is glad you're here so that he can escape my predicament for a while." She gave a weak laugh. "Besides, I've been wanting to talk to you about some ideas that I have for the nursery."

Frank coughed. "This is where I make my escape and let you ladies chat away. I'll be in my office if you need me, dear," he said, then leaned over to brush Ginny's brow with his lips. "Grace, before I leave, how's the courting going with Warren?"

"The best word I can use is . . . *slowly*," she admitted. "He doesn't seem to be around a lot lately, but I have to say, he's a talker."

Frank laughed. "Well, take your time. There's no hurry, is there? If you need anything, ladies, I'm at your service."

As soon as he left, Ginny started her litany of questions.

"I heard that Robert moved to the boardinghouse. You must be lonely without the children," Ginny said.

"Oh, Ginny. I'm missing them terribly, but . . ."

Ginny leaned forward. "But what? I can tell something is bothering you."

"Oh, I don't know . . . Maybe I miss Robert as well, though I doubt he misses me." Grace stared out the window and saw two bluebirds on the fence. A male and a female. The male was feeding the female a worm. *How wonderfully sweet. That's the way life should be. Commitment—living out your life with the one you love. Will it ever happen for me?*

"How do you know?"

Ginny's question brought her back to the present. "Because he told me he'd taken another job at the mercantile working for Eli. I wasn't happy about it, but I think I understand his situation. We talked a little, and he plans to work for me in the morning, and Eli when he's through. But what could I say? He wants to get the children in a house soon."

"That's very admirable of him, Grace."

"Yes, until he pulled me aside and kissed me right in front of the entire town!"

Ginny laughed until her eyes misted with tears, but Grace didn't think it so funny. "That's not so bad. Frank once kissed me right outside the front door of the church, after he proposed. I was mortified but exuberant at the same time."

"You never told me that story."

"Didn't I? Well, men sometimes forget where they are when a woman has befuddled their mind. But it sure *seems* as though Robert misses you."

"Don't be funny! I doubt anyone has befuddled Robert's

mind. He's still angry at his first wife. Which brings to mind . . . How in the world did he marry a woman who didn't tell him about her children?"

"Perhaps they didn't know each other long. You know it's not uncommon for people to marry quickly out here. Don't be too hard on him. Besides, you're still seeing Warren, aren't you? It must be nice to have two men chasing you."

"I see Warren when it's convenient for him. If he had his druthers, he'd have me sign away Bidwell Farms and live in town so I could be at his beck and call at a moment's notice. That's not for me, and I couldn't leave my father. What do you think of Warren?"

"He appears to be nice enough, but he and Frank were at odds yesterday. Frank is usually a good judge of character. This is changing the subject, but you are going to the Bozeman Ball?"

"I haven't given it much thought, really. But before I forget, could you give me the address of the place you ordered Bluebelle? I'd like to get another duck for companionship. A male, preferably."

"I'll see if I can find it. Or better yet, I'll order it for you . . . if you'll help me decorate the nursery."

Grace clapped her hands. "Oh, you know I would love to help you. I must be getting back to the boardinghouse where I left Pop. He and Stella, the proprietor, have taken a shine to one another," she said matter-of-factly.

"Oh, I didn't know. What a terrible hostess I've been. I should have had Frank make us a fresh pot of tea." Ginny started to rise from the lounge.

Grace held out her arm. "Please don't get up. I really need to get going. Let me know when you feel better and we'll talk about decorating. You have plenty of time left."

"I shall. Give my best to Owen, and think about going to the ball. It should be loads of fun and gives us women a chance to dress up for a change."

"I can't promise I'll come, but I'll consider it. I'll let myself out. You stay right where you are and rest." And with that, Grace excused herself and scurried back to the boarding-house.

25

Robert kicked at a rock with the toe of his boot, furious with himself. That's what women did to him. *No, that's what* one *woman does to me!* When had he let her get under his skin? *How could I let that happen? She'll either fire me or hate me for sure now.* He was so deep in his thoughts that he walked right past the boardinghouse, then decided to continue walking to clear his head.

Soon he was leaving Bozeman behind and stepping into the cool dampness of the forest. The quietness of the woods suited him and his frame of mind, and there was nothing around to disturb him other than the sound of the rushing Gallatin River. He went off the trail and sat on a downed pine log by the river's edge to think.

Never would he have guessed that he would have married and lost his wife and gained three children, half-grown. Never would he have guessed he would lose his farm. Never would he have guessed he would have feelings for another woman. *Never!*

But that's how love goes in this crazy world, he thought.

When he'd least expected it, gentle and gracious Grace had waltzed into his heart, cracking it open. But from the horrified look on her face just now, she didn't return those feelings. Oh, she loved the kids sure enough, but not him. When his lips made contact with hers, there was instant fire in his belly that made his hands shake even now as he thought about it. Had he felt that with Ada? Hard as he tried to recall, he couldn't. Best that he remember what had happened with Ada instead of fancying himself with another woman.

A twig snapped and he heard voices. As Robert stepped back onto the trail, he saw Warren speaking with another man. Both were on horseback and turned when they heard him approach. The men shook hands, and the other man trotted off in a hurry. Warren didn't smile, but turned his horse around to face Robert.

"What are you doing walking in the woods when it's so soggy? Name's Richard, isn't it?"

"Wet or dry—matters not to me. I feel right at home in the woods."

Warren gave him a skeptical look. "Then you can have these woods all to yourself," he remarked. He kicked his horse in the flanks and flew past Robert.

Definitely an odd man. What did Grace see in him? A comfortable life, maybe? Prestige? Could be. Plus, Robert could have sworn Grace had said Warren was out of town.

By the time Robert returned to the boardinghouse, all was quiet and Grace and Owen had already left. Which was fine with him. He didn't want to have to face Grace just yet.

"Grace, are you mad at me about something?" Owen asked. "You've been awfully quiet since we got home."

Grace glanced over at her father. "Of course not." She went back to her mending, though her lack of concentration meant she'd have to rip out the seam she had finished on her blouse.

"Your face is telling me something else," he pushed. "Are you upset that me and Stella are courting?"

"Is that what you call it? I had no idea. You haven't so much as mentioned Stella to me. I thought you were just friends." Grace knew better but pretended not to.

Owen laughed. "If an old man like myself can call it courting, then I suppose it is. But yes, we are becoming friends, and to me that's a whole lot more important at my age. I'm sorry that I didn't fill you in. I guess it slipped my mind."

"I see."

"Do you, honestly? Grace, I have a feelin' you are worrying about me too much."

"I confess, I am concerned about you having a lady friend. Is she after your money? Will she care about someone whose health—?"

"A cripple, you mean? You have nothing to worry about. She is very interested in my illness and has asked plenty about it and sympathizes. As far as money—which I have little of—she has no interest in what she can *get* from me. She's a woman that requires little in life besides her books, cats, or long walks."

"My, but she sounds like a recluse. I'm surprised she'd have time to spend with you, then." Somehow her reply didn't come out the way she intended it to—her father's face made that clear.

"Thanks for your confidence in me. I'm going to bed."

He struggled to get up from his chair and Grace hurried to his side.

Grace could tell he was hurt. "Pop, I'm sorry. I didn't intend to sound so mean. I guess I'm more worried about living alone the rest of my life." She placed her arm under his to assist him and he stopped to look her square in the eye.

"Grace, have a little faith. You're still a good-looking catch for any man. Maybe your relationship will grow with Warren. And I don't plan on going anywhere . . . I don't think."

They both laughed at his comment. "Which tells me you're thinking it's a possibility, Pop." They continued to Owen's bedroom and got him comfortable for the night.

"I confess, I think about companionship too, you know. You don't want to be saddled with me the rest of your life," he remarked as she tucked the covers around him.

She smoothed the covers. "I don't think of you that way at all. I love you and want the best for you."

"And I for you, daughter. So back to my earlier question. Why were you so withdrawn tonight?"

Grace sat on the edge of the bed. "On my way to Ginny's Robert told me that he's going to work for Eli."

"Oh no. Not now. Just when things are starting to fall into place around here. Did he tell you why?"

Grace fingered the satin on the blanket's edge. "He explained to me he must earn more money. He promised he'd still be around to help but will work part-time in the afternoons for Eli."

"Then that's not so bad, is it? . . . Is it?" he repeated with a quizzical look at Grace.

"I suppose it could work, but . . ." She didn't want to say more. "I'll still have to hire extra hands at harvesttime."

"What are you not telling me, Grace?" He sighed heavily.

"Pop, he kissed me!" she blurted out.

"Whoop! That surprises me. After what his wife did to him, I thought he'd written women out of his future."

"Maybe. He apologized, so he probably didn't mean it, I'm thinking."

"Ha! Don't be too sure of that. I've seen him look at you with a gleam in his eye."

"Pop! You're joshing me!"

"Nope. I think the only one who hasn't noticed is you. How did that kiss make you feel?"

She thought a moment. "Confused. Surprised."

"Look, it never hurts to have two eligible men sparking one woman. It gives you a chance to compare." Owen leaned back on his pillow, his lids visibly heavy.

"I'll keep that in mind, but I think you're wrong. I believe the kiss didn't mean anything. Warren travels quite a bit so I'm not sure what to make of him. He loves talking about himself—" Grace clamped her mouth shut when she noticed her father was asleep. She leaned over and kissed his brow, turned off the lantern, then tiptoed out of the room, shoving down the lump in her throat.

Grace was hanging the morning wash on Monday, thankful that the rain that had drenched the valley was past them now. She heard the sound of a wagon and looked over the clothesline to see Robert coming up the lane with the children with him. Would he say anything about the kiss yesterday?

When he stopped the wagon, the children scrambled down, so she put down the pillowcase she was about to hang and walked over to them. Sarah came running up and hugged her, leaving Becky timidly hanging behind, but Grace waved her to come and enveloped her in a warm hug. "I'm glad you came today."

"I'll help you hang the laundry," Becky offered.

"I'd be very happy to have your help, Becky. Later we can make lunch . . . that is, if you're all staying."

"I hope we are," Sarah said, then turned when she saw Blue-belle. "Hello, my friend. Are you happy to see me?" She bent down and stroked the neck of the duck strutting around her, then went traipsing out of the yard with Bluebelle following.

"Don't go too far, Sarah," Grace reminded her.

Tom waved at her, then followed Robert, hoe in hand, to the field where the potatoes were thriving from all the rain they'd been having. They ought to have a good crop this year, and the money would come in handy.

She and Becky continued to hang laundry under the clearing skies for the sun to dry. "Becky, what's it like living in the boardinghouse?" Grace asked.

Becky shrugged her thin shoulders. "Okay, I guess. It sorta feels like we're visiting someone's big house, but at least the bed is nice."

Grace laughed. "I think I know what you mean. Is Stella kind to you?" Grace was hoping the child's innocent appraisal could shed some light on the character of her father's friend.

Becky bobbed her head. "Oh, yes, ma'am. Sort of like a grandma."

"That's good then, isn't it?"

"Yes, but Papa said we'll have our own place very soon."

"I hope you do, Becky, and remember you and Sarah and Tom are welcome here any time."

It took a while to finish hanging the laundry. Grace noticed how meticulous Becky was and praised her. Becky's upturned face glowed under the compliment.

"Could you run down the lane and get Sarah? We can make lunch now that the menfolk are coming back from the field."

"Yes, ma'am." Becky skipped happily out of the yard calling for Sarah. Grace started for the house.

A few moments later, Becky came running into the yard and grabbed Grace's hand. "Please, come quick, Sarah has fallen into the creek! I can't reach her and neither of us can swim!"

26

Panic seized Grace's heart. The river was ice-cold this time of year and swift from the recent rains. She lifted her skirt and whirled around to run full tilt in the direction of Gallatin River. When they reached the riverbank, Grace yelled to be heard above the noise of the rushing creek. "Where? I don't see her, Becky."

"I see her—floating downstream. There!" She pointed up ahead. Grace rushed farther down the stream's bank, hair falling from its pins and tree limbs scratching her arms and snagging her clothing. Finally, she saw Sarah holding on to a dead branch with the roaring water swirling about her. Her head was nearly underwater as she gulped in a copious amount of water.

"I'm coming, Sarah. Hold on!" Grace flung herself, skirts and all, into the icy creek. Her skirts billowed about her, and the weight of her garments made it difficult to swim. She wished she'd removed them and her boots, but there wasn't time. Grace wasn't a very skilled swimmer, but she was willing to die trying to reach Sarah. She lost her balance when she hit her foot hard against a rock or log that threatened to take her down deeper. She bit her lip instead of crying out, so as not to scare Sarah.

"Please hurry, Miss Grace!" Becky was running to and fro, yelling from the creek bank.

The strong, swift current left Grace struggling to reach Sarah, until she felt her lungs would burst. *God, please help me get her. Don't let anything happen to this precious child who's like my own.*

Grace heard a splash from behind and first thought Becky had jumped in, but it was Robert who quickly had his arms about her, dragging her to a boulder. He secured her there, then swam toward Sarah, who still wasn't saying a word. *Poor thing, she's scared to death. Please, God, help him now!*

Grace turned back toward the riverbank and saw that Tom and Owen had now joined Becky. They stood watching with anxious faces. Soon Robert reached Sarah, and in one swift movement, pulled her onto his back. Her thin, little arms hugged him tightly about the neck. *Thank You, God!* Grace breathed deeply.

When Robert drew closer to her, he stretched out his arm, indicating for Grace to latch on. With his arm hooked under Grace's, he slowly swam, pulling them to safety until the floor of the river could be felt and they were able to stand. Shouts of joy sounded from the three observers above them.

"Sarah, are you all right?" Robert said with a heaving breath.

Sarah nodded, her eyes wide in shock and her face pale. "I knew I'd be okay, 'cause an angel told me not to worry," she said through chattering teeth.

Grace was shivering too, but she was too focused on the

pain in her foot to care. "Sarah, I'm so thankful that you didn't drown."

Sarah's bright blue eyes glistened and water droplets clung to her eyelashes. "Me too. I couldn't keep up with Bluebelle, though. I don't know where she went."

Grace kissed Sarah's pale face. "Don't you worry about Bluebelle. She's a great swimmer and she'll show up when she gets hungry for supper."

Robert hugged Sarah hard, then quickly released her. "I'm glad it wasn't any worse, because it could have been. Sarah, you can't go to the river alone anymore. It's too dangerous. You hear?" It was a reprimand, but given gently with a tender voice. Sarah nodded back, sniffing.

Finally, reaching the edge of the riverbank, they joined the others. Tom had gone back for blankets and Owen wrapped the shivering little girl quickly. "Thank God you are okay, little one."

Robert eyed her. "Grace, are you limping?"

"Maybe a little. I hit my foot on a rock or something." Becky placed the other blanket gently around Grace's shoulders.

"Sit down on that log and let me check out your foot."

"I'll be just fine," she protested.

"We'll see about that." Owen tried to guide his daughter to the log, struggling to keep his balance on the uneven ground.

"I can take care of this, Owen." Robert took over. "Tom, Becky, why don't you walk Sarah back to the house with Owen and get her warm. Tom, let Owen hang on to your arm. We'll be behind you as soon as I check Grace."

"Yes, sir." Tom offered his support to help Owen up the slope, and Becky wrapped her arm about Sarah's shoulder, hugging her tight before starting for the house.

Grace sat on the huge pine log while Robert unlaced her boots. His fingers gently felt around her foot until she whimpered aloud. "Is that where it hurts?" He indicated the side of her ankle.

Grace nodded, thinking how odd it was that he had his hands on her foot.

"I don't think anything's broken, but you're going to have a badly bruised ankle. So I suggest you stay off your foot for a few days to allow that swelling to subside," he informed her. As he looked up at her, his face softened. "We'll wrap it tightly and that'll help."

Grace wrinkled her nose in disgust. "I suppose you're right. I don't swim very well and thankfully you showed up."

He glanced away. "I hate to think—"

Grace touched his sleeve, water dripping from her cuffs. "Then don't. My prayer was answered."

Their eyes locked for a brief moment. "Do you think you can hobble back with my support or shall I carry you?"

Grace struggled to stand. "I think I can." But that failed to be true when she stood on her foot and winced.

That's all it took for Robert to swoop her up in his strong arms. Wet against wet, heart to heart, he carried her. Grace rather enjoyed this close look at him. She slipped an arm about his neck and they sloshed up the hill, his boots making squishy sounds, to the road. His jaw was clean-shaven, tight and lean, his face darkly tanned. Without his hat, his hair was curling and matted from the river. It didn't seem fair that his lashes were longer than hers. She swallowed, closed her eyes and enjoyed the manly scent of him. She thought he might bring up the stolen kiss, but neither said a word on the way back to the house.

Once they reached the others, Owen told Robert where to find bandages for Grace's foot. "Tom, get some wood to build a fire, then drag two chairs near the hearth. Becky, would you please go find them some dry clothing?" Everyone scattered to do as Owen asked while he set the kettle on to boil for hot tea.

Becky had already helped her sister peel off her wet dress and underthings and dressed her in Grace's nightgown. Sarah took a seat, still shivering, while Becky covered her with a dry blanket.

Grace watched how she tenderly cared for Sarah. "You're a great help to your sister, Becky."

"I have to. Tom and Sarah are all I've got." Becky sniffed back the tears.

"Well, yes, but you have Robert too."

"I don't think he really wants us." Her voice quivered with emotion.

Grace finished buttoning her blouse then tucked it into her skirt. "Becky, do you really believe that? Because I don't." The kettle whistled and she hobbled over to remove it from the stove. "I'm going to make us some hot tea." She glanced over to where Sarah sat huddled under the blanket. "Are you feeling all right now?" Returning her gaze to Becky, she said, "Please tell Tom we're dressed so we can get that fire going. Sarah's shivering."

Sarah sneezed and wiped her nose on the back of her sleeve.

"Then go to my bureau and bring your sister a handker-chief," Grace added with concern.

"Yes, ma'am." Becky scurried out, letting the menfolk back into the kitchen.

"Grace, I'll fix the tea. You sit down and let Robert wrap that ankle," her father ordered.

Grace did as she was told, then looked down to see her foot had indeed swollen, but not too badly. She propped it up on a footstool and Robert began wrapping it. When he was done, he stood back and looked. "Try standing now and see if that gives you some support. I've seen worse sprains and bruises, but still I know it hurts."

Grace found that she was able to stand and walk without too much pain, so she returned to her chair. Tom had the fire going and the room was warming up.

"Here you go." Owen walked slowly over and handed Sarah and Grace mugs of steaming hot tea. "That'll warm your insides."

"Thank you, Mr. Owen," Sarah said, taking the mug to warm her hands. Becky wouldn't leave her side.

"Gosh, who's going to fix our lunch now?" Tom looked around. "I'm pretty hungry."

"You and I will, Tom. It's time you got a little working knowledge of the kitchen," Robert teased. "If you'll tell me what you were going to have, Grace, we can get started."

"I'm not totally incapacitated." Grace started to rise, but Robert gently laid his hands on top of her shoulders.

"No, you aren't, but you do need to stay off of your foot a couple of days to help with healing and swelling."

"Yes, sir!" Grace saluted and the girls giggled.

When lunch, which consisted of leftover chicken soup, was over and chores finished for the day, Robert told the children that it was time to leave.

"Oh, Papa. Can't we stay here tonight with Miss Grace?" Becky pressed. "Sarah is tired."

"Please, can we?" Sarah whined. "Besides, I have one of Grace's nightgowns on."

"I can wait on Miss Grace while she rests her foot," Becky added with a smile directed at Grace.

Robert paused a moment to think through their request. He was struck with the realization the outcome could have been terrible—and he really *did* care for the children. Flashing a look at Grace, he quirked an eyebrow and she nodded her agreement.

"It might be best, Robert. She was in the icy water for a while."

Robert suddenly noticed how pretty and dewy-fresh Grace's skin looked. The towel-dried hair falling about her shoulders in curls made her appear at this moment much younger than her years. He dragged his eyes away and looked at his daughters. "All right. You two can stay. I'll be back in the morning."

"Yippee!" the girls shouted in unison.

"Okay, it's settled. Tom, let's go. I have work to do for Eli and so do you."

Owen followed Robert to the door. "Thanks for letting the girls stay, Robert. Grace loves having them around."

Robert paused, his hand on the doorknob. "I think I see that now. I'll bring them a change of clothes when I come to work in the morning. I think Sarah is fine, but send Becky for me if something changes," he said wearily.

"I will. Don't worry about a thing here. See you tomorrow."

Owen waited until they left, then returned to the kitchen. "How about a game of checkers, Becky, while we let those two rest?" He motioned to the sleeping Sarah curled up with her blanket in the chair. His daughter was content to have them back in her home again. He was so glad that Sarah had been rescued from the river's clutches. He'd already grown fond of the children and privately hoped that his daughter and Robert might grow to care for one another. Owen was a good judge of character, and after observing Robert the last couple months, he was convinced he was a good, stable person. Just the kind that Grace needed.

27

Eli's store was filled with customers by the time Robert and Tom arrived shortly after lunch. Miners, farmers, and more—all waiting to be helped.

Eli looked flustered. "I'm so happy to see both of you." He handed Tom and Robert separate lists. "I've got customers waiting for these items, so see if you can rustle these up while I attend to others." He hurried off to help the next customer in line.

Tom shrugged. "I'm not sure if I know what some of this stuff is." He frowned as he scanned the paper.

"We'll find it together. It can't be that hard. Most of the building supplies will be located in one place. Come on. Let's see if we can make a dent in this for Eli."

After a few hours, Robert decided that he and Tom had more than earned their salary for the day. There was barely a minute to take a break between customers, but Eli made sure when there was a slight lull, they stopped long enough to have a cup of fresh coffee and some gingersnaps Dorothy had baked. Robert let Tom have some coffee too. He figured if he was man enough to work as hard as he was, then he was old enough to drink coffee.

"The cookies are scrumptious!" Tom gobbled down three in the time that it took Robert to eat one.

"I believe Tom has a hollow leg, Robert." Eli chuckled, then downed the rest of his coffee.

"I think that's called a *growing spurt*," Robert surmised.

"I'm always hungry. I can tell you that." Tom smiled up at them.

"Changing the subject, I'm running low on supplies." Eli's smile was replaced with seriousness. "My last two shipments haven't showed up, so I wired my supplier, who told me they were shipped and signed off on. I don't know what to make of that."

"Then you need to ask him to produce the signed copy," Robert urged.

"You're right, I never thought of that. I just kept waiting for them to show up. Never know if a wagon broke down, or if they ran into those hostile Indians I keep hearing rumors about."

"Why not telegraph him and ask him to send you a copy of the shipping label? You could do it now. Me and Tom will take care of things for you."

"Good idea," Eli said, removing his apron. "I'll only be gone a few minutes." He rushed out the door.

A few minutes later, Robert saw Virginia enter the store. "Tom, why don't you take the cups back to the kitchen?"

While Tom gathered up the empty plate and mugs, Robert advanced toward Virginia. "Miss Virginia, what can I help you with today?"

She looked at him with her usual friendly smile. "Hello,

Robert. Grace told me you would soon be working here, but I must admit I'm somewhat surprised that you've left her with a load to bear, what with the potato crop and all."

Robert grimaced. *So Grace's talked to her about me.* "I haven't abandoned her. I'll do as much as I can to help when harvesttime comes. I couldn't ask her for an increase in pay, but I needed more income with three others to care for." *Why am I explaining myself to her?*

She blinked. "I'm sorry. I didn't mean that as a condemnation. I do understand. You are to be commended for trying to single-handedly raise three children. I shouldn't have mentioned it." Her soft Southern way of speaking could warm the coldest of hearts. "Where's Eli?"

"He'll return momentarily. He had an errand to attend to, and I told him I would watch over things."

"I see. I wondered if the fabric I ordered for the nursery had arrived. Do you think you could check for me?"

"I'll be happy to. Follow me to the counter where Eli keeps his orders and we'll see about it." Robert strode in the direction of the counter. He lifted the pile of shipping orders, shuffling through the stack. Shaking his head he said, "I'm sorry, but I don't see it here, Miss Virginia." He wasn't about to mention the missing shipments.

She blinked. "I don't understand. I ordered it weeks ago. It's for the nursery."

Robert's eyes discreetly traveled down to her midsection. She indeed was showing signs she was pregnant. "My congratulations." It struck him that one day he might want to have his *own* child, and he wondered what that would feel like . . . knowing he'd loved one woman deeply enough to have a baby with her. He swallowed hard. He wasn't used to these thoughts filling his mind. What was wrong with him? He already had three children.

Her face blushed pink. "I thank you, Robert. I have plenty of time to do the sewing before the baby arrives, but I was anxious to get started."

"I can see that. Will there be anything else?"

"No, but you can tell Grace to come see me."

"Mmm . . . it's best if you ride out to see her. She injured her ankle yesterday."

Ginny drew in a sharp breath. "Oh no!"

"It's not too bad, but I suggested that she stay off her foot for a few days, so I left Becky to help out."

"How did she do that?"

"She swam into the river to rescue Sarah and somehow hurt her foot."

"What? My goodness! Is Sarah all right?"

"Yes, ma'am. She is. She was going after Bluebelle, but the river was swift and Sarah doesn't know how to swim."

"In that case, you can fill one of those little bags with some bathing salts for me and tie it with a pretty ribbon. She can soak her foot in it to increase healing. I'll go check on her in the morning."

Robert measured the bath salts into a bag, then cut a length of ribbon long enough to tie at the top. "Here you go."

"Maybe this will help reduce the swelling. We have the Bozeman Ball coming up and I've encouraged her to go."

"Maybe Warren will take her."

Virginia nodded. "Yes, I suppose. You should go too. It's a big event for our town." She handed him the change for the salts. "I have an idea. You're going back there first thing in the morning, right?"

"Yes, I am. I work there first then come to work here. Why?"

"Why don't you give her the salts?"

"Sure. I could do that, but I'm sure she'd much rather see your face than mine."

Virginia giggled. "Oh, I doubt that," she said with a sly smile. She handed the salts back to him. "No need to say they're from me. She'll think you're very thoughtful."

He took the sack and replied, "Why would I do that?"

Virginia shook her head and said, "I'll be going now, so you can wait on others behind me. Oh, and Robert, please call me Ginny, everyone else does."

"Yes, ma'am." He bade her good day and stood there puzzled by her comment until another customer tapped him on the sleeve and said, "Are you here to help or not?"

"Yes. Yes, of course. How may I help you?" Robert tried to refocus, but was still wondering about Ginny's pushing him toward Grace. Wasn't the man courting Grace the one who worked for her husband? *Women! They're too hard to figure out!*

After Stella's hearty supper, Robert told Tom to get his bath and then he'd take his. The business at the mercantile had kept them hopping, and Robert could see the tiredness reflected in Tom's eyes.

"Tom, if you think the work is too hard or we need to change how many hours a day that you work, then let's talk about it."

Tom gazed at him through sleepy eyes, holding his towel and bar of soap. "I'm okay. Besides, what I earn can help us all find a place to live."

Robert was surprised and touched by his answer. "That's not your responsibility, Tom. It's mine. You can keep what you earn. I already told you that."

"I remember, but what else am I going to do with the money? And sometimes, I recall you didn't want us. I've done some thinking and I really want to help since it's my sisters we're talking about."

"I'm sorry I acted the way I did with you and your sisters. I know none of that was your fault. Seeing Sarah nearly drown today made me realize just how important you all have become to me." Robert watched Tom's face for a sign of emotion. "Maybe I'll let you contribute a small amount, but not until we find ourselves someplace to live."

"Fair enough. Before I forget, I didn't get a chance to tell you something today."

"Oh? And what was that?"

"Remember I told you that I saw a man stopped on the road to town talking with someone with a wagon load of stuff?"

Robert jerked his head around. "Did you see what was in the wagon?"

"No, and it may not mean anything, but I thought I'd mention it again." Tom shrugged. "I didn't think it was anything important or any of my business, but something seemed odd about the two men."

"Have you seen them around town?"

"Not that I recall."

"Okay. Better go get cleaned up before you fall forward."

Robert thought back to his walk in the rain when he'd seen Warren briefly. Who was it he'd been talking to? He'd seemed curt and anxious to ride past him, but Robert thought that

191

was because Robert worked for Grace. *He bears watching if our paths cross again.* Something didn't sit well with Robert about him, and it wasn't because he was courting Grace. Maybe he'd go to the ball just to keep an eye out for her.

28

It became quite evident by morning that Sarah had caught a cold from the river's icy waters. Or at least that's what Grace thought. She could've easily swallowed too much water that got into her lungs. Grace wondered if she should have the doctor check her out just in case.

Sarah sneezed again, then coughed and lay back on her pillow. "I'm not feelin' too good, Miss Grace. I'm sorry that I caused so much trouble and you hurt your foot."

Her pitiful look made Grace's heart swell. "Sweet girl, things happen . . . sometimes for a reason. I'll be fine in a couple of days and I'm sure you will too." Grace walked gingerly on her sprained foot as she placed a pot of tea and toast next to the bed. "Perhaps you'll feel better once you have something in your tummy."

"Where's Becky?" Sarah asked weakly.

"She's washing dishes for me. She'll be in to see you in a while. Here, try some tea. It'll make your head feel less stuffy."

"Okay." The little girl took a sip from the teacup. "Mmm.

I'm glad you put sugar in it for me. That's the way I like it. My mama—" She abruptly stopped while a big tear rolled down her cheek. Grace had never seen Sarah cry. Bless her sweet heart. She always tried so hard to be tough because she felt she had to.

Grace sat on the edge of the bed and put her arm about Sarah's thin shoulders. "It's okay to be sad. Sometimes when we feel bad, emotions come to the surface when we least expect it." Sarah leaned her head against Grace and warmth from her small body could be felt through her nightgown. Did she have a fever? Grace laid her hand on Sarah's forehead. It felt warm, but she wasn't too worried since a cold can bring on a fever.

"Would you like to try some toast?"

"All right. I'll try. Miss Grace, you're so sweet to me that sometimes I wish you could be my mama."

Grace's heart squeezed tightly in her chest. "What a sweet thing to say, Sarah. I'll always be your friend, even if I'm not your mama."

"You could be my mama if you married Rob—I mean, Papa," she said matter-of-factly.

The door opened, and Becky scurried in and plopped down on the bed, taking Sarah's hand. "How are you feeling this morning?"

"I'm better now that my two favorite people—" she stopped to sneeze—"are here."

Becky's eyes flashed to Grace. "It's just a little cold, Becky," Grace reassured her. "Why don't you read to Sarah while she finishes her tea and toast?" Grace picked up a book from the nightstand and handed it to Becky. "I'll come back in a little while."

Grace hobbled away and returned to her room, removing her robe and gown before changing into a simple yellow morning dress. Echoing in her head were Sarah's words about wishing she were her mama. *I do too, sweet Sarah.* But that wasn't to be, so she shoved those thoughts and longings away. She brushed her hair, then wound it into a tight chignon at the back of her neck. She had work to do but first she wanted to see what Robert thought about Sarah's sniffles.

By the time she was back downstairs, she heard Owen's and Robert's voices coming from the kitchen. She entered the kitchen, hobbled over to her apron, and put it on. "Good morning, Pop, Robert."

"Morning, Grace. How's Sarah?" Robert stood as she came near the table. She noticed a small valise by his chair, which she figured contained fresh clothes for the girls.

"No worse for wear, I think, but she has a few sniffles."

Robert cast a glance toward the upstairs. "I'll go see for myself."

"I'll come with you."

"You don't need to be going up and down stairs. Why not sit and rest your foot?"

"As you wish. First door on your left is the girls' room. Becky is with her now."

Robert picked up the valise and started out, then turned around, pulling a small bag from his pocket and tossing it to her. "Try soaking your foot in this. It's bath salts. It may help soreness and swelling." Then he strode from the kitchen, leaving her and her dad.

"Well, what d'you know? Your first gift from Robert." Owen chuckled.

"I wouldn't call it a gift exactly, but I will put it to good use after I do a few chores. I'm worried that Sarah may have a little fever. Do you think I should send Robert for the doctor?"

Owen scratched his head. "I'm not sure. Let's wait and see what Robert thinks once he sees her. How's the foot feel?"

"Better, I believe. I'm sure resting it the remainder of the day and evening helped, and I'm really glad it was not any worse."

It wasn't long before Robert returned to the kitchen. "Sarah definitely has a cold, but I don't believe it's in her lungs so she doesn't need a doctor—at least not yet. Thank you both for taking care of her."

"Maybe this afternoon she could sit out on the porch in the sun. It'll do her good," Grace said, ready to pour him a cup of coffee. Robert held his hand up.

"None for me, thanks. I want to get all the chores done by lunchtime. The mercantile was really busy yesterday, so I can't be late."

Owen stood, taking a minute to get his legs. "None for me either. I'll see what I can do to help out, Robert. By the way, where's Tom?"

"Oh, he's already mucking out the barn. He worked so hard yesterday at Eli's, he was plumb tuckered out before bedtime."

Owen nodded. "Work's good for the lad. Keeps him outta trouble." They started out the door.

"Tell Tom to stop in and say hello before he leaves," Grace said.

"I'll do that. Don't forget to soak your foot, now." Robert gave her a long look.

"Thanks for the salts. I intend to use them after lunch." Grace wondered why he was staring at her like that. Maybe it was the old faded-yellow dress she was wearing. She hadn't wanted to wear a nicer dress when she had gardening to do. That was at least something she could sit and take care of without being on her foot. It was such a clear, cloudless day, the kind that called to her to be outdoors as much as possible. In between times, she'd keep checking on Sarah.

Thirty minutes later, Grace looked up to see a carriage coming up the lane. *Who could that be?* Ginny? She struggled to a standing position, shaking her eyes from the bright sun's rays. As the carriage drew closer, she could see that it was Stella and not Ginny. Grace opened the garden gate to greet her as she pulled up.

Stella stepped down from the carriage as quickly as she drove up. "I hope I'm not interrupting your morning, Grace. Robert told me about your injury and I thought I'd drop off dinner for you today," she said while reaching into the back of the carriage seat to lift a large basket covered in a checkered cloth.

Grace removed her dirty garden gloves, stuffing them in her apron pocket. "That's mighty nice of you, Stella, but you shouldn't have. Becky's been helping me." She walked over to the carriage. "Can I carry anything?"

"Land sakes, no! It's all right here in one basket. Is Owen around? I hope to get a chance to see him today."

She was so tall that she towered over Grace—Grace had to look up to meet her eyes. "Yes, he's out in the field with Robert, but I'll ring the dinner bell. Believe me, they'll come running once they know it's time to eat." Grace glanced at the watch pinned to her dress. "Oh my, how time flies. It's almost dinnertime, isn't it?"

They made their way to the house, and Grace rang the

triangle that hung off the end of the porch. "Why don't we take this inside to the kitchen?"

"I hope I brought enough. Robert's children are here too, I understand." Stella followed her inside.

"We'll make it enough." Grace stepped inside the foyer and called up the stairs for Becky. When Becky appeared at the top of the stairs, Grace told her to come down to eat and bring Sarah if she felt up to it.

"I'll see, but I believe she's asleep right now." Becky hurried away, then returned, rushing down the stairs. "I didn't want to wake her, Miss Grace."

"That's perfectly fine. She needs her rest," Grace reassured her.

"Miss Stella, what are you doing here?" Becky asked, seeing her standing near the kitchen door.

"I brought dinner so Grace wouldn't have to cook today. I hear you've been a big help to her."

"I try to." Becky rolled her eyes at Grace and they laughed. Then she sniffed. "It smells wonderful."

Tom burst through the kitchen door. "What smells so good? Oh, hi, Miss Stella." He gave her a quizzical look.

"I brought dinner today. It's chicken pie and apple crisp," Stella answered.

"Go wash up, Tom," Grace ordered, then tousled his hair as he passed her. She spied Robert and her father slowly walking from the field. It was so good of Robert to take his time for her father's sake, and she was glad to see their friendship and respect for each other growing.

"Let me help you set the table, then once I say hello to Owen, I'll be on my way. I left Biddy, my housekeeper, in charge while I'm out."

"Let me show you where things are," Becky said, taking her by the hand. "I wanted to tell you that I've been reading to Sarah and it helps her to rest."

"Is she sick?" Stella inquired, flashing a look at Grace.

"We think it's only a cold, but I'm watching her closely."

"Perhaps she'd like a visit from KatyKat this afternoon. If that's all right with you." Stella looked at Grace.

"I suppose it would be all right." *What harm could it bring?* "I don't want to put you out."

"No trouble at all. KatyKat loves to take rides and she's grown an attachment to Sarah, I've noticed. Now, let's go ahead and set aside a plate of dinner for Sarah when she wakes up. You know how men can eat!" Stella laughed as she went about placing food on the table in her no-nonsense fashion.

Owen was surprised but happy that Stella had come bringing dinner, Grace noted, though she didn't stay to eat with them, but promised to return with the cat to cheer up Sarah. Owen walked her out, then returned with a happy look on his face.

Grace had to admit that Stella was a nice lady and settled on the idea that whatever happened between her father and Stella could be a good thing. It could take some getting used to since no one could ever replace her mother, but Grace was adult enough to know that wasn't what this was about.

By early afternoon, Tom and Robert were gone, and Sarah said she felt good enough to sit in the sun and wait for Stella. Since she had no fever, Grace allowed her to have a bit to eat with the sun's warmth for healing—which Owen insisted aided in curing most anything. Grace figured if anyone would know, it would be her father.

Becky helped clean the dishes but later settled into an over-sized wicker chair at the other end of the porch, her head stuck in a book, while Owen sat with Sarah to wait on Stella. Grace was feeling a little lazy herself while she elevated her foot, and stifled a yawn before Stella's carriage came rumbling into the yard.

Owen stood to greet her and walked to the front steps waiting for her. In her arms, she carried a small box with holes. "Everyone looks so comfy and cozy this afternoon that I feel like I'm disturbing your peace." Stella chuckled.

"You're not interrupting. We were all enjoying the warm sun and the benefits of it." Owen grinned broadly at her, and Grace couldn't help but smile at the unspoken affection that passed privately between them. She wondered if they knew how obvious their mutual regard was.

"Oh, I've been waiting for you, Miss Stella." Sarah got up from her chaise lounge. "Is that KatyKat in the box?" Meows sounded as the cat scratched on the box.

"Yes, it is, and as you can tell, she's anxious to be released." Stella bent down to remove the lid, and Sarah reached in and lifted the cat out.

"Sweet KatyKat," she murmured with a sniff and her thick-sounding voice from the head cold. "You didn't like that dark box, did you?" KatyKat nuzzled Sarah's cheek as she held her close, and she spoke soothingly to the cat who purred in contentment.

Becky got up and petted the cat too, then Sarah carried her back to the lounge chair to sit with her. "She's such a sweet kitty," Becky commented, "and she really likes you a lot, sister."

"Can I get you some tea or coffee, Stella?" Grace asked as they watched the interaction between Sarah and the cat.

Stella glanced at Owen. "I wanted to have a word with Owen first if you don't mind. And I'd love a cup of tea."

Grace sobered. "Well, of course. I'll go start—"

"But coffee for me, Grace."

She nodded at her father. "Why don't you two go sit in the parlor where no one will bother you?"

"Good idea. Come on, Stella. We can talk undisturbed there."

As the two walked off, Grace wondered what was so important that Stella needed time alone with her father. Surely, they hadn't formed that kind of relationship yet, had they?

29

Owen guided Stella to the parlor and shuffled them over to the settee. He selfishly wanted to sit next to her, so he turned sideways and she moved to face him. The look on her face was somber—not the look of a lady who couldn't wait to be alone with him—and his ego deflated.

"Stella, is everything all right?"

She took a deep breath and reached for his hand. "I need to explain something to you."

"What do you mean? You don't sound like someone who's happy to be with me right now." *Here it comes . . . She's going to say I can't get over the death of my wife and have gotten sick instead of dealing with it.*

She caught his look and sighed, staring him straight in the eye. "Don't pretend you know what I'm about to say because I doubt that you do."

"I'm sorry. I thought I was about to get discarded in lieu of your cats and books. I never want to interject myself where I'm not wanted, and we are both set in our ways at our age."

"Good heavens! Please hush and listen to what I have to

say or I'll have to hit you with a fireplace poker!" She laughed and he joined in.

"I'm sorry," he said. "Please go ahead."

Stella stared down at his hands. "Owen, you know, I've been doing a little research in my medical books, and I think I may know what ails you."

Owen drew back. "How would you know?"

"Something I've never told you—I started medical school at Women's Medical College of New York, thinking to become a doctor or nurse. My parents died when cholera hit in Montana, so I returned home and never went back. But I still love to research medical things and correspond with the professor back in New York that I maintained a friendship with. I've stumbled upon something that might explain the weakness and pain in your legs and arm."

He tried to follow her but was lost. "What do you mean?"

Stella bit her lip. "Well, I took it upon myself to write her about your condition—your odd motor symptoms and having no feeling in your feet when you walk. I read about a mysterious ailment in some medical research papers that my professor uncovered. She believes you have multiple neuritis, a type of peripheral nerve condition. Then I spoke with your doctor about our thoughts and he seems to think we are right."

"Gracious! That sounds very serious." Suddenly Owen's tongue felt dry, and he swallowed, but so what? He wasn't a young man. Something would kill him sooner or later. Maybe sooner, with all this serious talk.

"It can be, but I believe we can fight this chronic condition."

"We?"

Stella actually blushed right before his eyes. "Yes, we. I want to help as much as I can."

"You mean you'd still want to be with me with all this I have going on?"

"Yes, Owen. Your legs don't change who you are inside."

Her voice was sincere, and he didn't quite know what to say, so he squeezed her hand. "Now that you think you know what it is, what can I do about it?"

Stella smiled. "I'm getting to that. Dr. Avery suggests trying hot springs and drinking quinine water for leg pain. Also rubbing liniment."

"Why didn't Dr. Avery ride over and tell me this?"

"He was planning to, but since I was leaving and Matilda was in labor, he asked me to tell you. I grabbed the cat and came as fast as I could."

"Let's go find Grace and tell her."

———

Grace wondered what was taking her father and Stella so long. The tea and coffee were lukewarm at best now. She'd taken the tray out to the porch to wait for them. Between sneezes, Sarah was happily playing with the cat with the string from her shoelace. But at least she seemed to be feeling better.

Someone was coming up the road to the house. *More company?* Soon she could see it was Warren. Grace wasn't sure why he always just showed up at random, but she'd be a kind hostess anyway.

Warren dismounted and hurried up the steps. "Good afternoon, Grace." His huge smile faded into a thin, tight line when he glanced about the porch and saw Becky and Sarah. "I see you have company."

Becky glanced up from her book, then went back to reading. Sarah eyed him shyly for a moment, and the cat scrambled from her arms.

"Hello. Yes, they've come back to stay for a few days." She wasn't going to go into the reasons why right now.

"Oh, I never knew they left."

"Come have some coffee that I made for Stella and my father."

He frowned. "I saw the other carriage. You have another visitor?"

"Stella is a friend of my father's, and she brought us dinner today." She limped back to the coffee to pour him a cup.

"What's wrong with your foot?" he asked, sounding irritated.

"Oh, nothing much . . . just a little sprain." She handed him his coffee, but he never sat down. He stood looking about, frustration written all over his face. "Then you have quite a houseful. I was rather hoping to have you all to myself, but I can see you'll always be too busy taking care of others to have any time for me," he complained, staring at her with an unpleasant expression.

"I'm sorry. I had no idea you might drop by." She felt flustered by his criticisms about what she did with her time.

He leaned closer, and whispered, "I told you that I didn't care very much for children, and you'd be so much better off if you'd live in town away from all this work."

"And I told *you*, I love children and have no intention of moving into town. Ever."

"I should be going. I'm sorry I dropped in unexpectedly." Warren whirled around, red-faced, and his boot heel came down on KatyKat's tail. The cat screeched, causing him to jump forward and dump his coffee down the front of Grace's dress. The cat, in her scrambling to get away, got between Warren's legs, tripping him, and the teapot and tray went crashing to the floor. He bent down and scooped the cat up in a rage. When he did, KatyKat's claws came out. Hissing, she swiped his neck, leaving three long claw marks.

He swore under his breath, then tossed the cat at Sarah, who was crying now. Grace stood in utter shock as Becky came running. Warren pulled out his handkerchief, finding blood when he dabbed his neck.

"Let me put something on that for you, Warren. It was all an unfortunate accident." Grace moved toward him, but he withdrew. Becky and Sarah were watching both of them, with a look of irritation directed at Warren. Sarah continued to stroke KatyKat with a soothing sound.

"What's all the commotion?" Owen came as fast as his legs would carry him through the front door and onto the porch with Stella holding his arm.

"It's none of your affair, ol' man," Warren snapped.

Grace stepped close. "Warren, no one speaks to my father that way in my presence. Please remove yourself from my property. You are not welcome here."

He stared down at her, and she could almost feel his pent-up anger. He snorted, turned on his heel, and strode down the steps, hopping on his horse faster than a buzzard landing on a carcass.

Owen threw his arm about his daughter's trembling shoulders. "I'd say you got rid of him permanently."

"He's a cad, Pop, *and* mean. I saw the anger in his eyes . . . and this wasn't the first time."

"But it's his last time," Owen reassured her, staring down the road as Warren disappeared from view.

Stella turned to Sarah. "Is KatyKat all right?"

"Yes, ma'am. That man stepped hard on her tail and she scratched him."

"Humph. Maybe he deserved it." Stella chuckled and then stroked the cat's head. She bent to pick up the dishes.

"I'll go get the broom." Becky hurried away.

"I'm sorry about your tea, Stella." Grace picked up the broken pieces of her prized rose teapot.

"Another time, Grace, but thank you. After we clean this mess up, your father and I would like to talk with you."

Goodness! Are they planning on getting married so soon? Grace cleared her throat and muttered, "Okay."

"Don't look so alarmed, Grace. It's probably not what you're thinking about," Owen added.

She breathed a sigh of relief. Her father knew her very well. "I see. Well, then. Let me finish cleaning this up," she said as Becky returned with the broom and dustpan. "Becky, could you go put the teakettle back on?"

"Oh, please don't bother," Stella said. "Soon as we talk, I must get back to town."

"I understand. Let's go inside then. Becky, will you finish here for me?" Grace asked.

"Yes, ma'am," Becky replied, already sweeping up the pieces.

30

The warm salt bath felt soothing to Grace's foot as she soaked it in a small wash pan—so much so that she almost decided to soak her other foot. She thought back to the conversation she'd had earlier with her father and Stella. If Grace was suspicious of Stella before, all doubt was swept away when Stella shared that she'd been researching her pop's illness. The tone of Stella's voice and the affection she had for Owen was real, and this impressed Grace.

"Grace, I remember seeing a poster about hot springs near Helena last time I was in town," Owen said as he steadied himself and eased into a side chair. "Maybe I need to go and see if those hot springs would help me. I've heard they're good for rheumatism."

"I say there's no harm in trying, Pop. Why don't we ask Dr. Avery what he thinks?"

"I will. I've been praying about my health to the Man Upstairs." Owen's tone became serious. "It may not be a cure, but maybe God's pointing me in the right direction for help."

"I hope so. God sometimes answers in ways that surprise us, doesn't He?" She dared not tell him that she'd overheard him praying privately, but she had been praying too.

"By the way," he said, "your foot is not nearly as swollen, but the bruise sure is turning blue."

She looked closely at her foot as she took it out of the water to gently pat it dry with a towel. "I think you're right."

"It'll be healed in time for you to go to the Bozeman Ball." He grinned.

Grace giggled. "You forget that I just sent the man who was courting me packing."

"True, but there's Robert." Owen gave her a level gaze.

"I don't think he's interested in me or going to any ball. He keeps to himself and seems to like it that way." She slipped on her sock and shoe.

"You don't know that," he countered.

Grace shrugged, and picked up the pan of water to dump outside. "I think you're dreaming."

"You can't tell me you aren't attracted to him. He's a good man." He continued talking as she went into the backyard to throw out the water.

When she returned, she saw Ginny arriving in her carriage. "Ginny, dear. How are you?" Grace hurried to open the door for her friend. "You look much better than when I saw you on Sunday."

Ginny smiled. "Oh, I am to be sure, especially by each afternoon. I heard about Sarah and your foot from Robert, but I needed to see for myself how everything was."

"I'm doing much better. I just soaked my foot in bath salts that Robert got for me. Sarah has a little cold but seems better today. But tell me, how are you feeling overall?"

"Robert bought some bath salts. How thoughtful." Ginny shot her an endearing look, then continued. "Some foods don't always agree with me, or the very thought of them makes me queasy. For instance, coffee. I can't bear to drink it now."

"I poured her a cup and she turned a pale shade of green." Owen laughed, and Ginny giggled.

"Let me fix you some hot tea then." Grace moved to the stove.

"That would be nice. Becky mentioned something about Warren. What happened?"

Grace and Owen told her about the fiasco with the cat.

Once Ginny stopped laughing she said, "I'm sorry. It sounded so funny when you told it, but I think you did the right thing, Grace. This is very concerning about Warren's attitude. Do you mind if I tell Frank about this?" Ginny said, then took a sip of her tea.

"Not at all. There's something about Warren that I can't put my finger on. He wants me to be focused totally on him and no one else."

"I agree, that's odd."

Owen pushed his chair back. "I'll leave you two to chat—"

"Wait, Pop. Before you leave, tell Ginny what Stella told us today about your health."

"I don't want to bore her with my health," Owen replied.

"You won't be boring me. You know I consider you like a second father. Please, tell me. Have you received some bad news?"

"Maybe. Dr. Avery hasn't been sure I had a stroke, and now we might have an idea what is wrong with me."

"Then I want to hear about it, Owen," Ginny said.

Owen explained what Stella had told him, summarizing the details as best he could. "I don't think it'll kill me, but it will impact my life."

Ginny shook her head sadly, then looked at him and Grace. "But at least you may be closer to knowing what to do about it, right?"

"That's just it. It's rare and not a lot of research has been done. We're going to town tomorrow to talk with Dr. Avery. He's busy today because Matilda is in labor."

"Then please, let me know what you discover," Ginny said. "Perhaps I can come by and help you with the nursery too."

"Not yet, the fabric hasn't been delivered last I checked. I need it to pick a paint color." Pushing back her chair, Ginny set her teacup down and rose from her chair. "Thanks for the cup of tea. I'm glad I came to check on you and you as well, Owen. You know you're like family to me." She reached over to hug Owen and Grace noticed tears in his eyes—which was the case more often than not anymore with him.

"I'll walk you to the door," Grace offered, standing up.

"Uh, you mean you'll hobble. Don't trouble yourself. I can let myself out." Ginny squeezed her hand. "Please take care of that foot so you'll be fit as a fiddle to go to the ball."

"*Ginny*. I haven't said I was going. You know I haven't a dress to wear to a ball." Grace expelled a deep breath.

"We'll see about that when you're in town." Ginny glanced at her watch dangling from a gold chain. "Oh, goodness. Look at the time. I must get home before Frank or he'll be worried about me. Toodle-oo." She gave a tiny wave, then left.

As Ginny left, Becky burst into the kitchen with Sarah trailing a little slower behind her. "I'm hungry. Can we start supper now?" Becky inquired.

211

Grace motioned for Sarah to come close. She wanted to test her forehead for fever.

Sarah leaned against her. "I'm tired."

"Does she have a fever?" Owen watched as Grace felt her face and arms.

"I believe she may, Pop. Sarah, why don't you go back to your room, and we'll bring you supper in bed?"

"I'm not hungry," she answered with glazy eyes.

"Then, I'll make you some chamomile tea and bring you some crackers."

"Okay. Can Becky come with me?"

Grace nodded. "Yes. That's a good idea."

"But I was going to help you so you won't be on your foot," Becky reminded her.

"Not to worry. It's feeling so much better. Get Sarah into bed and then come help me."

Owen piped up. "No, you sit still. I can still walk, you know—just not fast. Why don't we see what's left over from the dinner Stella brought?"

"Thanks, Pop. That will be fine, if we have enough."

He winked at Becky. "It'll be plenty, especially when I whip up a pan of biscuits."

Spring quickly turned into summer and Grace's flowers were blooming, but more importantly, the potatoes showed signs of a good crop when she'd walked through the field yesterday. They'd do well at harvesttime—thanks in part to Robert's help and Tom's. She was so glad that Ginny had told Robert about her need, especially since that brought the children and Robert into her life, which was richer than it had ever been.

She was up early and stood kneading dough for bread by the kitchen window—which offered a pleasant morning view—thinking over the last several months. Tomorrow, at Dr. Avery's urging, she would take her father to the hot springs to help him manage his ailment. She hoped it would help. Even if it didn't, Stella had energized him better than any medicine could.

Her foot had healed and Sarah was back to her happy self, full of smiles and giggles, although Robert still lived in town with the children. Many times they would ride to the farm when Robert came and help with baking or laundry. Neither of the girls liked pulling weeds, so she enlisted Tom and got to know him better. She found him to be smart and eager to please. His sullen looks were replaced with an ever-warming smile and inquisitiveness to learn everything he could. Somehow, Stella had gotten him interested in the medical field, and he told her he was determined to be a doctor.

She punched down the dough, then patted it into two loaves. She could feel totally peaceful . . . *if* . . . If her father was better . . . If she was able to get a good price at the market for the harvest . . . If she had a nice dress for the Bozeman Ball . . .

She admonished herself. Too many *ifs*. *Why am I so ungrateful when I have so many blessings in my life?* An unexpected tear fell down her cheek. She knew why. She was in love with Robert *and* his children, but what could she do about it?

Grace set the dough aside, covering the loaves with a muslin cloth, then stepped outside. Smiling, she watched as Bluebelle came waddling up to the porch. She bent down and lifted the duck to her arms. "You silly duck. What would I do without your companionship? I'm hoping to have a companion for you soon. No one should be all alone without someone to love." Bluebelle pecked her on the face and she laughed.

"Does that apply to you as well as Bluebelle?" Grinning, Robert strode into the yard and stood watching her and the duck. "I see you talk to your duck quite a bit." He chuckled.

Grace turned around. She hadn't realized he'd arrived. "I talk to Bluebelle because she doesn't talk back," she quipped.

Robert couldn't resist teasing her. "That's the way it is with most women, they want to do all the talking."

"I beg your pardon?" She arched an eyebrow at him. "If we didn't have to read minds, I think conversation would be a whole lot different." She put Bluebelle on the ground and watched her waddle off with a quack.

"I've always answered you."

"Yes, usually with one-word answers."

He gazed down at her and she looked at him, her hands on her hips and chin lifted with a fake defiant look that he'd come to know. All he could think about was the kiss he'd stolen and the softness of her lips beneath his. "I'll try to do better."

"That would be a nice change indeed."

"I try to please."

"Then maybe you could start today."

"All right . . . about that kiss—"

"I know. It was a mistake." She lifted her skirts to leave, but Robert touched her arm and she paused, lifting her gaze to look at him through warm honey-colored eyes that went straight to his heart.

"No, it was not a mistake. What I wanted to say was I'm not sorry that I stole that kiss."

Grace blinked. "It's much too early to be talking about such things."

"I thought you wanted me to talk more."

"I—I do, but—" Her eyes flittered away.

"But what? Are you still seeing Warren? Owen told me what happened after me and Tom left that day."

"I haven't seen him since that day, and I don't intend to."

"Well, then. Maybe you'd like to take a turn down the lane on a proper courting ride." He waited, stiff shouldered.

"Well . . . I don't know what to say."

"Don't let me twist your arm. Either you do or you don't."

Grace stood gazing back with a blank look. Apparently, he'd gotten the wrong impression that she might actually *like* him in that way. "Forget it. I've got work to do." He twisted on his boot and strode in the direction of the barn.

"Where are the children?" she asked.

"They're not coming today," he tossed over his shoulder. He couldn't get away fast enough. How stupid of him. Why did he think she'd share his feelings? He had absolutely nothing to offer her. When had he decided he was looking for another woman in his life? He felt foolish. He'd hurry through his chores and get back to the mercantile. There was plenty of work to do there that would take his mind off her and get his focus back on the children that he'd promised to care for. *Permanently.*

31

Grace almost went after him. *But what would I say?* She hurried back inside, knowing she may have just ruined any chance she had with Robert.

She picked up the basket to gather eggs. Hopefully her mood would improve before her father asked questions.

Owen took time to pray, sitting on the edge of his bed, regretting that he couldn't get on his knees before the Lord. Many times, he felt the need to humble himself before his Creator in prostration, but it had become too hard for him. He prayed about the visit to the hot springs and thanked God for Stella's friendship and concern for his health. He also prayed for his daughter's future. After pouring his heart out, he rose and shuffled his way to the kitchen where breakfast smells assailed his nostrils, realizing that he was hungry for a change.

"Good morning, Grace," he said, making it to the stove for coffee.

"Morning," she replied, tight-lipped. She didn't look at him but continued frying bacon.

"Anything amiss?"

"No. Why?"

He scratched his unshaven face. "Oh, I don't know. You seem a little grumpy."

"Well, I'm not. I've been trying to get my chores done earlier today so I can get us packed for tomorrow's trip." She laid the cooked pieces of bacon on a plate, then viciously cracked two eggs to cook sunny-side up for him.

He knew her well enough to know something was bothering her, but it was up to her if she wanted to talk about it. "I was thinking of asking Robert to go along with us. What do you think?"

"No," she answered through clenched lips, then she flipped the eggs. "We don't need him. Besides, who will watch out for the children?"

"I hadn't thought of that, but I'm sure Stella would keep an eye on them for the day."

She placed his breakfast before him, then poured herself a cup of coffee and sat down.

"My thought was he could help me in and out of the springs. He's a lot stronger than you. I don't think he'd mind." Owen watched her face while he ate. Did her mood have something to do with Robert?

Grace sighed. "I didn't think about that. I believe I made him angry this morning, but you can ask. Just don't be surprised if his answer is no." She stirred the sugar in her coffee.

Owen washed down his eggs with a swig of coffee. "A fight so early in the morning?"

"Oh, Pop. I think I made a mistake. He told me he wasn't

sorry about the kiss that I told you about, and I didn't answer him right away so he took it to mean that I didn't want him to court me. I've probably lost any chance of his courting me." She blurted out the string of sentences without taking a breath.

Have mercy. How his daughter could talk when she chose to. He shook his head. "My goodness, Grace. You can't ride a horse in both directions. I've watched you. You give him different signals, and unless I've missed the mark, I think you care more for him than you let on. It's no wonder he hasn't said anything to you before."

He watched her face crumple and she started to cry. "There now, sweet daughter. I didn't mean to make you cry," he soothed, covering her hand with his own.

She pulled her handkerchief out of her apron and sniffed into it. "I'm just so confused, Pop. Remember, he didn't know much about his first wife and wound up with three children. How do I know he has *real* feelings for me?"

"Well, a man don't have *real* thoughts about women till he's thirty-five. A'fore then, all he's got is feelin's. I'd say since you're both older, thoughts are worth a whole lot better than just feelin's," he reasoned, then tipped his cup for the last bit of coffee and waited for that to sink in.

She winced, her face softening, and said quietly, "I never knew I was giving off any signs to him. He's a man of few words so I didn't know he might want to get to know me better."

Owen crackled with laughter. "I could see how he looked at you when no one was watching. Did it ever occur to you that he wanted to proceed with caution after what happened with him before?"

"Yes, but it also made me think he might be the kind of man who went from woman to woman."

He shook his head in disbelief. "Grace, listen to yourself. Robert would have been long gone from here soon as he had two coins to rub together if it weren't for you, *and* he'd have dumped those kids off back on their aunt, or he never would've taken them in. What kind of man do you think he is?"

She breathed a long breath. "I suppose you're right, like you always are, but after the way Warren acted, I wasn't sure."

"Then you must see how hard it was for Robert to entertain the idea of trusting anyone, much less a woman."

"How did you get so smart?" Grace sniffed, a weak smile crossing her face.

"Years of living with your mother. Take the time you need, but don't take more. I should know. Time is precious."

"Are you speaking about you and Stella?"

"I guess so. I'm not saying your mother wasn't the best thing I ever had. She was, just as you felt Victor was, but they're both gone and we have to see others as a gift while we live out our last days, don't you see?"

Grace walked around the table and kissed his half-bald head. "Yes, I do see. I love you. Thanks, Pop. Why don't you ask Robert to come along tomorrow? I'll be all right with that."

Owen squeezed Grace's hand resting on his shoulder in response. "I love you too, daughter."

The Saturday ride to the hot springs wasn't long, just fifteen miles south of Bozeman. Robert had agreed to come along, and Owen had given him the reins of the carriage, so Grace sat behind them. Neither she nor Robert gave one another direct eye contact, but her mind was saying a lot—just not out loud. In fact, she was deciding she would try to find a time when she could talk to him alone.

"I sure am glad Eli let you off today. I know Saturday's a busy day at the store," Owen said.

"It is usually, but Tom will pitch in and do whatever he can to help. Tom is a lot smarter than I used to credit him. He's been reading some of those books of Stella's on medical stuff. At least it's keeping him outta trouble."

Grace listened to the conversation without adding to it, studying the back of Robert's broad shoulders, his taut muscles pulling his shirt tight against him. Working on the farm had toned his muscles, and he looked leaner than when she first saw him. He sure wasn't afraid of hard work—but what impressed her most now was he seemed to genuinely care about all the children like they were his. She not only saw this, but also heard it in his voice just now when he talked about Tom. Her heart lifted and she was reminded how God answers prayers. Now, as they traveled to the springs for her father, she prayed silently that the minerals from the waters would be beneficial to his weakened body.

"We're here." Robert slowed the horses to a walk as they came upon crude wooden buildings hastily constructed for patrons of the springs. He found a spot where several other wagons, carriages, and a couple of horses stood tethered.

Robert helped them both alight, then picked up the carpet-bag holding the men's change of clothing. Grace saw a sign posted on the porch that read ENTER HERE. From somewhere behind the building, voices could be heard that she assumed

220

were patrons "taking the waters"—the term Dr. Avery had used.

"Follow me and we'll find out what we're to do," Robert instructed while holding Owen's arm for balance.

They were greeted by a robust, bearded middle-aged man with a toothless grin.

"Right this way, folks." He waved them in. "How many tickets for the baths? Three?"

"Two," Robert replied, then looked at Grace. "Unless you plan to enjoy the springs."

"No. I won't be going in. Perhaps I can watch?" Grace asked the proprietor.

"Yes, ma'am, you can. There's a few benches to sit on outside." He looked to Robert. "That'll be three dollars for the two of ya, and you'll find a place to change right down the hallway there." He nodded in the direction of the men's changing room at the end of the short hallway. "When you're done, come back and I'll show you out to the baths. The springs are a nice 105 degrees today."

Grace took the money from her reticule and handed it to him. "I'll wait for you here, Pop."

Owen and Robert walked in the direction of the changing room, and after a few minutes, Grace meandered to the large area at the back of the log house. Where windows would normally be placed there was an open frame to the outside for viewing. The springs were vast pools resembling a swimming hole, and steam formed above the pools. Both ladies and gentlemen in bathing attire were in the springs, but the men were separated from the women.

Grace stood watching as a woman about her age attempted to persuade a young girl to step into the bath. The child was frightened, and when she finally stood, Grace gasped at the sight of her deformed lower legs below her bathing dress. The mother caught Grace's stare through the open space and gave her a look of frustration.

Grace couldn't help herself. She hurried outside. "Is there anything I can do to help?" she asked, hoping she hadn't overstepped her bounds.

"Do you mind taking her arm? Susie isn't sturdy on her feet, and that's why she's afraid she'll fall in. Isn't that right, Susie?"

"Yes, Mama. Please, Mama, don't let go."

"Susie, I promise I'll keep holding your arm, but if you want the springs to help your legs, you must get in."

Grace pushed up the sleeves of her dress, then bent down to take Susie's other arm. The little girl reminded her of Sarah. She looked up at Grace with trepidation and Grace gave her a smile of encouragement. "You can do this. I was told by the proprietor that the water is nice and warm."

Susie gave her a lopsided smile, and between the child's mother and Grace, they helped her walk to the edge of the pool.

"I'll get in first, so keep holding my hand," the mother instructed. She stepped down into the pool and said, "The water's warm and feels good. Come on, now."

"Okay. Here I come," Susie mumbled. She got one leg in the water, but held a death grip on Grace's arm and wouldn't let go, and as she took a sudden leap into the pool, she pulled Grace right in with her with an enormous splash.

Grace's dress and petticoats were immediately soaked, and she lost her hat in the mêlée.

The girl's mother was horrified. "Oh my goodness! Susie, you were supposed to let go of the lady's arm."

Embarrassment hit Grace as other patrons chuckled. Mortified, but trying to cover her embarrassment, Grace wiped the water from her eyes and face. "I'm okay, really," she said good-naturedly, laughing. She didn't want the little girl to get upset.

"I'm sorry. I was only afraid I'd fall in and drown," Susie whined. "I'm sorry."

"We wouldn't let that happen, Susie." Her mother tsked, shaking her head at her daughter and then turning to Grace. "I'm so very sorry. You've ruined your dress. You must take my dress and change."

"I couldn't do that. You're much tinier than I am. Anyway, the water does feel very nice, don't you think?"

"It does," Susie agreed. "Can you stay in here with us?"

"No, she can't," a firm voice from the pool's edge spoke. It was the man in charge. "The pools are for paying customers and bathing attire is required. I told you that, miss," he griped.

The three of them laughed. "I'm afraid I yanked her in," Susie explained, "but I didn't mean to, sir."

"Makes no difference to me. Just get out," he ordered Grace.

"I'm coming." Grace didn't like his bossiness. Her father and Robert came outside as the burly man was pulling her by the arm out of the pool.

"Grace!" Owen yelled. "What happened?"

Grace tried to ignore Robert's open stare as she stood dripping. "It was an accident."

The lady in the pool looked at the proprietor. "Please, my key is by the towel next to the bench. Give it to her so she can dry off and change into my dress."

"No, I'll be just fine drying right here in the sun for a while, but thank you—?"

"Nadine Johnson."

"I'm Grace Bidwell. Please go on and enjoy your time in the pool."

Nadine nodded, saying, "Thank you for your help."

Grace walked over to a bench placed in the direct sunlight and plopped down. She leaned forward to squeeze out the water from the bottom of her skirts. Someone from the pool had retrieved her hat and had given the soggy, limp mess to Robert, who handed it to her. She could tell he was stifling a laugh, but she didn't care.

"Grace, are you all right?" Owen had a worried look, but the corners of his mouth twitched.

"Go ahead you two and have a good laugh, then get on in the pool while I dry out. I assure you I will *not* melt."

Robert smiled at her, his face softening, she supposed, because of her predicament. Then he and her father walked slowly to a pool nearby. She watched for a few moments after they got in.

The sun was hot and though her clothes stuck like glue to her, she endured the stares of the patrons. Leaning her head against the log wall, she closed her eyes to the sun's rays while the afternoon passed.

32

On the way home from the springs, Grace sat up front with Robert so her father could stretch out and doze on the back-seat. Owen seemed worn out, so Grace knew they wouldn't know immediately whether the one visit helped. Grace's dress was still damp when they finally left the hot springs, so she wrapped a blanket about her that she kept in the carriage when they left. In the shade, the dampness of her dress chilled her.

"Your father really enjoyed taking the waters, but he's tuckered out. We could stop in town and have a light supper at the boardinghouse or somewhere before I take both of you back to the farm," Robert said, keeping his eyes on the road.

"That won't be necessary. Besides, I need to get into some dry clothes."

He glanced sideways to look at her. "I suppose so. Tell me what happened back there."

Grace rolled her eyes. "Okay, but no laughing." Before she finished with her tale, Robert was chuckling while trying to keep his laughter down so as not to wake Owen.

"I said no laughing," she reiterated.

"Ah, but I didn't promise. I can't help it. That was funny, but I'm sorry you had to sit around in wet clothes."

"The nice lady, Nadine, offered me her change of clothing, which I hadn't a prayer of fitting into. I wouldn't have used them anyway since she needed them herself. Thank you for coming with us. I fear my dad is heavier than I can manage sometimes."

"Glad I could help out. Anytime, just let me know. I believe he'll have to make more than one visit to the springs from what the other men said today. They swear by it."

"I hope you're right. I guess he told you what Dr. Avery and Stella believe he has?"

"Yes, he did. But what's the prognosis?"

"I'm not sure they know, but it does answer some questions the doctor and we had. I don't think there is a cure."

"I see. At least he has you and Stella. She's very important to him, I gather."

"And you, Robert. He admires you and I can't thank you enough for being his friend."

They were nearing the outskirts of town, and he took the fork in the road toward Bidwell Farms. "It was a natural thing—me and your father. He's more like my own father."

"What happened to your father? I've never heard you speak of any family."

Robert sighed and answered, "I was just a teenage boy when my parents died. I wound up fending for myself. I was angry. Maybe that's part of the reason me and Tom got off to a bad start."

Grace was glad that he was opening up to her. "I can understand that, especially since the children were thrust on you the way they were."

226

"Yep, but the truth is, they've been good for me. Made me think about my own youth and foibles. I want to do what's right by them."

"That's very admirable of you, Robert. I've come to care about the children like they were my own."

"I can see that, but I'm not surprised. It's the way you are, caring and giving."

They continued on in silence for another mile until Grace became braver to broach the subject on her mind.

"Robert, about yesterday morning . . . I think we have a misunderstanding and I want to explain, if you'll let me."

He jerked around to look at her. "There's nothing to explain, Grace. I know I'm not what you're looking for, and I have little to offer so forget I even said anything."

"Who says I'm looking for anything? Or anyone? I'd like love to happen naturally. Wouldn't you?"

"I haven't been too lucky when it comes to love. I'd like love to come with commitment—you know, someone I can grow old with. That didn't happen for me the first time. Shucks! I'm *already* getting old."

"I'd like to believe that's what all couples want and need. Both of us have loved and our lives were suddenly changed forever, but I'd like to think we still have years ahead of us. You're not that old. Anyway, I started out by trying to explain about yesterday—"

"You said the kiss was a mistake."

"It's because I was taken by surprise. I didn't mean that the way it came out, and I wasn't sure that it meant anything at all to you. I believe you took my hesitance as a rejection when you asked me about a proper date. Pop made me see that sometimes I give off the wrong impression."

Robert harrumphed, staring ahead at the dirt road. "I guess I don't understand women at all."

She turned in her seat to look at his profile. "I was upset with how things had gone with Warren the other day. I came to the realization that I couldn't trust him and was wasting my time. I have a feeling that you don't trust women since you married without knowing your first wife had children."

"I wish you would give me the benefit of the doubt." He clenched his jaw. "I'm not that shallow. Just so you know, I knew Ada long enough to know that I loved her, but it was very unfortunate that she kept such a big secret from me. It changed me for the worse for a while, I agree, and I was angry. I felt I was either duped or just plain stupid. To make it all worse, my own town scoffed at me. That's the real reason that I left."

"I'm really sorry for that. Please don't think I'm judging you. I hope I didn't sound that way." Grace turned back to face forward in her seat again and saw that they were nearing the farm. *Did I only make things worse now?*

"Listen, Grace. Why don't we call a truce and see where this leads? We're not youngsters anymore, but adults with a past that we've been trying to mend. In many ways, sometimes I feel God must have led me here at this time and place because of how you love the children . . . I mean, *my* children."

Grace considered Robert as he spoke, and nodded briefly. "I agree, and I'd love it if you'd take me for a turn down the lane . . . alone," she answered.

Robert chuckled. "Then how about tomorrow?"

Owen had awakened a few miles back, but in his drowsy state he continued to lie still and listened to their conversation. He looked at the two of them through a slit in one eye and thanked God they had reached some sort of agreement. *Thank You, Lord. It's been a good day.*

After assisting Owen back inside the house, Robert put the carriage and horses away. He set off on horseback for town again, thankful he had time alone for reflection. It had been a productive day in his mind, in more ways than one. Owen had become like a father to him these past few months, and he was honored to be able to help him out today in the hot springs. While they were sitting in the hot springs, Owen had told him how worried he'd been about his health and his concern over his daughter.

Owen revealed that meeting Stella had taken the focus off of his own health. "I think God's had a hand in all this, Robert—me meeting Stella—you and Grace. You see, I've been praying someone would come into her life that was dependable and stable who may be able to give her children. Your children were proof of that," Owen had told him. "She adores them, and I think she really cares for you, although she won't be the first to say it."

Robert was surprised and hadn't answered, so Owen added, "Don't look at me like you have no idea what I'm talking about because I think you do."

Could it be that Owen was right? After their talk on the way home, Grace not only had apologized, but wanted a truce of sorts. He wouldn't deny that he was beginning to care for her but he was shocked that she might even have the tiniest feeling about him.

Out of the blue, he let out a whoop, and his horse skittered sideways. Robert patted his neck. "Sorry about that. Guess this is the first time I had something to look forward to in a long time." His horse snorted, then tossed his head in agreement, making him chuckle.

Days later, the potato vines were growing well, but keeping the weeds down was a continuous aggravation. It was backbreaking work, but Robert knew he had to stay on top of it if they were going to produce a good crop. He'd dusted for aphids a week ago, and today he took his time checking for cutworms, removing them when he spotted them. The fat worms could destroy a plant in a matter of hours.

It was nearly noon, so he stood up to stretch his back, shoving his hat back to see better. From across the field, Grace and Tom were busy doing the exact same thing. The more he thought about it, he decided wheat farming was somewhat easier, but this lush valley held perfect conditions for growing beets and potatoes. Grace waved, and he lifted his hat in a wave—their signal that the morning's work was done.

He almost wished he didn't have to go to work at Eli's today. Since their talk, he wanted to be around Grace more. It had been hard for him to open up to her, but they'd seemed to come to an understanding of sorts. He couldn't help but smile when the vision of Grace sopping wet at the hot springs in her pretty dress and hat came to mind. One thing he had to say—she had certainly dealt with it in a ladylike fashion. He had a lot to learn about her, and he was so glad that she was part of his children's life. Robert was beginning to have a good feeling about the future.

33

Owen lingered over his morning coffee. Was it just his imagination, or were his legs somewhat stronger? He still had weakness and fatigue, but some days he was a little more stable when he walked. Either way, he and Stella were going to go back to the hot springs. He might just make this a routine—as long as he thought it was making a difference.

"Hello, Mr. Miller, are you here?" Tom called from the front door. "Grace said I'd find you in the parlor. Should I come back later?"

Owen set his cup down. "Tom, come on in. I'm just relaxing and ruminating."

"Good. I can't stay but a minute or Robert will come looking for me. I have to muck the barn this morning, but I wanted to give you something I made." He brought his hand around from his back, holding out a cane in front of him. "I hope you like it."

Owen took the cane with surprise. "You made this?" He ran his hand over the smooth carving of wood with a crook at its top for his hand. "I'm mighty impressed, and of course, I'll get a lot of use out of it. Let me try it out."

It took a moment for him to stand after sitting so long, but Tom immediately assisted him from the chair. The cane was sturdy and the smooth, hooked neck fit nicely in his palm. Owen walked across the room, leaning on it for support. Tom's broad smile told him that he was very pleased with his workmanship.

"Tom, this is just about the nicest thing anyone has done for me." Owen paused next to him, then gave the youth a bear hug. "I wasn't aware that you liked carving, and you did a great job, my boy."

Tom's face flushed and he shrugged his scrawny shoulders. "Aw, it started out with whittling a long time ago to pass the time, then I got the idea to try something larger and I thought you could use a cane. I read somewhere that you should use it on the side that is the strongest. I think that's what you did."

Owen stared at him. "Right you are. Makes sense to me. You should consider apprenticing to a wood-carver."

Tom shook his head. "No, that's just a hobby to pass the time. I think I want to be a doctor. Miss Stella loaned me a couple of medical books, and I like reading about all that stuff."

"Is that so? That's a noble occupation—but remember it's a lot of hard work."

"That's exactly what Miss Stella said, but she also said anything worth pursuing will involve hard work."

"Smart lady, that Miss Stella. Where are your sisters this morning? In town?"

"No, they came this morning to help Miss Grace bake cookies." Tom started for the door. "I gotta run or I'll get yelled at."

Owen lifted the cane with a wave as he left. A deep warm feeling flooded him. *He might be the grandson I always hoped for.*

A week later, dressed in her pop's overalls, Grace stirred the buttercup-colored paint in the pail until it was smooth. "Ginny, this room will be transformed in a few hours between me and Becky." Ginny sat knitting nearby with her feet propped up, while Sarah held a ball of yarn.

Becky giggled. "I hope I can paint. I've never tried it before," she said. Becky's hair was tied up in a kerchief, with a strand or two peeking out from beneath. She wore a pair of Tom's pants and his old shirt. Grace smiled, wondering how despite all she'd been through, Becky had turned into such a sweet, eager, young girl, always willing to help when asked, no matter what the task.

"You'll do just fine, just watch how I do it." Grace carried the pail over to the ladder with her paintbrush to start. "I'll start at the top, so you aren't on the ladder. You can start lower nearest the door."

"I wish I could help," Sarah grumbled.

"But you are helping, Sarah. Sitting here with me when I'm not allowed to help *is* a help. Besides, you've helped by carrying in all the paint supplies." Ginny unwound the ball of yarn that Sarah held. "Soon, this will become my baby's blanket."

Sarah uttered, "Oh, can I please hold her?"

Ginny giggled. "Well, I'm not sure if it's a girl or boy, but yes, you may if you're very careful."

Sarah's head bobbed. "Oh, yes, ma'am. I'll be extra careful."

Grace glanced down from the top of the ladder, glad that Sarah was there too. The children needed a sense of family, and Grace considered Ginny like a sister.

A half hour later, the two women stood back on the other side of the room, surveying the wall. Ginny put her hands together. "It's perfect. I wanted it to look like warm sunshine, and I think Eli helped me find just the right shade."

"He did. I wish I could paint faster, but thankfully, this isn't a large room. I have supper to cook, but I can come back for a few hours tomorrow, if you can, Becky."

"I'll ask Papa, but I think he'll say yes."

"Girls, I really appreciated your help today. We'll put things away while you go to the kitchen. Nell has some cookies and milk waiting."

The girls whooped, darting from the room to see who could get there first.

Grace cleaned the paintbrushes and set them aside for the next day, while Ginny waddled over and put a lid on the paint pail. "Thank you for taking over for me today. Frank is so busy with work, he couldn't find time to paint."

Grace shot a glance at her friend. "Do I detect loneliness in your voice?"

Ginny sighed, then looked at her. "Not really. It's more than that. Frank is worried about something at work but doesn't want to bother me."

"That makes sense. He wants you to concentrate on taking care of yourself, and I agree."

Ginny's brow furrowed. "I guess. Do you have time for a cup of tea?"

"One cup, but then I really do need to leave," she replied.

Over tea, Ginny talked about her excitement about the

234

baby. Then she asked, "Are you feeling more settled about your father and Stella? Last time we talked about it you had your doubts."

Setting her cup in the saucer, Grace was thoughtful for a moment before answering. "You know, I was wrong about her. She's the genuine thing, and I believe she really cares for my father. If it hadn't been for her, we'd still be wondering what is wrong with him."

"I'm happy to hear that for him, and for you as well. Which leads me to ask, now that Warren is out of the picture, do you think there's a chance for Robert?" Ginny arched a brow when she looked at her.

"You do like the details, don't you?" Grace giggled.

Ginny laughed. "I do. Let's just say that I believe in romance, and I believe there is something there."

She shook her head. "Ginny, you are a hopeless romantic."

"Maybe so, but one thing I learned from the War between the States was that you mustn't take anything for granted, or ignore what's right under your nose. And I've been praying for you."

"Okay. If you must know, Robert and I have cleared the air, and we're going to see where it leads."

Ginny clapped her hands together. "I knew it! Tell me all about it."

The afternoon was slowly winding down without a customer, so Eli and Robert spent time going over the status on back orders and current ones. "I have no idea where those two orders went, Robert, but I can tell you this—they didn't make it to Bozeman." He pulled out a bill of lading from the supplier that had come in the mail as requested. Sure enough, there was Eli's signature. Eli fumed. "Someone forged my signature. I don't have a leg to stand on, and now I owe for the items. I simply don't have extra cash floating around to pay for those loads."

Robert tapped the pencil against the paper. "Is it possible the clerk that left signed one day while you were gone?"

"No, I never leave the store when I know shipments will be arriving and I never gave him that privilege. Besides, I can't recall any time I've left the store, except the time you told me to send a wire to my supplier."

"You're too trusting, Eli. Towns are sprouting up everywhere. You have miners in Alder Gulch, and Gold Creek. I've been thinking—if your goods have to arrive by steamboat coming up the Missouri River to Ft. Benton, along the Overland Trail, it's an open opportunity for road agents or any dishonest person to hijack a wagonload of goods."

Eli rubbed his chin back and forth. "I reckon you're right."

"I'd let Sheriff Mendenhall know about your next shipments just in case they arrive."

"Yep. I'll stop in and have a talk with John after I close up here."

"Good idea. I better go see how Tom's coming along restocking those canned goods."

"Why don't you two go on home and I'll close up here?" Eli suggested.

Robert looked up at the large clock. "I hadn't noticed it's quitting time. See you tomorrow then."

Striding out the door, Robert and Tom nearly walked straight into Grace and the girls, who were making their way through the folks on the sidewalk.

"Whoa! What's the big hurry?" Robert steadied Grace by her arms.

"I'm so sorry. I wanted to walk Becky and Sarah back to the boardinghouse before I left for home." Grace straightened her sleeves as Robert let go of her arms.

"We'll walk with you. Did you get the painting done?" Robert fell into step with her, and the kids raced on ahead, betting who'd get there first.

She laughed. "Hardly. I'm not a fast painter, nor very good, but I promised to come back in the morning for a while. For now I must get home. How was your day?"

Robert stared down at her. Her laughter, rich and velvety, eased his mind. "Same as always, busy."

"Busy is good. It makes the day go faster."

Robert cleared his throat for what he was about to ask. "So do you think I could come by and see you tomorrow afternoon? We could take that ride and see all the wildflowers blooming on the mountainside." He held his breath while he waited for her answer.

She paused on the sidewalk to look up at him. He hadn't noticed before how many freckles were sprinkled across her nose and cheeks. It made her look cute and fresh like the buttercups he'd spotted in Stella's backyard.

"I look forward to it, Robert."

"That's great. Say, where is your wagon? At Stella's?"

"I rode Cinnamon today and left her at Stella's. Since Ginny had all the supplies we needed, there was no need for the rig."

Near the boardinghouse, Robert watched the children slip through the door. "I'll go get Cinnamon for you, unless you want to stay for a while." He stopped in front of the porch.

"No, truly, I've got supper to prepare and I need to check on Pop. Oh, did you know that Tom made a beautiful cane for him?"

"Yes, I knew he was carving one. It's taken him some time, and I'm proud that he would think of someone else."

Grace smiled sweetly. "I'd say your parenting skills are improving."

Robert stuffed his thumbs into his pockets. "Thank you. I surely hope so. I still have a lot to learn when it comes to children. I'll go get your horse and be back in a flash."

Grace rested on the front porch to wait and plan the evening meal in her head. Leftovers from the potpie she made yesterday would be just fine with her, and her father never complained. Hearing the front door open, she turned around. Stella started down the steps.

"I saw you from the window after the children came barreling in. I wanted to ask you about something." Stella sat down next to her.

"Hello, Stella. What did you need?"

"I didn't want to overstep my bounds, so I felt I should ask you first. Would it be okay if I took your father for weekly baths at the hot springs? I know how busy you are taking care of the farm and your father and wanted to offer my help." The older lady smoothed the front of her apron, splattered with spots of berry stains and flour, as she talked.

"Why, I don't mind at all, if it's okay with him."

Stella grinned. "I've already asked him and he said yes, but I still wanted to get your approval."

Grace chuckled. "My father doesn't need my approval, nor do you, and truly it would be a big help for me. But won't that be a burden for you?"

Stella's face colored a dusty pink. "I . . . I'd want to do anything I can to help Owen."

"Then I'm very grateful. Stella, I know I wasn't so friendly the first time I met you, and I'm sorry. That was very unkind of me. I guess I thought I was protecting my father."

Stella patted her on the hand. "No need to apologize. I understand. But I must tell you I feel a connection to your father that I've not felt before . . . not entirely romantic—comfortable too." She blushed again. "I'm sorry, I'm talking too much."

Grace was surprised that Stella had said as much as she did. Somehow Grace never thought about romance and her father at his age. It might take some getting used to. "It's okay. I'm glad you told me. I promise not to get in the way."

She was relieved when Robert showed up with Cinnamon.

"Want me to ride with you back home since it's getting late?" Robert asked, handing her the reins.

"That's very sweet of you, but I think I'll take a shortcut so I'll get there sooner."

Grace waved goodbye, comforted by knowing that someone cared about her.

34

As Grace traveled her shorter route home, she realized that she'd taken a wrong turn at some point. She hadn't gone far—how had this happened? Her mind had been on something else, and to make matters worse, dark clouds were closing in over the mountaintops. She should've left Ginny's sooner and foregone the tea. It was dusk now, and there would be no moon to light her way.

She came to a crossroads and pulled hard on Cinnamon's reins until she stopped, giving her time to contemplate which way to go. *This is what I get for thinking I could find a short-cut. I thought I knew these parts like the back of my hand.*

A loud snapping branch behind her caused her to turn around in her saddle. She squinted to see in the waning daylight. Something didn't feel quite right. A strong gust of wind rustled the pine and cottonwood trees, and alarm ran down the back of her neck. Through the shadows, a rider and another man were talking about something and she strained to hear.

She whispered to Cinnamon, "Easy girl. Quiet and slow."

Edging closer, she saw a man in a wagon, which appeared to be loaded down with goods, hand the other man a big envelope. Large drops of rain pelted the dirt road between them.

"Until next time," the man perched on the wagon said.

"This is our last exchange, I'm afraid. Too many in one location and someone will be on to us," the man on horseback responded.

"Keep in touch, then, and we'll see what we can work out." He clicked the horses' reins and took off, disappearing with the wagon into the rain.

Grace didn't move a muscle for fear of being noticed. When the other man turned his horse around, her heart caught in her throat. Warren!

Warren spied her and trotted his horse toward her. "Well, now look who we have here."

Heart pounding, Grace moved to pass him. "I was just on my way home—"

"I think you'd better come with me. It's dark and you shouldn't be out alone. Are you lost?" Warren's voice was menacingly tense. He reached over, grabbing Cinnamon's reins from her tight clutch.

Grace was so surprised her jaw dropped and fear clinched her insides. "I'd rather get on home," she rasped with a dry mouth, while trying to retrieve the reins from his grip.

"Yes, you must get back to your *father*. Well, too bad. He'll have to fend for himself tonight." His tone held a warning.

The rain was beginning to come down harder. Shouting above the noise, Grace tried again. "Let go of my reins, Warren, or I'll—"

"Or you'll what? Do you really think I'm afraid of a thin

241

gal like you?" he scoffed. He dismounted, dragged her down from the horse, who cantered away, then pulled her close. Rain dripped from his hat brim and trickled down her blouse. His finger followed the dripping rain to the top of her blouse, then back up her throat with his thumb, pressing it firmly against the pulse that beat there. "I know you saw me with Jack a moment ago, so I think you might need someone to teach you a lesson about eavesdropping."

A slow thud of dread sent a chill down her spine. She'd have to think of something fast. "What you do in your free time is your business, Warren. Now let me go. I promise I won't say anything." Adrenaline raced and she tried backing away, but he struck a quick blow to the side of her head, stunning her and making her sway on her feet. She felt a trickle of blood slide down the side of her face. *I don't believe I've ever been hit.* Did she hear herself say that or was she thinking it? *Too hard to think clearly.*

Twisting her arm hard, he yanked her against him and she grimaced in pain. "Don't worry, I'll make sure of that. Grace, with all her sweetness . . . Grace, loyal and helpful to everyone—except for me." He swore.

It was hard to see his eyes through the dimness and the rain, but she felt more than saw his unleashed anger through the grip in his hands. *I have to get away from this man. He's gone crazy!* Her mind screamed, *Think, Grace! And pray.*

Robert had stood for a moment when Grace cantered off. Could it be that one day she'd be riding toward him, not away? *Is that what I really want and have wanted for so long? Someone who I could join at the hip—soul to soul—with the*

truth and openness that I'm beginning to have with Grace?
He scratched his head, thinking about the two of them and
for some reason not really wanting to go inside. Maybe he'd
take a ride. But no sooner had he thought about it than the
rain began, so he changed his mind.

He turned to go inside for supper, but stopped short when
he saw Cinnamon loping down the street, stopping in front
of the boardinghouse. Robert walked up to the horse, patting
her flanks. "Cinnamon, where's Grace?" Cinnamon snorted,
shaking her mane. Something wasn't right. Robert felt it in
his gut.

He picked up Cinnamon's reins and threw his leg over the
horse's back just as Tom came out to call him in to supper.
"I think Grace is in trouble. Run to get the sheriff and then
let Stella know where I am," he shouted at Tom, who took
off running to the sheriff's office.

Robert had been concerned about Grace leaving so late
with rain threatening, especially when she mentioned a short-
cut. He didn't know of one, and he knew the foothills could
harbor road agents and occasionally Indians, though the
Blackfeet had been relatively quiet lately. Still he prayed for
her safety.

He spurred Cinnamon into a gallop in the direction she'd
just emerged from with urgency. A gnawing feeling rumbled
within him. Whatever it was, he hoped he wasn't too late.

With Cinnamon gone, Warren held Grace's wrist so hard
that it burned as he pulled her behind him, mounting his
horse, and then in one swift movement, pulling her up in
front of him. "I know a nice place where we can have some

time alone . . . no one to interrupt," he whispered in her ear above a clap of thunder.

Grace couldn't think straight with her head throbbing. They hadn't gone far when a small, run-down log cabin appeared through the darkness ahead. Warren stopped the horse and pulled Grace off, then kicked the cabin door open. An old, musty smell was strong and overpowering. Someone had left a coffeepot and mug on the table, and the smell of smoke from a recent fire in the grate filled the one room.

How was she going to get away from this monster of a man she used to think was a gentleman? *Oh, God, please help me!*

Flinging her onto a lumpy bed in the corner, Warren gave an eerie smile. "Don't move," he ordered. He reached behind her, retrieving the pillow, then took the pillowcase and tore it in half. Dread filled her soul. Her mouth was so dry with fear that she couldn't move a muscle, much less utter a cry. She watched, horrified, as he wound two long strips around one of her wrists, tying it tightly to the iron bedpost before doing the same to the other.

Finally finding her voice, Grace begged, "Warren, please don't do this. Let's talk about why you're so angry with me—"

A sharp slap on her cheek silenced her with pain and filled her with rage. In that moment, Grace knew talking wouldn't matter. She'd have to fight against him. She twisted and struggled against the ties, and kicked her legs, sending a hard blow to his stomach. Unflinching, he clamped his hand hard over her mouth, causing her teeth to cut her lips as he eased himself on top, his full body weight nearly crushing her.

Despite his hand over her mouth, Grace tried to scream— knowing she wouldn't be heard anyway out here in this desolate area. His other hand fumbled with her skirt and petticoats. Having his eyes piercing into hers was too horrible, so she closed her eyes, held her breath, and prayed.

The cabin door crashed open as someone yelled, "Stop! I have a bullet aimed at the back of your head!"

Grace couldn't see over Warren's large body, but instantly he tensed and looked around. "This is none of your business, *hired man*. This is between me and the little lady," he spat.

Robert! Thank God. Grace was finally able to take a breath as Warren removed his hand.

"But it is *my* business," growled the sheriff, "and if you don't turn around and let go of Grace, I can promise you'll be dead in less than a minute."

Hearing the sheriff's voice, Warren backed off Grace, lifting his heavy body and turning to face him. "She came willingly," he lied.

Robert moved in and hit him with a right hook, sending Warren sprawling backward against the iron footboard. "You liar. I should—"

Sheriff Mendenhall stayed Robert with his hand. "Easy, Robert," he said with his gun pointed at Warren. "Cuff him."

Robert reached into the sheriff's back pocket and took the cuffs out, but Warren lunged at him, pulling a knife from his boot, and Grace screamed, "Robert, watch out!"

The two wrestled on the floor until a shot rang out, hitting Warren in the arm as he held the raised knife to Robert's throat. With a yelp, Warren dropped the knife, held his arm, and sat on the floor like a whipped puppy.

"Lucky for you that I didn't shoot you when I had the chance, you lily-livered piece of a man!" the sheriff said. "But I'm sure you won't be hurting anyone else for a long time."

Warren glared at him, his face twisted in anger. Robert

clipped the cuffs about Warren's wrists and yanked him off the floor.

"I got it from here, Robert," Sheriff Mendenhall said, shoving Warren toward the door. "See to Grace, and I'll see you back in town," he tossed over his shoulder.

In two strides, Robert was at Grace's side, and she saw the fury in his eyes as he bent to untie her arms and set her free.

35

"Robert, thank God you came!" Grace cried.

He untied her wrists while she sobbed, then she threw her arms around him.

"You have your horse to thank for that. Cinnamon came back to the boardinghouse, and I knew something was terribly wrong. I'm glad we got here in time." He wiped her tears with his thumbs, then cradled her face between his hands. He winced when he saw her cheek was cut, and a nasty lump above her brow was swelling. It might have turned out so differently . . . His prayers for Grace earlier had been answered.

He held her while she cried, clinging to him. "Don't leave me."

"I won't." Robert stroked her hair, which had fallen from its pins and was now a tangled mess about her, and his heart softened. He almost never saw her hair down. It made her appear feminine and vulnerable. "Sweet Grace. I'm so sorry this happened," he soothed.

When she was all cried out, she looked at him through swollen eyes. "Warren was angry because I broke it off with him, but he also didn't like me finding him with someone in the woods. I don't know what it was about. Still, he wouldn't let me go." She hiccupped.

"Is that right? We need to tell the sheriff about that. I have a hunch he'll get to the bottom of this after we tell him, but we can talk about it tomorrow. Let's get you home now." He yearned to sit right where he was, holding her to his chest, listening to her breathe. But Owen would be worried by now that she hadn't returned home.

It was drizzling rain when they made their way to the farm with Grace and Robert both on Cinnamon's back. Robert talked about the weather to keep Grace's mind off the last hour with Warren until he noticed her head nodding from his shoulder to his chest. Sometimes that was the way the body dealt with a bad experience or bad news. He'd seen it before.

Owen was standing at the door, looking out with a worried face when they arrived. Grace woke up, and when she saw her father, started to sniffle as Robert carried her to the front door. He knew she didn't want to break down in front of Owen and was holding back the tears.

"Land of Goshen, Grace. I was worried sick when you didn't come home," Owen sputtered, running his hand through his hair.

Robert carried Grace past Owen, whose mouth had dropped in question as he followed them both inside. Once Robert had placed her on the settee, Grace spoke.

"Pop . . ." But she could say no more.

Owen stepped to his daughter's side. "Grace, please tell me what happened." When he got closer and saw her cheek and head, he gasped. "Lord, have mercy. Who did this to you?"

"I'm okay now, Pop, only a little bruised and frightened," she answered.

Owen sat next to her, taking her hand. "Robert, what happened to my daughter. Did someone try—?"

"Yes. I can vouch for that. The man is in custody. It was Warren." Robert watched as Owen tried to process what he was telling him.

"That low-down scoundrel! I knew there was something strange about that man the last time he was here," he said after Robert relayed the events to him. "Thank you, Robert, for being there."

"I'm glad that I was, and with the sheriff's help." Robert looked at Grace. "Owen, if you'll tell me where to find something to clean her cheek, I'll do that before I leave."

After he'd cleaned Grace's wound, Robert said, "I think I'll go on back to town now, Grace, and tell the sheriff what you saw before Warren attacked you. It's the same thing Tom saw weeks ago, and I have a feeling that the wagon was loaded with the goods meant for Eli's mercantile. Warren must've made a deal with someone to sell the shipments and pocket the money."

Robert squeezed her hand, then turned to Owen. "Can I borrow a horse? I think Cinnamon deserves a rubdown and a rest, and I'll do the rubdown before I leave."

"No problem, Robert, and thank you again." Owen blinked a tear away and blew his nose.

Robert, still concerned for Grace, said, "Get some sleep. You're safe now."

Grace nodded numbly.

Despite the late hour, Robert thought he'd stop by and let Ginny know about Warren. It'd be good to have her here with Grace tomorrow, and they should know the facts about Warren, if they didn't already. Giving Owen a pat on his back, Robert went to take care of Cinnamon, who still stood patiently in the yard, before he took a fresh mount.

"Just a minute," Ginny called out to the loud knocking at the door. She and Frank had just retired to the parlor after dinner to talk about his business. Who could be here at this hour? She pushed the lace curtain aside on the door and saw that it was Grace's hired man. What in the world did he want at this time of the evening? She hoped it wasn't Owen taking a bad spell suddenly.

She opened the door. "Robert, come in. I'm surprised to see you."

He had a somber look on his face as he stood in her foyer with his hat in his hand. Frank came into the hallway where they were. "Anything wrong with Owen, Robert?"

"No. It's Grace."

"Grace?" Ginny inhaled sharply. "Is she all right?" Frank grabbed her arm protectively.

"She is now, but she's a little shaken up. I thought you should know that on the way back from town after she did some painting for you, she was attacked by Warren, your employee." He looked from her to Frank.

Ginny's hand flew to her face. She could hardly believe it. "Oh no," she cried, trying not to think the worst.

"For goodness' sake! Robert, I was about to tell Ginny that I fired Warren today, but I never knew he'd do something so horrendous."

"You did?" Ginny jerked her head around to look at her

husband. "I must go to her." A knot coiled in the pit of her stomach, and she prayed Warren hadn't . . . No, she mustn't think that. Robert said she was all right.

"I'll take you," Frank said to her. "I won't let you go alone."

"No," Robert said. "I mean, she's resting now, but could you go in the morning? I think the sheriff is going to want to talk to you tonight, Frank."

"Me? I don't understand," Frank barked.

"There's a little more to what Warren might have been up to besides working for you." Robert donned his hat. "I'm going over to the sheriff's now. If you want to come along, I'll explain on the way."

"Yes, of course. I won't be long, honey." Frank kissed her brow.

They left and Ginny returned to the parlor but couldn't sit still. She paced the floor and moved knick-knacks around while her mind whirled. Was it Frank's firing that caused Warren's attack on her friend, or was it the other mysterious issue that Robert referred to? Either way she was glad that he would be out of their lives. She was sorry she'd ever set Grace up with him. She eventually sat down, rubbing her abdomen with soothing strokes. It was growing larger every day. The rhythmic movements seemed to calm her and the kicking baby inside her womb. She lowered her head, praying for Grace, and waited for her husband to return.

"Have a seat," the sheriff said, indicating the chairs in front of his desk. Robert and Frank sat down. The building they were in housed the small jailhouse and sheriff's office. A portrait of Andrew Johnson hung behind the desk. Down the tiny hallway to the back was where the prisoners were kept, but Robert didn't hear a sound coming from Warren's cell. Which was a good thing, or he might be tempted to take care of him—for good. *Heaven help me.* He struggled to hold his temper in.

"John, I can't believe what's happened tonight, and if what Robert told me on the way over here is true about Warren confiscating Eli's supplies, then I'm shocked," Frank sputtered in anger. "I felt he was up to something else besides working for me, but I couldn't imagine this!"

Sheriff Mendenhall harrumphed. "You mean there's more to the story?" He glanced over at Robert.

"Yep, but it's actually another story. Grace told me she caught Warren tonight exchanging what she thought might be money for a wagonload of goods. That's when Warren got furious. I don't know who he might have sold them to, but Tom mentioned seeing the same sort of thing a while back."

"Why do you think the goods are stolen?" the sheriff asked.

"Because Eli has been missing deliveries for a while now, and he thinks his name has been forged on the receipts."

"It bears checking out. Is it okay if I go speak with Tom?"

"Sure. I think he'll corroborate Grace's story."

"Could be Warren was selling supplies to the Blackfeet or the miners in Alder Gulch—he could make a big profit," Frank inserted. "I wanted you to know, John, that I fired him this morning. He was always gone hours from the office and alluded to the day he'd be wealthy, but I thought he meant with his own law practice. Little did I know . . . I thought I'd checked his references well enough." Frank sighed.

The sheriff had been taking notes, then looked up. "Thank you both for coming to tell me this. You can rest assured that

I'll get to the bottom of it. He'll be transported to Virginia City where he'll face trial, so he won't be back. That's almost certain."

"I need to get back to Ginny, who I'm sure is worried," Frank said. "Thanks, John, for the good teamwork with Robert."

Sheriff Mendenhall stood, shook their hands, and walked them to the door. "I'll lock up here, then walk over to talk to Tom to verify his story. He's not in bed, is he?"

Robert laughed. "I doubt it. I'll see you over there. I need to get a bite to eat, if there are any leftovers, and I'm sure Stella wouldn't mind feeding you too, John."

"Sounds good. I'll see you there."

36

Grace woke to a throbbing headache and realized she'd slept late. As she swung her legs out of the bed, dizziness overcame her for a moment.

"Morning, sleeping beauty," Ginny greeted her.

"Ginny, I didn't expect to see you here." Grace slipped on her robe. "Why did you let me sleep late? I have to fix breakfast for Pop."

"That's all been taken care of. Robert and the girls are taking care of things. Eli gave Robert Saturday afternoon off. How's your head feel?"

"Like I was clobbered with my garden hoe. It was so horrible, Ginny."

Ginny came to sit on the edge of the bed and slipped an arm about her shoulders. "I know, and I'm sorry this happened. I feel partly responsible since I more or less pushed Warren on you."

Grace looked at her. "Please, don't blame yourself. Warren became a different person . . . or he was hiding his true nature the first time we met."

Ginny looked her square in the eye. "Did he—"

Grace shook her head. "No, he didn't, but he tried. If it wasn't for Robert's intervention, I'm certain he would've." She tried to shut out the image of his body looming over her with his hand over her mouth. "I'm sure God saved me from a worse fate."

Ginny squeezed her hand again. "Then we have much to thank the good Lord for. Now, let's get you something to drink and eat. It'll help your headache, I'm sure. Do you feel like going downstairs, or shall I have Becky bring you something?"

"I'd rather go downstairs, if you don't think I look too ghastly."

"No. You have a cut on your cheek, but let me comb your hair. I think I can hide that large knot on your forehead. It might upset them to see that. Oh, I nearly forgot. I've brought you another duck so Bluebelle will have a companion." She picked up the brush as she talked. "I ordered it almost two months ago."

"You did?" Grace clapped her hands together. "I can't begin to thank you enough. Bluebelle has been a lot of company for me and follows me everywhere. Sarah will be happy, I know."

Ginny laughed. "I've already introduced them. So now you'll have to come up with a duck name for him. They could have little ducklings."

Grace laughed. "Wouldn't that be something?"

Once she was downstairs, the girls fussed over her, bringing her toast and coffee. Grace felt cherished, and soon her headache was better. "You're all too sweet to me, but I have to say it's nice to get a little attention for a change," she said, smiling at all those gathered in the kitchen.

"Ha! Are you saying I never give you attention?" Owen grumbled.

They all laughed good-naturedly. Robert winked at her and Grace smiled back.

"Did Miss Ginny tell you that she brought you another duck? He's beautiful," Sarah said.

"She did." Grace smiled at her. "Isn't she the sweetest friend?" Sarah nodded.

"What should we name him?"

"I think we should call him Paddy," Sarah offered.

Grace thought a moment. "You know, I like that. Paddy it is."

"I think I'll take my leave now. It looks like you're in good hands, Grace." Ginny rose to leave.

A knock at the door interrupted their goodbyes. "I'll go see who it is," Ginny offered.

"I'll walk you to the door," Grace said, feeling steady now. "I'm so glad that you came in spite of your condition." She smiled down at Ginny's midsection.

"That's what friends do. You would do no less, I'm sure." Ginny opened the door.

"Is there a Robert Frasier here?" a well-dressed woman in a tweed traveling suit inquired.

Grace was embarrassed to be standing in her robe looking like she'd been in a fight. The woman's eyes traveled down Grace's full length and back up to stare at her. She looked to be about her age with clear blue eyes that were oddly cold.

"Well, yes, he is. And you are?" Grace inquired.

The woman straightened her shoulders and with a drawn mouth answered, "I'm Mildred Nelson, the children's aunt, and I've come to take the children home with me."

Grace was stunned, and she heard Ginny's sharp intake of breath next to her. "I beg your pardon? I'm Grace Bidwell." She held her hand out but the lady didn't reciprocate.

The woman dismissed her with a wave of her glove. "Really, it's none of your affair. Could you tell him I'm here?"

Ginny looked at her narrow-eyed, indicating she could stay, but Grace shook her head. "I'll talk with you later, Grace. Goodbye." Ginny marched past the woman to her carriage parked in the yard and quickly left.

"Please come in. I'll show you to the parlor and go find him."

"He *is* up, isn't he?"

"Why do you say that?" Grace thought the woman was being presumptuous.

"Well, I see you're still in your dressing gown this time of the day." She frowned.

Grace felt her face flame. "I assure you, it's not what you think. If you'll have a seat, please."

"I'd rather stand."

"Suit yourself." Grace scurried out of the room and back to the kitchen. Everyone stopped chattering when she walked in, nearly out of breath from her nerves. "Robert, your sister-in-law is here to see you."

Robert stared back at her with an incredulous look. "What do you mean my sister-in-law?"

"I think you better go see for yourself," Grace replied.

Owen, Tom, and the girls sat with blank expressions on their faces, not making a sound. Grace led Robert to the parlor where Mildred stood ramrod straight.

"I'll leave you two so you can talk privately," Grace said.

"Robert, I'm sure you remember me—Ada's sister Mildred."

Robert gave her a slight nod. While his heart skipped a beat at the sight of her resemblance to Ada, this was not the Mildred he'd briefly met when she'd dragged the children through his front door. This woman was very well-dressed and her hair was perfectly coiffed. "How could I forget?" he said sarcastically. "Are you here to see Ada's children?"

Tilting her head toward him, she gave him a strange look. "No. I'm here to take them back home with me now."

Robert let out a resounding laugh. "You must be kidding. You were the one who couldn't wait until I took them off your hands because you couldn't feed another three people. Now suddenly you've changed your mind?"

Mildred squared her shoulders. "That's exactly why I'm here. I've married a wealthy businessman and can now afford to give the children a good home and an education as well. They will enjoy the best of everything."

"Is that so?" Robert mused, taking in the fancy traveling clothes, the jewelry hanging about her neck, and rings adorning her hands. Maybe she was telling the truth.

"Yes. They will have the finest of everything, the way Ada—" Her voice caught.

"They may not want to come with you. We're a family now, you know."

"But I'm their only blood relative. Could I please see them, if only for a moment? I know it's hard for you to believe, but I've truly missed them."

Robert hesitated. "I guess there's no harm in that. Follow me."

As soon as they entered the kitchen, Sarah ran to Grace's

side and hopped up into her lap, while Becky leaned against Owen's shoulder. It was evident they hadn't missed Mildred, but Tom was cordial. "Hello, Aunt Mildred. Never thought we'd see you again."

Mildred walked over and tweaked Tom's check. "Dear Tom, I've so missed you all."

Robert watched as tears flooded her eyes, and he tried hard to understand how she might be feeling. "Mildred, this is Grace's father, Owen Miller."

Owen nodded but didn't smile. Mildred turned to Robert. "Then Grace is your wife?" she asked innocently.

Robert cleared his throat. "Uh, no . . . I'm the hired man for Bidwell Farms, which belongs to Grace."

"Mmm, I see." She looked back at the children. "Your stepfather and I are discussing you children returning home with me in a day or so. Won't that be nice?"

The term *stepfather* sounded odd to Robert's ears. He didn't feel like one.

"I want to stay with Miss Grace," Sarah said, her bottom lip trembling.

"But you children need a good home and schooling," Mildred continued. "Becky, I can take you shopping for the latest girls' fashions. Won't that be fun?"

Becky slowly answered, "I guess." She looked over at Grace with sadness in her eyes.

"See there, Robert." Mildred glanced at him. "And Tom, you will have the best education that money can buy. I heard that you want to be a doctor."

Tom flashed her a half-smile. "I plan to when I finish high school."

"They have a home with me," Robert said drily.

"You have to admit—living in a boardinghouse and holding down two jobs doesn't make much of a home life," Mildred reminded him. "Don't look so shocked. That information was quite easy to obtain in town."

"I'm wondering how much you had to pay to find that out." Robert glared at her. It was one thing coming for the children, but it was another thing for her to snoop around in his business. "You could've asked me and saved yourself money and time."

"I know it's none of my business, but why don't you let Robert and the children have some time to think about your offer?" Owen asked.

Mildred directed her gaze to Owen. "You're right. It's not." She fished inside her reticule and handed Robert a card. "This is where I'm staying. I leave on Monday to return to Cheyenne. Perhaps we can meet for lunch tomorrow to discuss this. But do keep in mind that I'm their only flesh-and-blood relation. Ada would want that."

Robert showed her out, then came back and plopped down, suddenly tired. He could feel Grace's eyes on him. She hadn't said a word during the conversation.

"We aren't going to have to go with her, are we?" Tom asked.

"Let's talk about it after we get home, but right now we have chores to do, or poor Miss Grace will be hobbling around trying to do it on her own." Robert tried to sound cheerful.

Sarah hopped down from Grace's lap and went over to him. "Papa, we won't leave you. Don't worry," she soothed in her babyish voice. Robert's heart melted. He was in a quandary.

That evening, Grace readily agreed to a ride, sensing that Robert wanted someone to talk to. He'd said very little all day, but went about the chores avoiding any conversation. She was scared that he might agree to let the children go live with their aunt, but she would only give her opinion when asked. In her mind, they hadn't seemed too keen on going to live with her, and she couldn't tell what Robert was thinking.

The gentle breeze that swept across them made their ride in the buggy more enjoyable on a warm summer night. Tall mountain lupine, harebell, and monkshood danced with the wind. They rode in silence for a mile or two until they got to the ridge overlooking the Gallatin Valley.

"This is the most spectacular view to me, looking down at the town's glowing lights below us. Ever wonder what folks are doing after the day's work is done?" Robert asked, staring straight ahead.

"Many times. I spent a lot of time alone up here after Victor died. It was the only place I could think about life and my circumstances." Grace moved a stray hair from her eyes.

"I'm sorry if it brings back sad memories—we can drive farther." Robert swerved in his seat to face her.

"No. It doesn't bother me. I find it quite peaceful. How about you? I know you have a lot on your mind."

"You are beginning to know me well." His slate-colored eyes latched on to hers. "I talked with the children, and they don't want to go with their aunt. I keep thinking they would have everything that I'll never be able to give them. Tom wants to go to medical school, and that's very expensive. I can't afford piano lessons, or anything else more refined for the girls. Maybe Mildred is right. They'd be better off with relatives."

"Do you really think so? I got the impression they were

beginning to grow on you. Am I wrong?" Grace was so glad they were alone to talk so she could study his handsome face.

"No, you're not wrong. That's just it. After Sarah almost drowned, then seeing Warren hurt you—I realized how much I care about the children and you. But let's face it, I'm no great father."

Grace took his hand in hers. It was big and strong and calloused. "I thought that's what you might be thinking. Remember, having everything given to you on a silver platter doesn't guarantee happiness. And the children really care a lot about you."

He smiled and said, "They care more about you than you know, Grace. What should I do?"

"You need to do what you think is right and fair for them. If you want to be a father to them, then do it. With Mildred they'll be starting over with another new stepfather. I don't see how that can be good for them, no matter how wealthy they are. You must figure their happiness in there somewhere. You could try not focusing on the past, but look forward to what the future holds. Trust me, I know how hard that is to do."

An owl on the tree branch near them hooted several times, breaking the seriousness of their conversation, and they laughed. A full moon slowly rose over the valley, casting a yellow light around them. "Thanks for your advice. I'll work on doing that." Robert leaned in closer, whether to see her better in the moonlight or to kiss her, she didn't know.

"Do you want to kiss me, Robert?"

"Well I was thinking about it. But after last time—"

"Then go ahead," she whispered. She closed her eyes and waited. As he drew closer, his cologne pleasantly filled the air between them, and her heart pinged. His lips touched hers, pressing lightly at first, almost timidly, then firmer as if drinking nectar from a flower. He lingered there a long moment.

He pulled back and she opened her eyes, breathlessly looking into his. His eyes held a softness she didn't know he possessed. Had Victor ever kissed her that way? She thought not.

Robert seemed a little uncomfortable. "I hope that kiss was better than the kiss I stole from you a while back," he said.

"Much better . . . and one that I encouraged."

He reached for the horse's reins. "I suppose we should be getting back." He sounded reluctant to leave. "I want to keep your father as a friend."

Grace giggled. "Remember, I'm a grown woman, not a young lass," she reminded him as he turned the buggy around.

"That's just the problem—we both know what love is about, and we don't need any temptations."

37

Sleep refused to come as Robert thought about the day's events with Mildred and the ride with Grace. Hands behind his head and eyes wide open, his mind in turmoil, he ruminated on his answer to Mildred and felt cornered. The truth was the children *would* be better off with their aunt and all that she had to offer, and yet . . . when had he gone from not wanting them to wanting to be their father? In the beginning he'd been angry and thought his future bleak, believing no woman would want him with three half-grown children.

But after tonight, he wasn't so sure. He knew that Grace had grown to love the children, and while he might not call it love yet, what he felt for Tom, Becky, and Sarah was a deep affection. Grace was right, happiness didn't consist of material things. *So keeping all that in mind, how could I send them back? I can't . . . I just can't do it.* Once he'd reached that decision, he breathed a deep sigh of relief. He hoped his tossing and turning hadn't disturbed Tom on the other side of the bedroom.

Chilled, Robert pulled the covers over his shoulders, closing his eyes, allowing the image of Grace's face waiting for his kiss to fill his thoughts.

After church the next morning, Grace fixed a quick lunch for herself. Owen and Stella had gone on a picnic, so she took her coffee outside to enjoy a relaxing few hours alone.

Alone. She wasn't used to having any time when it was quiet and still, unless she took a ride by herself, but even then she felt the pressure to be back soon to take care of her father. The silence was comforting in some ways, she thought as she sipped her coffee.

Briefly after church she'd talked with the children and Robert. He seemed in a hurry for his meeting with Mildred, so she never asked him what his answer to the children's aunt would be. He'd tell her when he was ready. But now she wondered how life would change. If she thought it was quiet now, well . . . It would be hard to let them go, but if that was what Robert considered in the best interests of the children, then what right did she have to say otherwise? She wasn't his wife . . . yet. But what if Robert liked things as they were between them? One or two kisses didn't create a meaningful relationship. Good thing they'd become friends now.

It surprised her that he'd been somewhat shy last night when he wanted to kiss her, but at the same time she knew how he'd been duped into marrying Ada. That was the very reason he'd shied away from having any feelings toward her, she guessed. Maybe she felt like he couldn't trust her either.

Whatever the outcome with the children, she'd have to be content, but she'd felt that God had given them as a gift to satisfy her longing to be a mother. Now she wondered if she was only being selfish, since they had living relatives.

She prayed the answer to the situation would be clear to both parties involved. After all, they would be deciding on three people's lives that might forever be changed. By tomorrow, she'd know the decision.

She finished her coffee and leaned back in her chair, enjoying the warm sun, thinking about the feel of his lips against hers. That kiss could last her for a long time . . . forever etched in her memory. But she hoped it wouldn't have to.

Monday morning after breakfast found Grace with one eye on the lane leading to her house, and one eye on the tomatoes she was picking. Where was Robert? And the children? Fifteen minutes later, she saw Robert coming up the lane for work, but he was alone. She swallowed hard, blinking back the tears. So he'd given in to Mildred's demands. As he drew near and stopped in the yard, she searched his earnest face and clenched jaw but wasn't able to read him. Was he so upset that he couldn't look at her?

She set the basket of tomatoes on the ground and walked over to him as he jumped down from the wagon's seat. "Robert . . . the children . . . are they . . ." She couldn't finish the thought, her heart ached so badly. Her hands tightened on her apron as she watched his face.

"I'm sorry, Grace. I let the children decide."

"So they—" She choked.

"SURPRISE!" Three heads popped up from underneath the tarp in the back of the wagon. "We're staying," Sarah yelled.

"Oh my goodness! This is such good news." Grace fought

back the tears, clasping a hand to her chest as the children scrambled out of the wagon to crowd around her. She hugged Sarah and Becky, and while Tom held back, she reached for him and he allowed a hug from her.

"I take it you like the news?" Robert said, grinning as he watched them.

"You're all so sneaky." Grace laughed. "I was certain when I thought you were alone they'd left with Mildred." She wagged her finger at Robert.

"We didn't want to go live with Aunt Mildred. She was never mean to us, but we like living right here in Gallatin Valley," Tom said.

Grace nodded. "And I couldn't be happier for you if that's how you feel."

"We did agree they could visit her for a week or two every year, *if* they wanted to," Robert confirmed.

Grace smiled at all of them. "That's sounds fair enough. This calls for a celebration."

Sarah clapped her hands. "What?"

"Why don't you girls and I bake some apple pies, and if you can't stay for lunch when Robert leaves for Eli's, then I'll let you take one home. How does that sound?"

"My mouth is already watering." Tom rubbed his hands together in anticipation.

"Then you men get started, and we'll bake the pies." Grace's heart was singing inside, and when she glanced over at Robert, he winked.

"Let's get going, Tom. We've got plenty to do this morning."

Owen watched the interaction from his usual view at the parlor window and smiled. Thank God, this was a good turn of events. He didn't know what he would've done with Grace if the children had decided to go with their aunt. One thing he knew for sure, God did answer prayers—maybe not the way everyone expected, but He did on this one. Owen loved seeing his daughter happy, and when she was quiet yesterday he knew she'd been worried.

Owen saw Tom at the doorway. "I just wanted to tell you that we are not going to live with my aunt." He was beaming.

"I thought that was the case as I sat here watching, and I'm glad, Tom. I've gotten used to having you and the girls, and it'd be mighty lonely around here without all of you now."

"Thank you, sir." Tom cleared his throat and although it looked like he might cry, Owen knew better. "You're like the grandfather I never had."

He turned, scooting out before Owen could reply. Owen chuckled, then said aloud, "A merry heart doeth good like a medicine." And he needed all the medicine he could get.

Becky rolled out the dough for the piecrust while Grace and Sarah sliced apples, then mixed in sugar and cinnamon together for the filling. They chatted and laughed as they worked, enjoying their time in the kitchen together. Anyone walking in would've thought this was a natural family occurrence. Grace starting humming a tune and the girls joined in while Becky folded the crust in half then laid it in the pie pan the way Grace demonstrated. Grace showed them how to use their fingers to crimp the edges of the crust, while they giggled throughout the entire process.

"The oven is hot, so let's get these pies in," Grace instructed. "Becky, you keep an eye on the pies while Sarah and I make lunch, so the men can eat early before leaving for the mercantile."

"Men? Are you calling my brother a man?" Sarah laughed.

"He is nearly grown and he's doing a man's job. So we should respect that," Grace answered.

Becky's eyes narrowed. "I never thought of him that way, but I reckon you're right."

Sarah looked thoughtful. "He's been our protector since Mama died too. That's because he loves us, huh, Miss Grace?"

"Yes, I'm certain of it. And now you have Robert to protect you as well."

"I'm so glad we didn't have to go live with our aunt," Becky added.

Grace beamed at both the young girls. "Me too. I would have sorely missed you."

"Then maybe you could be our mama, 'cause we love you," Becky leaned near and whispered.

"Now wouldn't that be something? I love all of you too. I couldn't ever replace your mother, but I can be your best friend for now, and be here whenever you need me." Grace hugged them to her while the smell of baking apples filled the kitchen, much as their love had filled her heart.

"I think that's about the best pie I've ever tasted," Robert commented as Grace followed him out the door to where the children waited in the wagon. "Thank you for lunch."

"I assure you it was my pleasure. We had so much fun baking them, and I hope I taught the girls a thing or two."

"We need to get going, but while I'm in town do you want me to ask around for extra hands to help with the harvest?"

"That would be an excellent idea," she said. "I don't think we can do it all."

"If I have anything to do with it, we'll get enough help so you won't have to and leave the hard work to us. But maybe you can feed us and the girls could help."

"We could manage that."

"Grace—" he stammered.

"Yes, Robert?"

"I . . . uh . . . wanted to say thank you for everything these past few months. You've helped to make our lives bearable."

"I'm happy I could help." Grace squinted up at him in the noonday sun.

He seemed to want to say more but instead doffed his hat, then climbed up onto the seat of the wagon and took off while the children waved goodbye to her.

After dropping the girls off at the boardinghouse, Robert and Tom went on to the store, ready for their afternoon work. From the looks of it when Robert entered the store, Eli was having a busy Monday.

When there was some free time between customers to talk, Eli turned to Robert. "I can't thank you enough for solving the puzzle of the missing shipments."

"I had help from the sheriff, but I'd had a suspicion for a while that there was something odd about Warren. I'm so glad that he didn't do any more harm to Grace than he did," Robert said.

"Me too. John told me how he roughed her up. Is she doing okay?" Eli asked.

"I think she is. We're glad that it's over and you should start getting your shipments now."

"I heard from Stella that the children's aunt showed up on your front doorstep to take them with her. What did you do?" Eli asked.

"After a lot of soul-searching, I said no. I'm their father by marriage legally now and will take care of them. I won't be able to give them what she could, but the kids said they'd be happier with me."

Eli clapped him on the back. "Son, you did the right thing, and I could tell those kids were starting to be your family."

"Family. I never thought of it exactly that way, but you're right. Now if I can find them a mother, they'll do even better."

"I have an idea you've already thought about that, but I promise not to pry." Eli smiled at him.

"Changing the subject, could you help me put the word out that Grace wants to hire some extra help for the potato harvest? I want to get some men lined up to help us with that."

"Will do, Robert. I'll send them to you. There's always someone passing through looking for money until they find steady work. I'll loan her an extra plow for digging too. Maybe that'll help out."

"It certainly would." Robert glanced over to where Tom was busy trying to wait on customers. He chuckled. "I guess we'd better get to work before Tom runs away."

38

The first week of August the harvest was suddenly upon Bidwell Farms. The weather was hot but bearable. Robert had been able to secure several extra hands to help them and Grace prayed the harvest would bring enough to pay them with money left over to live on. It would be a very long day for certain.

She watched Robert, in his broad-brim straw hat with his sleeves rolled up, at the end of one plow turning over the soil to expose the potatoes while workers came behind him, lifting the potatoes gently with pitchforks or shovels to place them onto the wagon Tom drove. Owen was at the opposite side of the acreage in charge of carrying out the same task with the borrowed plow from Eli. As Robert promised, Grace and the girls delivered water to the workers, but mainly worked on cooking up a big lunch for everyone.

Her father promised that he wouldn't stay out in the heat for long periods of time. Since he'd been drinking quinine as Dr. Avery suggested and taking the baths at the hot springs often, his legs had become stronger most days, and he had less pain than before.

He waved to her from across the field and Grace waved back to him. Stella had become a good friend and a great companion for her father, and Grace was grateful.

She turned and went back to the porch where she had Becky shelling peas and Sarah helping. "Are you nearly through? I'll need to get those peas cooking shortly."

"Yes, ma'am. But, goodness, shelling makes my fingers sore," Becky complained.

"Mine too," whined Sarah.

"Oh poo. You've hardly shelled anything. You're such a baby," Becky insisted.

"Am not!" Sarah stomped her foot.

Grace reached for the bowl. "Now, girls. I'll finish here. Why don't you go offer the men some water again? Then when you get back we'll start lunch."

"Do I have to?" Sarah asked. "I can't cook."

"Then I'll let you carry the plates and forks outside, and we'll set up some sort of tables to put the food on."

"Okay. I can *do* that." Sarah smiled up at Grace.

Her big sister shook her head and went to the well to pump the water with Sarah skipping behind her. Grace smiled to herself. She realized children loved to pick at each other, but she'd usually been able to keep them from fighting when an argument started. Never having a sibling when she grew up, Grace was fascinated at their interaction, knowing at the bottom of it all, love won out.

Grace and Becky carried out the platter of fried chicken, a bowl of peas loaded with ham, a large bowl of rice, and a pan of hot biscuits, placing them on a table made from sawhorses and boards that had been covered in a plain cotton tablecloth. Rhubarb pies for dessert sat cooling at the end of the table. Sarah rang the triangle—proud that she was able to reach it with the aid of a footstool.

The men dropped their tools and made their way from the field to the well to wash up. Grace had left soap and towels for them to use next to the pump. Most of them splashed cold well water on their faces to cool themselves off as much as to clean up.

Robert was last to take a plate, while the extra men sat on the porch steps to eat. Grace fixed one for her father before she got her own, and stood behind Robert while he filled his plate.

"It's going good, and we should be finished before dark, so I told them they'd get paid when the work was done, if that's okay with you. The men are hard workers."

She nodded in agreement. "I'll have that ready then."

"I asked Eli if I could have the week off to transport the crop to Virginia City for you, if you'd like. Your dad said he'd go too, but I fear it's much too far for him. Tom can drive the other wagon, but it's up to you." Robert picked up a piece of chicken to add to the rest of the food on his plate.

"I don't mind at all, if you'll let the girls stay here. I must confess they are good company for me, and you're right, Pop would have a hard time taking a long trip. But how can you afford to take that much time off?"

"I can, so don't worry. I'm sure the girls would love to stay here with you. We'll be here early in the morning since it'll take us nearly two and a half days to drive the wagons to Virginia City." He bit into his chicken as they sat on the grass under the shade of the cottonwood.

"Our first picnic," Grace teased and looked over at him.

"Ha-ha! Yes, but not one that I would choose." A smile twitched at the edge of his mouth.

"And what kind would you choose?"

"One that was far away from all this." He waved his hand at everyone else. "A place where it was quiet except for the sound of the wind in the trees or a gurgling creek."

"Sounds lovely." Grace's heart skipped a beat at the thought. "What else might it include?"

"Oh, perhaps a pretty woman to keep me company." He bit into a biscuit with a grin.

"Have anyone in mind?" She flashed him a smile.

"Oh, she's tall with a sprinkle of freckles and a cut on her cheek and bakes a mean rhubarb pie."

Grace laughed. "You know, you're about the only one that can make me laugh."

He bowed slightly. "Then I'm happy to oblige." When he fixed his gaze on her and lingered, Grace's breath caught.

With the men on their way to Virginia City, Grace planned to teach the girls to quilt. In the evenings, she'd been quilting a baby blanket for Ginny, so when she pulled it out to show them, they oohed with awe at the beautiful pattern.

"It's lovely," Becky whispered, fingering the quilt. "And soft."

"Would you like to help me finish it? Then this week we can take it to Ginny and surprise her."

"Oh, yes, ma'am," Becky exclaimed.

"Me too?" Sarah asked.

"I tell you what—I'm going to give you both a scrap of fabric and show you how it's done. The stitches are very tiny so we'll see how you do." Grace handed them each a needle and thread along with a scrap of material.

After several attempts, Becky began to sew tiny stitches but not in a straight line. "Very good, Becky, but you have to keep the stitches nice and tidy. See, look at my piece."

"I'll try." Becky bent her head over the piece with her tongue sticking out between her lips in total concentration, while Sarah looked on with serious interest.

"That's much better, Becky. Let me see you try, Sarah."

Sarah's little hand held the material underneath as she stuck the needle through the scrap. Then she winced. "Ouch!" Jerking her hand from underneath, blood spouted on her small finger. She immediately put her finger to her lip, sucking the blood away with tears in her eyes.

"Let me see." Grace reached for her hand. "Oh, that's not so bad. Let me kiss it." She touched the little hand and fingers to her lips.

Sarah smiled and said, "It feels better now, but I think I'd rather watch."

"That's okay, but sometimes there's pain to go with learning a new skill. For now, you can go feed Bluebelle and Paddy if you want to. Just call their names. You know where I keep the feed in the barn."

Sarah hopped up and handed Grace the scrap. "I'll go look for them right now."

In a few days, Grace had finished the quilt, and she and the girls were quite pleased with the outcome. "Pop, we're going to go to town to see Ginny today and take the baby quilt. Would you like to come?" Grace asked shortly after breakfast.

"I don't mind if I do come, but not to see Ginny. No offense, but maybe you could drop me at Stella's?" Owen answered.

Grace giggled. "Of course. I didn't think you'd want to be with us girls talking about baby things."

"Whew! I'm relieved." Owen flashed her a teasing grin. "Let's get going, then," he said, standing up with the aid of his new cane.

They all piled in the buggy Grace had hitched earlier to Cinnamon and rumbled down the lane to town. *Just like family*, Grace thought. A bounty of potatoes was harvested, her father was feeling better most days, the children hadn't gone with their aunt, and her own life had been spared. Feeling grateful and very happy, she hoped things would slow down for a while.

Ginny, the ever-gracious Southern hostess, was tickled when Grace and the girls showed up and immediately sent Nell for refreshments. "I'm so happy that y'all didn't leave," she told the girls. "Grace would've been very sad."

"And so would we," Becky affirmed.

"We brought you something, Miss Ginny." Sarah looked over at Grace with a nod.

"Yes, we did, and the girls helped me finish it." She pulled the wrapped quilt from behind her back and handed it to Ginny. "It's just a little something for the baby."

Ginny asked, "Shall I open it now?"

"Yes, of course." Grace nodded.

They stood around as Ginny unwrapped the gift. Ginny's sharp intake of breath showed her surprise. "Why, Grace, it's beautiful." She stared down at the beautiful patchwork pattern in soft hues of blue, green, and pale pink. "I'll treasure it and the baby will love being snuggled under it." She hugged her friend, then the girls, with tears welling up in her eyes. "I couldn't ask for anything more special . . . something made with love."

"I'm glad you like it. Since we are in the dark as to whether this will be a boy or girl, I decided to use the soft pastels so it wouldn't matter either way." Grace was proud that Ginny loved her quilt and all the work that went into it late at night when she'd rather have been in bed.

Nell entered with a tray of refreshments. When she spied the quilt, she picked it up. "It's beautiful, Miss Grace. I wish I knew how to quilt but never had time to learn, what with working and all . . ."

"Then I can teach you like I did the girls. It's not hard, but practice makes the stitches uniform so the quilt becomes a work of art."

"What an excellent, idea, Grace. We should start a quilting circle," Ginny said, holding the small of her back. "Excuse me while I sit."

"I'd try to find time to come if it was after my work here was done," Nell said.

"I'll bet you Stella would let us meet in her large parlor at the boardinghouse," Grace said, thinking ahead. She liked the idea a lot. "Then you wouldn't have to drive out to the farm, Nell. I'll ask and tell you what she says."

"Better enjoy the tea while it's hot. I've got work to do. Please excuse me. Oh, and let me know whenever you decide on a quilting circle," Nell said over her shoulder as she scooted out.

Grace poured the tea and they all sat down, chatting. She told Ginny about harvesting the potatoes and Robert and Tom driving them to market.

Ginny's lip curled into a smile above her teacup. "Sounds as though Robert intends to be around for a while." She was careful to lower her voice while the girls were playing checkers in the corner.

"Oh, I don't know." Grace sighed. "He indicated that when the harvest was over, he'd be leaving, but that was right after he came to work for me."

"Do I detect a note of regret?"

Grace gazed at her friend with a frank look. "I suppose so." She told Ginny about their drive to the ridge one evening. "He still seems unsure of the thought of *us* but his actions reflect that he cares for me."

"He'll come around. Remember, his first wife hurt him pretty badly," Ginny commented, then shifted uncomfortably in her chair.

"Are you feeling okay?" Grace set her teacup down.

"I . . . uh . . . I'm not sure. I—" A sharp cry escaped her lips and the girls looked around. "Maybe not. Could you get me up to bed, Grace? I suddenly don't feel well."

The girls hopped up from their checker game. "Is Miss Ginny sick?" Becky asked.

Immediately, Grace was at Ginny's side, supporting her with her arm across her shoulder to help her from the chair. Ginny winced again, holding her abdomen. "I think it's the baby." Beads of perspiration popped out across her upper lip.

"Sarah, run to get Nell for me, please," Grace barked. "Becky, do you remember how to get to Frank's office?"

Becky nodded, her eyes wide in alarm.

"Then please go get him and tell him to bring Dr. Avery with him."

The girls took off with their assignments, eager to help.

39

Grace yanked back the bedcovers, then loosened Ginny's skirt and blouse—just then noticing a puddle of liquid by the bed. "Good heavens, Ginny, what's that?"

Ginny looked numbly at the floor. "My water broke. Could you please get a nightgown from the bureau for me?" she muttered through clenched teeth, then closed her eyes in pain.

For a moment, Grace couldn't move. *Lord, please don't let anything happen until Doc Avery arrives!* She found a nightgown and was pulling it over Ginny's head when Nell opened the door.

"Nell, her labor's started, I think, but I've never had a baby, so—"

Nell walked over to help Grace get Ginny into the bed. "I'm not surprised. The baby's right on time, if not a wee bit early."

"Have you ever deliver—?"

Grace's question was cut short by a scream that shattered the afternoon silence. Her heart gripped her. *Oh, Lord, what can I do?* She felt totally unprepared and inadequate.

"I'm sure the doc will be here any moment. Stay with her and I'll get clean linens and hot water—things I know he'll need." Nell hurried out and down the stairs.

Grace wanted to ask Nell to please stay, but that was being silly. There was time.

She walked over to the pitcher on the washstand and poured water over a washcloth, then wrung it out. The room was stifling hot, so she rolled up her sleeves and opened a window. Ginny was fretting more and breathing hard as Grace applied the washcloth to her forehead, then her face.

"Ooh, Grace . . . my contractions are hard and getting closer." Suddenly her abdomen tightened in a hard ball. "Oh my, oh my . . . I think the baby's coming."

There was nothing else Grace could do but pull back the cover exposing Ginny's lower half. Modestly peeking, Grace confirmed it with a gasp.

"VIRGINIA! I think I see the baby's head!" Grace spouted with excitement. "Where's the doctor?"

She looked around, then opened the door and scanned down the stairs. No one was in sight. *Oh Lord, please don't let me have to do this alone.* "Nell!" she yelled.

But Grace couldn't wait as Ginny hollered again. "Please, Grace . . . help!" Ginny thrashed and strained in the bed.

Instinctively, Grace did the only thing she knew to do. "Ginny, listen to me. Take a deep breath, then pull your legs up so I can help you," she ordered. She ran to the pitcher and washed her hands, quickly returning to checking the baby's progress.

"Oh, Ginny, your baby's coming! PUSH!"

It was all over in a matter of minutes. Grace witnessed the most incredible sight—the miracle of birth. Ginny cried out one last time, half-sitting, and with one big push brought her baby into the world. Grace cried with happiness as she held the tiny, slippery baby in her hands, its umbilical cord still attached. "It's a little girl, Ginny! A perfect little girl."

The baby began to wail, so she held her up for Ginny to see, and Ginny burst out sobbing without saying a word. Nell ran in with the hot water and linen, pure shock on her face. "In all my years, I've never seen a birthing happen that fast. A sweet baby girl, Miss Ginny." Nell fawned over the baby as she tied off the cord. "Here, you want to cut the umbilical cord, Grace? You deserve the honor."

"I can't do—"

Nell roared with laughter. "Honey, you just delivered a live baby. That's a miracle in itself, so I think you can cut the cord." She handed Grace the clean scissors. "Go ahead."

Reluctantly, Grace neared the baby and with shaking hands, snipped the cord, separating the little one from her mother. She blew out a sigh of relief, suddenly tired. Nell took the baby and began cleaning her up while cooing to her. Grace glanced at Ginny, who lay spent on the pillows, but smiling as she watched Nell.

"I'm naming her Grace," Ginny choked out through her tears, looking at Grace.

Grace took her hand. "Are you sure?"

"I'm perfectly sure. Frank and I decided on that long ago if the baby was a girl."

Grace squeezed her hand. "Then I'm proud to have a namesake. Very proud. Thank you so much." Her heart swelled with love.

There was a knock at the open door, and Dr. Avery entered. "I see I'm about five minutes too late. First babies can come very quickly sometimes." He walked over and checked out the baby with his stethoscope, then went over to Ginny's side. He nodded. "Mother and daughter are fine. You can go down, Nell, and let Frank know. I'll finish up here."

"Is there anything more I can do?" Grace asked the doctor.

"You did a good job, but from the look on your face, I'd say it was your first time to deliver a baby?" The doctor arched a brow at her.

She nodded. "That's true."

"Then I'm happy there were no complications. Not all births are this easy," he whispered.

They both looked over at Ginny, content to be holding her first child to her breast. If ever her heart felt fuller, Grace couldn't recall.

Once Frank had come back downstairs beaming with pride and shared his thanks, Grace told him she must go pick up her father, who by this time would be wondering what happened to her.

"Frank, I'm so proud the two of you decided to name the baby after me. I don't know what to say, really."

Frank kissed her cheek. "It was the right decision. Ginny loves you like the sister she never had."

Grace nodded, unable to speak, then shooed the girls toward the door to leave.

"Let me know if there's anything at all I can do to help out."

"We will, but I'm sure Nell will stay right by her side. Thank you again for being here, and for the quilt. Becky showed it to me. It's quite beautiful."

"You're both welcome. I'll come back and check on her once she's had a chance to rest."

With the sale of the potato crop behind them, Robert and Tom walked the streets looking for a place to get something to eat. Tomorrow they'd head back to the Gallatin Valley with empty wagons to haul. The potatoes had sold for thirteen cents a pound—a good price. Grace would be pleased.

Tom pointed out a nearby establishment. "This place looks good and I'm starving to death."

"Fine with me, son. I could eat the biggest steak this side of the Gallatin River."

Service was quick, and they soon shoveled in their supper. "Tom, thanks for coming along with me. This was a job for a man, but you stepped up to the challenge."

Tom sat up a little straighter with pride. "Told you I was growing up." He grinned, taking in another mouthful of potatoes. "Funny, I didn't think I wanted to lay my eyes on another potato until I got hungry." He laughed.

"I felt the same way after digging and hauling them, but they sure taste better than they look." Robert hesitated a moment, then added, "I'm glad things are square between us. If you keep working this hard, I'll help you in every way I can to go to medical school. You may even get a scholarship. Won't know until you're old enough to apply."

Tom put his fork down. "I know I was a rotten kid before and gave you a hard time. Reckon I was just mad at the world."

"And I understand that. It's okay. You were struggling and trying to find your place after your mother died. I'm really sorry that we started out on the wrong foot. But look at us now."

"Do you think you'll ever marry again? My sisters need a mama," he said matter-of-factly.

"I'm not sure. Don't take this the wrong way, but I'm a little gun-shy after your mother."

"No hard feelings. I guess she didn't tell you about us because she thought you wouldn't want her."

"That's understandable. But I loved her, and she didn't trust my love enough to believe that I would've accepted anything she told me—not until she was dying. I guess my reaction was not very gentlemanly either, and I apologize for that." Robert wiped his mouth, then laid his napkin aside. "I'm as full as a tick on a dog's back."

Tom laughed, then belched. "Oops, sorry."

Robert tried to cover a chuckle. "We'll work on those manners too while we're at it. Let me pay the bill, then we'll go help ourselves to a bath and a good night's sleep before heading back."

"I'm all for that," Tom responded.

Nearly a week had passed since Robert left, and every time she passed a window Grace looked for him and Tom. She was like a child looking for Christmas. She wasn't sure when they'd return, but it should be nearing that time. Everyday farm chores had kept her and the girls busy, and she realized how much she'd come to rely on Robert. Tom had been an enormous help with the harvest too.

It was well after lunch. The dishes were done, and Becky was reading but taking the time to help Sarah with unfamiliar words in her book. Grace smiled watching them. Such sweet girls, and what a blessing they'd turned out to be in her life and her father's.

Grace was mending and Owen was reading a week-old newspaper when she heard the wagons rumbling into the yard. Grace and the girls jumped at the sound and hurried out to meet Robert and Tom. Owen took his time with his cane, but stood on the porch and waved across the yard to them in greeting.

Grace and the girls walked over to the barn when Robert stopped the wagon. "I'm glad you're both back," she said. Tom was right behind him, driving the second wagon like a pro. Robert needed a shave but was still ruggedly handsome, and his tan was deeper. Tom looked tired but different somehow. She knew when you don't see someone every day when they're in the growing stage, it could appear that suddenly their facial features were rearranged or changed somehow. Had he grown? She hoped the trip wasn't too hard on him. He was tall, but not too muscular. Guiding the horse and wagon loaded down had to be a big change for him.

"Me too," Robert answered. "It was a pretty long haul, but we got thirteen cents a pound, and that's good in this market."

She smiled up at him. "Yes, I agree. Any trouble along the way?"

"Not a bit. The weather was good too." Robert climbed down a little stiffly, watching while Tom did the same.

Sarah rushed over and hugged Robert about the legs and he kissed the top of her head. "Sweet little Sarah. I've missed you and Becky."

Becky looked over at her brother, her arms crossed. "Believe it or not, I've missed you, even though you can be aggravating to me most of the time."

Tom poked his tongue out at her, then yanked one of her braids. "I take that as a compliment then."

"We'll get the horses rubbed down, then head on back to town if you don't mind. I think we're about out of steam for the rest of the day. Guess I'm not as young as I used to be."

"Not at all. Both of you deserve to get some rest," she answered. "I can feed and rub the horses down so you don't have to stay and do that."

"I'm not *that* tired." Robert flashed her a grin. "Do you have anything you can make sandwiches with? We had a beef jerky snack earlier, but other than breakfast that's all. We'll take care of the horses if you can get us something to eat."

"If you insist. Come on, girls, let's rustle up something to feed these hungry men."

While they ate, everyone sat with them in the kitchen, listening to tales about the trip. Grace poured coffee for her and Owen, then related how she came to deliver Ginny's baby.

"My, but that must've been quite an event. I'm proud of you. I'm assuming Ginny and the baby are doing fine?" Robert gazed at Grace.

Grace had a hard time looking away when he locked eyes with her like that. "Yes, everyone is well. Tomorrow, I'll go check on her again and hold the baby awhile."

"She named the baby Grace," Becky inserted. "Wasn't that sweet? I love babies."

Robert's gaze softened. "Now that is wonderful, and I'm not surprised one bit."

Owen chuckled. "Trouble is, now Grace won't be able to name her own child after herself."

Grace felt her face burn. "It doesn't look as though that's a concern anytime soon."

Robert glanced at Owen, then Grace. "You never know . . ."

"I'd love to help you with your baby when it comes," Becky said.

"If I ever marry again, I would be happy to have your help, and you too, Sarah," Grace answered, not wanting to leave her out. She avoided Robert's eyes, though she could feel them on her.

40

Something special happened when Grace held her namesake against her and felt the baby's heartbeat—an impact greater than that sweet smell that all babies have. A deep longing for a child hit her full force. "Ginny, she is so perfect and beautiful."

"Just like you, Grace, and I must add that you look very natural holding Grace."

"Is she a fussy baby?" she asked, not taking her eyes off of the baby's face.

"Only when she is hungry, but otherwise, a new mother couldn't ask for a better baby the first time around." Ginny folded diapers while they talked.

"That's good. It's obvious that Frank dotes on her already." The baby stirred awake, and Grace rocked back and forth with a soothing coo.

"Are you going to the ball with Robert?" Ginny asked.

Grace looked up with a sigh. "He hasn't asked me. Besides, I don't own a fancy ball gown and have no one to make one for me."

Ginny snapped her fingers. "I know exactly what you can

wear. I have a beautiful gown that I bought before I knew I was pregnant. There's no way it'll fit me now. My figure has changed, and it would be far too tight."

"Oh, I wouldn't dare take your new dress. You'll be able to wear it soon, I'm sure."

Ginny shook her head. "Not before the ball though. While you're holding the baby, I'll go get it for you."

She returned shortly with a gorgeous gown the shade of emerald. Grace drew in a deep breath. "It's stunning," she whispered above the baby's head.

"Grace is asleep, so why don't you put her in her crib and take a closer look."

"All right." Gently she placed the baby in her crib, then the two of them stopped momentarily to stare down at her precious visage. "I could hold her forever."

"Me too, however, I'd never get anything done, because it's hard to lay her down. I love the way she snuggles against me, contented after her feeding."

"I could only hope to be so fortunate," Grace murmured wistfully.

Ginny squeezed her arm. "You will be. Don't give up hope."

They tiptoed away reluctantly so Grace could examine the gown. It was actually two pieces. The bodice had black silk embroidery with black jeweled buttons. Black silk fringe was on the upper sleeves, and the skirt had silk edging sewn around the bottom. Scattered along the sleeves and above the silk trim at the bottom were tiny black embroidered flowers. A cream, lace-edged collar completed the neck of the bodice.

"This is much too beautiful for me, Ginny. I've never worn anything like this," Grace exclaimed, holding the bodice up to her.

"Then it's time you did. I guarantee you'll turn some heads wearing it. In fact, you and I have the same coloring, so it'll work perfectly for you. I insist you take it."

"But what if I'm not asked?"

Ginny giggled. "You will be. Trust me."

"Thank you, my friend, but I'm afraid you're a little prejudiced." Grace laughed.

The baby started to cry and they both made a beeline for the crib, forgetting all about the ball.

Stella served up a special supper for Tom and Robert the next day, and her boarders were beneficiaries of her excellent cooking. After everyone went their various ways, mostly to their rooms, Robert stayed behind to help with the cleanup. He felt it was the least he could do. Besides, she had become more like a mother to him than a friend, and she took a special interest in the children, which pleased him immensely.

"Stella, if you keep this up, I'm gonna have to buy larger trousers."

"The way I see it, Robert, you could afford to gain a few pounds," Stella teased. "You've been working too hard. Say, now that the harvest is over, do you plan to stay around these parts or move on?"

"I have no plans to leave yet," he said, stacking the plates at the sink.

"That sounds vague. Have you got something planned? Perhaps wooing a certain young woman?"

He gave her an intense look. "Maybe."

Stella dried a dish, then laid it aside. "Why not start by inviting her to the Bozeman Ball?"

"Nah. I don't even own a suit, and it's not likely that I can get one quick enough."

"But it's the social event of the season," she protested, hands resting on her hips. You must invite Grace. And as for a suitable suit, I know just the person to introduce you to."

"Well, I don't know—"

"Sure you do. Now don't argue. A young man like you shouldn't be hiding away at home when there's a ball here in his town. Come with me. It's just a short walk," she said, not taking no for an answer. "I'll walk you over there right now." She removed her apron and waited for his response.

What else could he do? He followed Stella down the street to a row of small, hastily built clapboard houses, until she stopped. "She hasn't hung out a shingle yet. But once folks discover how fast she is with her sewing, you can bet she'll be extremely busy. Here we are."

Stella continued to walk up the sidewalk to the front door of a clapboard house with black shutters. "Her name is Opal." Stella lost no time and rapped on the door. Momentarily, a comely young woman answered the door. "Good evening, Stella," she said hesitantly when she saw Robert with her.

"Opal, I don't mean to intrude, but I'd like you to meet Robert Frasier. Are you busy?"

Opal smiled. "Not at all, just cleaning up after supper. Please come in." She led them to the parlor and stuck out her hand. "I'm Opal Sloan."

"Nice to meet you," he answered, but wasn't sure what else to say.

Opal nodded, withdrawing her hand. "Why don't you have a seat?"

The odor of fried onions and liver wafted on the air. Robert glanced about the homey but untidy parlor. *Evidence of more family members?* She looked younger than he was, but he'd never been a good judge of age, especially in women.

Stella took over. "Thanks, but we won't be here long. Robert is looking for someone to make him a decent suit for the Bozeman Ball next Saturday, and I told him about you. Would you have time to accommodate such a quick request?"

"Mmm." Opal backed away, sizing him up. "I think I could do that. He's tall, but it shouldn't take me long."

"I guess I should be relieved?" Robert chuckled and glanced over at Stella, and she winked. "What do you need me to do? Go buy the material? I have no knowledge about those kinds of things."

"You have nothing to be concerned about. That's my job." Opal smiled at him.

Robert liked her warm friendliness, which put him at ease. He'd have to get busy and ask Grace to go to the ball.

He heard the sound of a baby crying from down the hall, and Opal glanced in that direction. "I'm sorry, but I need to take care of the baby now, so I'll need you to return first thing in the morning for me to get your measurements, if you don't mind." Her tone was apologetic. "Sometimes she can be a handful when I need to be working."

"I understand." Robert nodded. "Thank you, Opal."

Opal walked them to the front door. "Do you think you can stop by first thing in the morning?"

"I can do that on my way to work."

Opal gave him a warm but tired smile.

"Good. Could you please come to the back entrance? That's where I have my sewing area set up for now so it's away from the living area." The baby's wails began to get louder. "I'm sorry, I must go to her."

She scurried away and they stepped outside, closing the door. "I told you she'd be able to do it," Stella said.

"Can we keep this between us, Stella?"

Stella looked at him above the spectacles low on her nose. "Sure . . . but why?"

"I want to surprise Grace. She has never seen me in anything but trousers and a chambray work shirt."

Stella nodded. "I see. Then I'm sure she will be delightfully surprised."

They continued back to the boardinghouse. Robert paused before he went to his room. "Thank you for helping me out, Stella. By the way, are you and Owen going to the ball?"

"Yes, we'll be there. He may not be able to dance, but we aren't going to miss out on the fun. Almost everyone attends."

Robert walked to the back of Opal's house the next morning and tapped on the door and waited. Since the harvest was over, Tom was working all day for Eli, so he didn't have to explain where he was going. The girls didn't always go to the farm with him every day now. Summer would soon drift into fall and school would be upon them again.

The door swung open and Opal held a baby on her hip, measuring tape around her neck and a pincushion strapped to her wrist. "Good morning." She stepped aside for him to enter.

"Is this the little one that was crying last night?" Robert asked as he entered.

"I'm afraid so." Opal grinned. "She's sweet most of the time . . . unless I'm finishing a sewing project."

Robert decided she was cute as far as babies go, but never having been around them, he didn't really know. "What's her name?"

"Annie. She's six months old. My husband died in a mining accident before she was born. I'll measure you as soon as I can get her settled again in her crib with a toy or two for company, if you'll wait right here."

"I'm very sorry to hear that." Robert watched her eyes fill with tears.

"Yes, well . . ." She lowered her eyes and slipped down the hallway.

Robert took a moment to look around her sewing room. A scarred rectangular table held material, scissors, thread, and a small stack of thin tissue paper, which he assumed was to cut out patterns. Her sewing machine sat in front of the window where bright light flooded in, next to a dress form. She had all the makings for a dress shop. He hoped one day she'd have it.

A few minutes later Opal returned. "I'll need to take your chest, neck, and arm measurements and then your pants length. If you could hold your arm out for me . . ."

Robert did as asked while Opal started at the center of the back of his neck and measured from there down to the cuff of his shirt.

She marked the number on a small pad, then moved on to the next measurement. "Now if you'll hold both arms out a little, I can measure your chest." When she was done and scribbled down the number, she looked up at him with surprise. "Your chest is broader than I first thought."

"Is that a problem?"

"No, not at all. I was only thinking aloud." She continued with his waist and legs. Satisfied she had what she needed, she took a step back. "Do you prefer a dark suit in broadcloth or a pinstripe?"

"Whatever you have on hand is fine, since I have no suit at all."

"Okay—" Annie's cries sounded in the background. "As I was about to say, if you can drop back tomorrow late afternoon, I'll have the pattern cut and would like to check it against you."

"Will do. How much will I owe you?"

"Whatever you can afford to pay me, but if you could help spread the word, it would help me grow my business. It's been a real struggle since my Will died."

"I'd be glad to do that." The crying was getting louder as he opened the door to leave. "I wonder . . . would you like someone to entertain Annie while she's not asleep so you can work?"

Opal laughed. "That would be like a dream come true, but of course, I know no one who fits that description."

"I do. I have a daughter, Becky, that would love to help with Annie. She's free during the summer and she loves children. I can bring her with me next time."

Opal's eyes grew wide. "Oh my! That sounds too good to be true."

"Then it's a deal. I've got to get going and let you go handle Annie," he said, standing at the back door.

She reached out and shook his hand before he left. "I look forward to it. Thank you." She smiled broadly. He couldn't help but notice how her face had brightened, and it did his heart good. He strode back to the boardinghouse to get his horse from the barn before heading to the farm.

Grace looked closely in the mirror at her cheek. Only a fine line was visible now, but the scar on her heart from the episode was deeper. She was uneasy sometimes, and especially when she was alone, the nightmare of Warren clouded her mind. What if he escaped? Would he come back to finish what he started? She mustn't let those thoughts creep in. Ginny told her that it was the work of the devil in order to keep her from healing.

She's right. Warren was behind bars, right where he needed to be. Frank told them that Sheriff Mendenhall had heard judgment was swift and Warren was in prison for a long time, convicted of confiscation of goods, bribery, and attempted rape. Thank God!

Since the harvest, Grace had more free time on her hands to tend her flowers, pick berries, and can the vegetables for the coming winter. Becky and Sarah spent several days learning the process and sampling the jams as they helped. Other days, the girls were in town now that Tom was working at the mercantile every day. Robert tended to the cows and had removed the wilted potato vines left behind from the harvest.

Her father was spending more and more time away with Stella and going to the hot springs as often as time allowed. He still had bad days, but was encouraged when he would have an entire week when he felt like himself . . . almost. But Stella didn't seem to mind, and Grace was so happy that she was a part of their lives.

After gathering the eggs, Grace filled a bowl with peas to

shell and went to the porch to sit in the shade. Robert strolled from the barn to where she was.

"Just cleaned out the barn and worked on that loose gate." Taking a rocking chair, he dragged it close to hers. "Can I be of help before I leave to go to Eli's?"

Grace paused with her shelling. "If you'd like." She was curious why he'd sat so close but placed the bowl between them. If he got any better-looking, she wasn't sure what she'd do. When he was this close, her insides quivered.

He reached inside for a pod to shell and brushed her knuckles with his, then looked over at her. "Grace, I've been meaning to ask this all week, but time got away from me. Can I take you to the Bozeman Ball?"

She flashed him a smile of pleasure. "I've been hoping you'd ask but was beginning to wonder. I'd love to go with you."

He gave her a childish grin. "Great! Stella says anyone who is anybody will be there. I guess she means the staunch bedrock of our community."

She laughed. "I believe that to be true. It's at least something we can look forward to since there's little out here to do but work or farm."

He reached back into the bowl, but this time when his hand touched hers, he took hold of it. "Grace," he croaked.

"Yes?" She blinked.

"Uh . . . I'm glad you're going to go with me. I'm not much on dancing." His eyes searched her face, and she had a feeling he had intended to say something entirely different. But he didn't. Instead he leaned over the bowl, stroking her cheek with his fingers. Her heart began to hammer. She licked her lips, staring at his as he moved in closer to nibble her bottom lip until she tilted her head back with a sigh.

The screen door swung open and Owen hobbled out. The timing couldn't be worse. "You young'uns care for a glass of iced tea?"

They both jumped back, almost turning over the bowl of peas as Robert fumbled to grab hold of it.

"Yes, Pop. But I'll go get us some."

Owen chuckled. "Taking you a long time to shell those peas I see," he teased.

"Pop!" Grace protested. She'd been longing for Robert's kiss for days, and now the moment was past. She sighed and looked at Robert, who stood up, looking embarrassed, with his thumbs in his pockets.

"I'll pass on the tea. I really should get on to Eli's."

"Are you sure?" Grace gazed at him.

"I'm sure. I'll see you both tomorrow." He started down the steps, then paused. "Is there anything you need from town while I'm there?"

Owen scratched his head. "Nothing I can think of."

"I don't need anything either, but thanks for asking. Tell the children hello for us."

"Will do." He doffed his hat and strode toward the barn to get his horse.

Owen sat down and propped his cane on the armrest of the rocker. "I'm sorry if I interrupted a private moment, Grace."

Grace resumed the pea shelling with a shrug. "It's okay. How would you know? I certainly didn't. Sometimes he can be a bit impulsive."

"Either that or it's due to the fact that he caught you alone. You know the children are always around, or me. Plus, with him working two jobs, and that long drive to Virginia City,

I can't say I blame him. You're a pretty woman and good-hearted to boot!"

Grace patted his hand. "Thanks, Pop. Something nags me about him. If he really cared for me, other than kissing, why doesn't he just tell me?"

Owen sighed. "Only he can answer that, but I think it has something to do with his first wife, her sudden death, then inheriting three kids all at once. That alone could keep him a widower for a long time to come."

"Words of wisdom. But surely someday in the future he'll get over that, won't he?"

"It takes some longer to forget than others."

Grace had been piling the pea pods in her apron in her lap. After finishing the rest, she rolled her apron up and set the bowl full of shelled peas on the floor. "At least he asked me to Saturday's ball. I was afraid I was going to have to go with you and Stella."

"I'm glad he did. Just don't rush him, Grace. I have no doubt that he has other things in mind when it comes to you, but he's cautious."

"I'll try, Pop."

41

Ginny decided once she'd finished feeding the baby and before the day's heat became too much for her that she'd take Grace for a stroll in the baby carriage Frank had bought. Nell helped her take the buggy down the steps and met her with lively little Grace in her arms.

"Maybe the stroll will help her take a long morning nap," Nell commented.

Ginny nodded with a smile. "She really has gotten used to her morning outings, and it helps me to get out of the house for a while and stretch my legs."

"Let me know when you're back or just park the buggy by the steps, and I'll come get it for you."

"Thanks, Nell. I couldn't make it without all the help you've been." Ginny placed the baby in the buggy, unlocked the brake, and began their usual morning stroll. She waved to the familiar folks on the street going about their day. Most were friendly, hardworking folks just struggling to make a living for their families. She loved her life here.

As she rounded the block, between houses, she once

again saw Robert nearing the back door of a house whose owner Ginny didn't know. Probably someone new in town since she'd had little Grace. She paused, chewing her lip, wondering if she should mention this to Grace. It had been early morning right after breakfast this week when she'd first seen Robert at the house. Now she caught a glimpse of a pretty woman with blonde hair opening the door with a friendly smile and taking his wrist, pulling him inside. *Mighty friendly*, she thought. *Is that the reason he's never seriously courted anyone? Another woman? Heavens to Betsy, I pray not!*

Grace pulled out the emerald gown to make sure that no alterations were needed. She was in awe at the beautiful and intricate silk embroidery on the dress. Her friend had excellent taste, that was for certain. After slipping it over her head, she realized that she and Ginny were nearly mirrors of one another's shape, with Grace only a little taller. The dress didn't reach the floor but was only an inch above. No one would notice that small difference in length, and she was quite pleased when she wandered over to the cheval mirror and caught her reflection there. She was transfixed at how elegant she looked in the lovely gown of moiré silk. Ginny had probably ordered it from Paris, costing her a pretty penny. Grace felt bad that she would be the first one to get to wear it—she mustn't spill anything that night.

She pulled her hair up from the nape of her neck. Not too bad, but she'd have to work on taming those curls. *Will Robert think I'm pretty?* She scrutinized her face with a critical eye. Her skin was drier this year than ever before, a direct result from working in the fields with the harsh wind and sun. More freckles dotted the bridge of her nose and cheeks as well. *So much for trying to protect my skin. I'll never look like a real lady like Ginny does.*

Despite all that, a thread of excitement coursed through her as she anticipated the ball and Robert's arms about her as they waltzed. So much so that Grace waltzed about her room, her gown making swishing sounds across the hardwood floor until she was nearly out of breath. She stifled a giggle so as not to wake her pop.

For the third time, Robert hurried up the back steps to Opal's, surprised when the door opened and she quickly grabbed him by his wrists, pulling him in.

"I'm sorry, but Annie's in a foul mood from teething, and I didn't want the neighbors to hear her screaming. Do you think Becky will come today?"

"Yes, she's coming and plans to bring Sarah, so with the two of them, they should be able to give you some freedom."

"Oh, thank you! I have your suit ready for one final measurement—to hem the sleeves and pants. Then I'll press it and I should be done. Could you slip on the trousers and coat while I check on Annie? Then I can mark the hemline with my chalk."

"Of course, you go right ahead," Robert answered, thinking he would never want babies. The three kids he had were plenty. Still, it might be nice to see what a little girl would look like if Grace were his wife.

"I'll close the door for your privacy and be right back," Opal said before hurrying away.

Robert slipped on the pants first, then the coat. He'd never owned anything as fine as this pin-striped suit. He stared at his reflection in the full-length mirror and decided he liked it very much. Opal had outdone herself.

A knock sounded on the door, and Robert invited Opal to enter.

"Don't you look nice? With a bit of tweaking, it will be a perfect fit," Opal said. "I hope there's a certain young woman you want to impress." She arched a brow, standing back with her arms folded to size up her creation on him.

"There is. Grace Bidwell—but I'm guessing you haven't met. She's an incredible, resilient woman, very sweet natured. I'm sure you two would get along well."

"I'm sure we would. I've barely got settled, as Stella told you, but I'd like to meet her. Stella allowed me to stay at the boardinghouse rent free with Annie until I could get on my feet with a few clients. I owe her a lot."

"That sounds like something Stella would do. She's quite a woman and has been good to me and my children."

They talked further while she marked the cuffs and hems, chatting about Grace and her father before Opal spoke a little more about herself.

"There. I think that about does it. You can pick up your suit any time after tomorrow. I only need to sew buttons on the vest."

"I appreciate this so much. If I can help you out in any way, please keep me in mind."

She left the room so he could change, and he was soon out the door, riding toward Grace's with romantic thoughts for the first time in a long time—if one didn't count their interrupted interlude the other day.

Robert was in an exceptionally good mood when Grace spoke with him that morning and didn't seem to mind that he had fence line to repair. "I haven't seen Sarah or Becky in a couple of days. What have they been up to?" she asked while he loaded his tools in the back of the wagon to repair the fence.

"Aw, you know kids." He was quiet for a moment then added, "Uh . . . different things or reading every book they can get their hands on from Stella."

"Oh." Grace thought he sounded vague but didn't comment further. "You'll be gone by the time I get back from town. I'm off this morning to pay Ginny and the baby a visit and take some jam that I made."

Robert watched her climb on Cinnamon's back to leave. As she left, she turned in the saddle to wave. He was still standing there, gazing after her. She blew him a kiss, and knew her father was in good hands while she was away.

The warm bundle in her arms had finally drifted off to sleep, so Grace forced herself to put her namesake into her crib. "She has the face of an angel," she whispered as they quietly left the nursery.

"I couldn't agree more. Nell made us a light luncheon. Why don't we have it on the back porch in the shade?"

Once they were halfway through lunch, Ginny coughed and cleared her throat. Taking a big gulp of water, she looked at Grace intently.

"What is it? I know from the look on your face something's not right. Do you want your gown back?"

"I wish it were that simple." Ginny chewed her bottom lip. "I'm not sure if I should be telling you this at all."

Grace shook her head. "Please don't make me guess. Tell me what's wrong."

Ginny squirmed in her chair. "It's Robert. I . . . uh . . . saw him with another woman."

Grace's heart slammed against her ribs. "What do you mean saw him with another woman? Who? Where?"

Ginny sighed and her eyes were pained. "I was strolling with the baby, and I saw him going in the back door of a very attractive lady's house. The children were not with him either."

Grace laid her fork down, a rock in the pit of her stomach threatening to make her sick. "I'm sure there's an explanation. Perhaps he's taken on a third job."

"Like what? By slipping in through the back door?"

"I don't know, but we aren't engaged, so he's free to do whatever he chooses."

"How can you say that? He's kissed you more than once, and I thought you said you two had an understanding?"

Tears welled up and Grace croaked, "I thought we did too."

"It may all be purely innocent, but I have to say I've seen it more than once, usually after breakfast when I walk Grace. Once, the woman yanked him in quickly like she was very happy to see him. Remember, he married his first wife rather fast, and I don't know his intent, but you're my best friend, and I felt you should know. I'm sorry if the knowledge hurt you."

So much for the longing Grace thought she'd seen in his eyes lately. Maybe she misunderstood his look of sympathy when he'd really wanted to tell her that he was seeing someone else. She didn't know, but she knew she wouldn't play second fiddle to anyone.

"I'm sorry, but I must go. I can't eat another bite." Grace shoved her chair back and Ginny did the same.

"What will you do? I don't want Robert to think I was spying on him. It just happened that he was there when I was out with the baby," Ginny insisted.

Grace walked to the door. "I'm not sure, but he owes me an explanation."

"I'm sorry. Maybe it's not at all what it appears to be," Ginny said. "Let me know."

All the way home, Grace struggled with feeling betrayed—but how could one really be betrayed when there hadn't been any real commitment? Her heart felt it all the same.

When she neared the river, she pulled Cinnamon to a stop and slid off her back, dropping the reins to allow her to munch on sage grass. Any other time, she would be filled with happiness and wonder at the grandeur of the mountain peaks, the wildflowers, and rushing waters of the river, but not today. Tears fell and everything she'd stored up tumbled out. She cried about Robert—cried about her pop—cried that she had no children—cried that she'd given her heart away, and that she was an old maid, until she was thoroughly spent.

As the afternoon sunlight waned, she found Cinnamon dozing in the shade of a cottonwood. "At least *you're* faithful," she said to her.

"Gracious, you can't speculate on this situation until you talk to Robert, otherwise you're spending time wallowing in pity," Owen had said after she told him.

"Thanks, Pop. Just what I hoped to hear from you," she said sarcastically.

He threw his arm around her, and she rested her head on his shoulder. "I'm only trying to make you stop and think clearly. That's all."

"I know." She sniffed into her handkerchief. "But something doesn't make sense to me."

"Well, he did ask you to the ball, didn't he? Why in the world would he do that if he was seeing another lady? He could easily have asked her. Talk to him tomorrow. Now go to bed and try to sleep on it."

She kissed his wrinkled cheek. "I guess you're right. I think I let myself care for him a whole lot more than he cares for me."

Owen was up before Grace. He wanted to make sure he had a word with Robert before Grace knew he was there. As soon as Robert arrived, he asked him to walk to the barn under the pretense of milking the cows, but out of Grace's view from the kitchen.

"Owen, something troubling you?" Robert narrowed his gaze.

"You might say that. Grace came home pretty upset last night. I'm not going to get in the middle of it, but if you're seeing someone besides my daughter then you need to tell her. You got that?" Owen knew his body trembled with weakness when he got upset, and he was trying not to let that happen. He'd pegged Robert to be a decent man in love with his daughter.

Robert's head jerked back. "Another woman?"

"Yes, and if that's true, it's really none of my business what you do, but you need to be honest with her. I don't know this other woman, but my advice to you is, don't overlook an orchid while looking for a rose."

Robert sputtered. "Owen, I assure you I wouldn't do that. I'm going to tell you who the lady is, but trust is a two-way street. If Grace changes her mind about going with me to the ball, then I'll know she doesn't trust me. I've already had one woman that didn't trust me enough to tell me *all* the truth about her life, and I won't live that way again. Am I making any sense?"

"Maybe . . . But what do you plan to do?" *This better be good, mister.*

"Promise me you won't say anything to Grace, and let me handle this. I've got to find out if we can build a life on trust as well as love. Just so you understand, I love Grace."

Owen nodded, knowing it was best that he stay out of it. Robert clapped him on the back, and if it hadn't been for the cane, he would've knocked him off his unsteady legs. Then he told Owen his plan.

Robert wasted no time and knocked on the kitchen's back door before he entered. Grace had her back to him, washing dishes, with suds up to her elbows. She didn't turn around, evidence that she was miffed.

"How are you this morning? Mind if I have a cup of coffee?"

"Help yourself," she replied.

"I'm looking forward to Saturday night, how about you?" He decided to start the conversation that way to lay it all on the table. He was right. She turned around, snapping her towel as she picked up a dish. *Is she going to throw it at me?* Worse had happened to him in the past.

"I'm not going. At least not with you."

Pretending ignorance, Robert asked, "And why not?"

She eyed him sharply but continued drying the plate. "Because you were seen several times keeping company with another woman. That's why!" she snapped, her honey-colored eyes boring holes into him.

"Don't believe what you hear. You must trust me," he said, hands on his hips.

"So you're not going to deny your new friend?"

He made a decision right then not to explain the circumstances at that moment. *I need a trusting heart.* He repeated, "Trust me, Grace."

"I repeat, I'm not going to the dance with you, so you're free to take . . . your new friend. And you may as well look for another part-time job to go with the one you have." She turned and flounced out of the kitchen, slamming the door hard behind her.

42

Until Robert left, Grace did her best to avoid crossing paths with him. She was furious that he wouldn't tell her anything. And what did he mean by not listening to what she heard? Ginny would never make up something like that.

After weeding her vegetable garden, she went inside and found her father working on a crossword puzzle. He looked up at her approach.

"I couldn't help but notice Robert left without saying good-bye. That's not like him. Did you two talk?" He laid aside his reading glasses while waiting for her to respond.

Grace plopped down in her chair. "We did, but all he said was for me to trust him when I asked about the other lady. Not the kind of answer I expected." She leaned her head back, looking up at the ceiling.

"Then maybe you should."

"I told him I wasn't going to the dance with him, so I guess I won't go at all."

Owen grumbled, "Oh, yes you are. You can go with me and Stella."

She sat up, looking at her father. "I don't know . . . I also fired him. The harvest is over, and I don't really need his help now."

"You did what? Have you lost your mind, daughter? Don't you think you're being a little harsh?"

"Probably. I wasn't thinking rationally, but if he can't trust me enough to tell me about his new friend, then . . ."

"Oh boy, I hope you didn't make a mistake. But come tomorrow night, you may as well go to the ball. Sitting here will only make things worse. Besides, I'd love to see you in the pretty dress you borrowed from Ginny."

Grace folded her arms. She didn't want to talk about it anymore. "I won't promise."

"Grace, don't let your stubbornness create a wall between you and the man you love. It was Robert that saved you from Warren, remember?"

Her eyes drifted down to a place where sunlight streamed through the window, warming the hardwood boards beneath Owen's chair—much like his love and wisdom warmed her life. She knew he was right, as usual.

A while later, Grace peeled potatoes with a vengeance, releasing her frustrations. Maybe her father was right about letting Robert go, but really, she'd managed before he came, and she could do it again. She hadn't expected her father to take his side. Did he know something she didn't?

Grace took a long walk alone after supper. She was torn— half of her felt bad that she'd fired Robert, the other half wanted to continue to be obstinate. But if he *was* spending time with another lady, then why not tell her? *Is there a way to fix this?* As a solution nudged into her mind, peace flooded her torn heart.

Early Saturday morning, taking time to gulp down a cup of strong coffee for fortification, Grace told Owen her plan.

With a raised eyebrow but a look of satisfaction, he said, "That's my girl! What man could refuse an invitation to the ball that comes with an apology?"

Grace handed him her empty coffee cup when he followed her to the door. "I hope you're right. I shouldn't be long. I have a lot to do before tonight if he says yes."

Owen grinned. "Oh, he will."

Bozeman was slowly beginning to stir as Grace rode into town. Smoke curled from chimneys, and somewhere the scent of bacon frying wafted in the air, making her stomach growl. Grace wasn't sure what she'd say to Robert, but there was no turning back now. She looped the horse's reins to the hitching post in front of the boardinghouse. At the door she caught her reflection in the glass and stopped a moment to drop her hat to hang down her back, remove her leather gloves, pat her hair into place, and smooth her riding vest. Taking a deep breath, she opened the door to the foyer.

She heard voices chattering but doubted the children were up yet. A couple of folks nodded to her as they swept past her to the dining room for breakfast. She waited, hoping she hadn't missed him, but she couldn't stand here long looking like a fool or her courage would vanish.

Grace turned to look up the staircase and spied Robert looking down from the top stair at her. He paused a moment, clearly surprised, then headed down the steps.

"Grace, to what do I owe the pleasure of your company this early in the morning—or are you here to see Stella?"

Grace licked her dry lips, her palms perspiring as they clung to her riding skirt. "I . . . uh . . . could I speak with you privately for a moment if you have time?"

He moved closer, taking her elbow and guiding her to the parlor. "What is it? Is anything wrong with Owen?"

Inside the parlor, she turned to him. "No. Pop's fine. It's me."

"You? You look good to me, and that's an understatement." His lips curled into a rare smile.

She looked up at him. "Robert, I feel I must apologize for my childish behavior yesterday. I want to also thank you for saving me from Warren's brutal attack. I'm not sure that I ever did." Her mouth felt about as dry as parched grass in the middle of August as she gazed into his brooding eyes.

"No thanks are needed. I would do it all over again to save you from harm. As to yesterday's tongue-lashing—maybe I deserved it."

She shook her head. "No. No, you didn't. I know we both have had past heartaches, and I do want to trust you . . . if you'll forgive me."

Robert took a step closer and took her hands, his steely eyes holding hers with a softened gaze. "How could I not when you're pleading with me?" He lifted her hands, kissing their tops, then pulled her into his arms to envelop her in a sweet embrace.

Grace was soothed by the thumping of his heart against her, and it was comforting, oh so comforting. A moment or two later, she pulled back, forcing herself to lose all her pride.

"Robert, unless you've asked your *new* friend, will you go with me to the ball tonight?"

He laughed and tapped her nose. "Mmm, let me think," he answered with his chin cupped in his hand, pretending to be in thought. Then he chuckled again. "You *know* I'd love to be your escort. But first there is someone you need to meet." He grabbed her hand, pulling her out of the boardinghouse, then outside and down the sidewalk, despite Grace's protestations. She could barely keep up with his long strides and a time or two she stumbled over the toe of her riding boot.

"Robert, please. Let go of my hand." But he didn't seem to hear or care, nearly dragging her, breathless, down the block to stop at the back door of a clapboard house.

With a sharp rap against the door, he stepped back and waited, still holding on to her wrist, until a pretty lady opened the door with a smile. Grace swallowed the huge lump in her throat. This must be the woman Ginny had told her about. Surprised by her beauty, Grace tried not to stare. *She's a lot younger than me and prettier too.*

"Robert, so nice to see you. Won't you come in?" She smiled a little too much, Grace thought.

"No, thank you. It's early, but I wanted you to meet someone," Robert said, nearly shoving Grace closer. "Grace, this is Opal Sloan."

Why is he torturing me this way?

"Oh, I'm so glad to meet you! Robert can't seem to stop singing your praises," the blonde stated.

Grace didn't dare to look at him, but stared at Opal, whose face expressed real friendliness. With a cool tone she replied, "Really? That surprises me."

Opal glanced at Robert, appearing uneasy.

"Can I pick up my suit now if it's ready?" Robert asked.

"Oh, yes." She seemed relieved. "Let me get it. It won't take but a moment." Opal hurried away and was back momentarily. "Here you are."

Robert took the suit and thanked her, handing her a wad of bills in exchange as Grace watched.

"I can't thank you enough, Opal."

Opal nodded, beaming with pride. "Thank you! We'll talk soon. It's was so nice to meet you Grace, but if you'll excuse me, I hear the baby," she said. "I was about to feed her breakfast, so if you don't mind . . ." Robert nodded and she shut the door, leaving the two of them eye to eye, standing on the doorstep.

With a twinkle in his eye, Robert pulled her closer, and said, "It's not what you think, Grace. Look closely at this stitching on my new suit." He held it up for her to see. "Perfect, isn't it? Opal made this suit for me so I could impress *you*. She's a new seamstress in town and doesn't have a shop yet. Stella took me to her to see about making an appropriate suit for me in time for the ball. Hence the back door entrance." He paused, his eyes penetrating hers.

Robert pulled back his suit coat, and Grace inspected the tiny, perfect stitches that held the coat to the lining and the neatly sewn buttonholes. Robert continued, "Opal has a baby that Becky's been watching while she sews. Her husband died. So I told her all about you." He pulled her close to his face, lifting her chin, and gazed lovingly into her eyes, questioning and searching. "I didn't tell you the other day because I wanted you to believe in me. I need a trusting heart in the woman I love—not the kind of love I had with Ada. I didn't

316

want to make that same mistake again. I had to see if you trusted me, so I didn't tell you. Don't you see? I love you, Grace," he whispered huskily. "Only you."

Fighting hard to keep from crying, Grace found herself melting under his gaze and admission of love. "I feel like such a fool. I understand now." She began to sob and he crushed her to his chest, stroking her hair. After a long moment, she pulled back to see him clearly. "I will never mistrust you again," she murmured, overwhelmed at the love reflected in his eyes.

"Grace, I've been tortured with thoughts of love for you day in and day out. I never thought I'd find someone like you. Tell me you love me too."

"I do, Robert. I think I have from the very beginning, when you came to work for me." She hiccupped and he chuckled, then kissed her lips, and they both tasted the saltiness of her tears, until she was breathless.

"It's time to go, Grace," Owen yelled up the stairs. "We don't want to keep them waiting."

Grace rushed to the top of the stairs, nearly out of breath. "I'm coming," she answered, again patting the curls about her face and neckline. She was no expert in hairdos, but had pulled her hair off the nape of her neck, leaving a few trailing curls. Butterflies fluttered in her stomach as she wondered about Robert's reaction when he would finally see her in something besides a housedress. "It took a little longer than I expected. Social events are not an everyday occurrence for me."

As she descended the stairs, her father gasped. "Grace, you

look so much like your mother. So beautiful," he said, taking her hand. "Wait until Robert sees you."

Grace kissed his cheek. "You look very nice yourself, Pop." Before getting herself ready, she'd helped him dress in the suit he used for church and funerals. He'd refused to spend money on a new one.

"You'll make a striking entrance on Robert's arm." He smiled as he took his cane from the balustrade of the stairs and crooked his elbow. "Shall we go?"

Stella was waiting at the boardinghouse door when they arrived. Grace parked the buggy and looped the horse's reins about the hitching post, then helped her father down. The Stafford Hotel was only two doors down the street, so they planned to walk from the boardinghouse.

"You look marvelous, Grace," Stella exclaimed. "And who is this handsome man you have with you? I hardly recognize him," she teased.

Owen stepped back to admire her. "You look wonderful yourself."

"I agree." Grace loved Stella's lavender gown with its creamy lace collar. "You make a handsome couple," she remarked when Stella took Owen's arm.

"Thank you, my dear. And the weather couldn't be more perfect," Stella replied just as Robert strode over to meet them.

Grace's heart caught in her throat. He was so handsome, sporting the fine pin-striped suit Opal had created with a matching vest and four-in-hand tie around his stiff white collar. He'd never looked so dashing. He flashed her a broad smile, taking her hand in his large warm one.

"Grace, you look astonishingly beautiful!" Robert's eyes swept over her, and Owen and Stella smiled as they watched them. "I . . . my goodness. All I can say is a housedress doesn't do you justice." He took her arm, clasping the top of it with his other hand.

"Thank you. I do wash up pretty good, don't I?" she teased.

They joined the throng of folks walking to the ball. Most of the town had turned out for the event. Some had gathered outside the hotel to chat, while others were already in the building, where music could be heard.

Inside, they headed straight to find a chair for her father that was visible to the dance floor. Grace observed several admiring looks from old and young alike, and she smiled back while Robert squeezed her arm. *Must be Ginny's gown.*

"Come, Grace. Let's go get us all a glass of punch first." Robert steered her in the direction of the refreshment table past the floor of dancers, who were laughing and smiling at them as they swept past.

Grace scanned the floor, seeing the familiar faces of Eli and Dorothy, Dr. Avery and his wife, and Ginny and Frank. They were dancing to a waltz, Grace's favorite dance. The last time she'd danced was before Victor died. But tonight, the bittersweet memory of Victor was dimmed as she and Robert carried the punch back to where Owen sat with Stella. Grace couldn't be happier.

At the end of the waltz, Ginny and Frank ambled over to talk. "I declare, Grace, that gown suits you better than it does me." Ginny gave her a hug.

"Oh, I doubt that, but I'm so glad that you were able to

come tonight, Ginny." Grace had told her about the confrontation she'd had with Robert yesterday, and she knew from her friend's look that Ginny was surprised to see her with him. "I'll have to talk with you later," Grace whispered to Ginny, who nodded with interest.

"We wouldn't miss the ball," Frank commented, then leaned over to Grace's ear. "I'm still so sorry for what happened with Warren. Both Virginia and I feel responsible for pushing him toward you. For that I'm deeply regretful."

"You have nothing to be sorry for," Grace answered, shaking her head.

"In that case, would you like to dance?" Frank held out his hand to her.

Grace glanced at Ginny, who nodded, and then to Robert, who also agreed. "Yes, yes, I would."

After the dance with Frank, she agreed to dance with another gentleman who was one of the local druggists. As she listened to his labored breathing and endured his sweaty palms while they danced, her eyes swept back to where Robert stood talking with Ginny while they drank their punch.

"Want to dance the next one with me?" the man holding her hand asked.

"If you don't mind, I need to go check on my father."

The druggist bowed slightly. "As you wish."

Robert scurried across the floor to rescue her.

"Oh, thank heavens! I don't know how much more I could've endured." She giggled as he took her hand.

"You won't have to again. I'm here to see to that. I didn't think you could ever look any more beautiful than you did before, but tonight, you do."

It was hard to focus on his face through the tears blurring her vision. It had been a long, long time since she'd felt carefree. Robert took his handkerchief from his pocket, gently dabbing her tears.

"Shall we dance?"

Epilogue

September trees dotting the foothills with their beginning hint of color announced fall's arrival. Grace and Robert stood leaning against the fence, their arms draped across its top rail, lost in the companionable silence of the afternoon. School was already in session, but the quiet wouldn't last long.

Grace enjoyed this view of her farm, the curling smoke from the chimney, the freshly plowed fields, sunflowers nodding, cows grazing lazily, and a large stack of cut wood by the corner of the house, thanks to Robert. All of this, plus the music of the birds' tweets, comforted her soul.

Robert slipped his arm about her waist and gave it a squeeze. "We couldn't ask for a more perfect day," he commented.

"It's my favorite time of year—the cool snap—a fire in the grate—cozy blankets and wraps—with school programs coming up and apples to pick. We have so much in our lives to be grateful for, don't you think?"

"Yes, we do, Grace. We've come through a lot this year.

With your help the children have fared well, and I believe the future looks bright."

She turned to look up at him. "I hope so."

Bluebelle came waddling down the lane into their view, her baby ducks following in a neat line with Paddy bringing up the rear.

"I think they have the right idea—a family, don't you?" he asked, reaching inside his vest pocket.

Grace wasn't sure what he meant until he lifted her left hand. *Am I dreaming?* A thrill shot through her, and her jaw dropped as she watched him.

"This was my mother's pearl ring. I . . . Grace, I'd be honored if you'd marry me, and wear this ring showing the commitment of our love. Then we can become a real family."

"Oh, yes, Robert, I will," she murmured, looking down at the pearl ring as he slipped it on her finger. She quickly looped her arms around his neck, kissing him with longing and intensity. "Now, you have to make me that soufflé that you've bragged about," she teased, and he laughed heartily.

"I promise," he answered, stroking the side of her face with his thumb.

Suddenly a ruckus came from the chokeberry bush behind them. Turning around, they saw Tom, Becky, and Sarah emerge and shout, "Hooray!" The children rushed to Grace and Robert, and they all became a huddle of hugs, laughter, and tears.

"I told you the angel said my dream would come true." Sarah proudly beamed up at the couple.

Grace kissed the top of her head. "*No one* can argue with that."

Author's Note

It's no secret that I love the West and history, thus the reason I chose a Montana setting. Gallatin Valley was called "Valley of Flowers" by the Indians, owing to its many wildflowers. The Bridger Mountains and Gallatin Range surround the valley. The town nearest my heroine's farm is Bozeman, named after the famous guide John Bozeman from Pickens County, Georgia. He was known for creating the historic Bozeman Trail, which shortened the distance from Omaha to the gold camps in the West. His was the first house built in Bozeman. I chose a location in the Gallatin Valley near the Gallatin River, named by Lewis and Clark. Montana became a territory in 1864. The movie *A River Runs Through It* was filmed in Bozeman.

Potatoes and beets were the principal vegetables grown in the Gallatin Valley during 1866, but a variety of other vegetables also grow in the lush valley's rich soil. In pioneer times, potatoes were taken to either Helena or Virginia City and sold for thirteen cents a pound.

Sheriff John S. Mendenhall is a historical character who was the sheriff of Bozeman. Samuel Anderson, the school teacher, is a historical character, and William W. Alderson was a historic preacher and community leader at that time. He is noted for naming the town of Bozeman, Montana's oldest city, in 1864.

The Bozeman Ball, Bozeman's first big social event, was started in 1864 on Christmas Eve, but I took the liberty of moving it a few months forward for my story. The ball was held at the Stafford Hotel building. A log house known as the Masonic building was the meeting place for the church.

The Women's Medical College in New York, where Stella attended, was a real college and was established in 1863.

The Swedish duck, Bluebelle, did not arrive in the US until 1884; however, I took the liberty of adding her to my story because of her grayish-blue color.

KatyKat was named after my beloved cat of nineteen years, and Amelia, our calico cat, lived until she was seventeen.

My husband suffers from a rare disease, chronic inflammatory demyelinating polyneuropathy (CIDP), which is the same disease my heroine's father, Owen, contracts in the story. Little was known about the disease at the time it was first discovered by Robert Graves in 1843. They called it Multiple Neuritis then. In my research I found that some experts believe Franklin D. Roosevelt may have suffered from CIDP instead of polio. You can learn more about this debilitating disease at http://www.gbs-cidp.org.

Maggie Brendan is the CBA bestselling author of the Heart of the West series, the Blue Willow Brides series, and the Virtues and Vices of the Old West series. Her books have received the Book Buyers Best Award from the Orange County Chapter of Romance Writers of America and the Laurel Wreath Award. A member of the American Christian Fiction Writers Association, Romance Writers of America, Georgia Romance Writers, and Author's Guild, Maggie lives in Georgia.

She invites you to connect with her at www.MaggieBrendan.com or www.southernbellewriter.blogspot.com. You can also find her on Facebook (www.facebook.com/maggiebrendan), Twitter (@MaggieBrendan), Pinterest (https://www.pinterest.com/maggiebrendan), Goodreads (https://www.goodreads.com/author/show/1682579.Maggie_Brendan), and Instagram: https://instagram.com/maggiebrendan.

Connect with

Maggie Brendan

★ ★ ★

MaggieBrendan.com

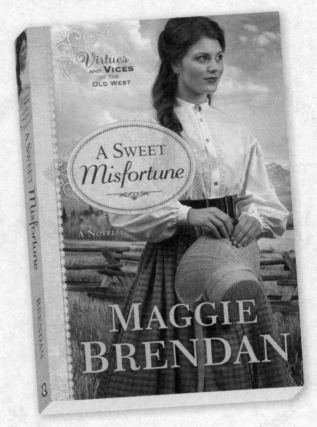

"*A Sweet Misfortune* will hold you captive with its colorful Western setting and cast of memorable characters. Woven within this heartfelt story is a beautiful thread of faith and love that is timeless."

—Laura Frantz, author of *The Mistress of Tall Acre*

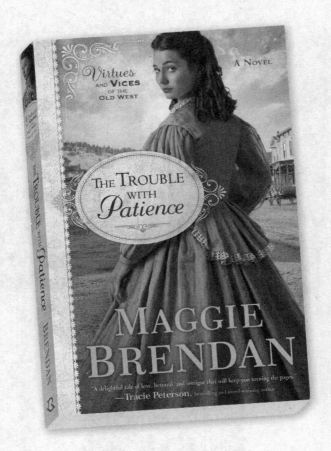

Life on the American Frontier Is Full of Adventure, Romance, and the Indomitable Human Spirit

Heartwarming Tales of Mishaps, Hope, and True Love